FIRST

BETROTHED #5

PENELOPE SKY

Hartwick Publishing

First

Copyright © 2020 by Penelope Sky

CONTENTS

1

DAMIEN

WHEN I ROSE FROM MY CHAIR, I BUTTONED THE FRONT OF MY SUIT. I held the folder of papers in my hand and left my office to head down the hallway. My footfalls were heavy on the hard wood, and my shoes were stiff because they were new. There was a slight squeak in the air, but since they were hand-picked by my designer, I ignored the sound.

His door was cracked at the end of the hallway, and as I got closer, the old rush of feelings returned.

Rage.

Ferocity.

Bitterness.

Resentment.

I hated that fucking asshole.

I walked inside when he was on the phone, noticing his wedding ring on his left hand and the watch Sofia gave him. I assumed my old birthday gift had disappeared in the bottom of a garbage can a year ago.

The last time we had a real conversation was when I told him to fuck off and have a good life. We were civil as much as possible, communicating at the bare minimum to get shit done. I tossed the folder on his desk. "These are my numbers for the week."

Hades stared at me with the phone to his ear. "Baby, I'll be home in an hour." He put the receiver on the base and stared at me like I was the bad guy who'd interrupted his extremely important conversation. "Alright."

It was his turn to do the business accounting, but judging by his attitude, he didn't want to waste time handling that shit. "I did it last time. It's your problem."

His eyes showed his annoyance, but he didn't argue.

I walked out again and didn't bother closing the door to the position he liked. Just looking at his face made me want to explode like a volcano. I'd never had a breakup so bitter, a falling-out that landed so hard. Sometimes I thought about leaving the bank just to rid myself of him.

But there was too much money on the table.

My assistant caught up with me in the hallway. "Sir, I have a client who needs to see you."

I held up my arm and looked at my Omega watch. "It's almost five. I'm leaving."

"She said it's urgent."

I'd had a really shitty day and didn't want to deal with any more bullshit. I still had a long night ahead of me at my second job. But my clients were big and powerful, and if it was urgent, it was truly urgent. "Fine. Name?"

"Annabella De Luca."

"Alright. Send her in." I went to my office and sat in front of my computer. Her name didn't ring a bell, so I had to look her up in my system to see what kind of funds she had. She couldn't be that important. Otherwise, I'd recognize her name.

When I finally located her in the system, it was clear that her husband was the one who made all the money.

A shit-ton of money.

I didn't recognize him either, so he must be a Hades client.

She walked in a second later, wearing a long-sleeved purple dress with over-the-knee black boots. With curled brown hair that reached past her chest and full lips that looked like pillows, she was not at all what I expected.

Sexy.

She was one of those women who spent a great deal of time perfecting her features, wearing the perfect makeup, styling her hair every morning even though she had to get up at the crack of dawn, and clearly hitting the weights to have an ass like that.

Fuck, I needed to focus.

She approached my desk with her black purse hanging in the crook of her elbow. "Damien, Annabella." She stuck out her hand to shake mine.

It took me a second to process her professionalism because I'd already made an assumption about her character based on how fucking pretty she was. I expected her to be stupid...shame on me.

I got to my feet and took her hand. "Pleasure to meet you."

She smiled before she dropped my hand and sat down.

After the initial high passed, I sat down again and tried to pretend she was a man. "How can I help you?"

She crossed her legs and set her purse on the table beside her. Her dress rose slightly, and the outfit was provocative in those boots. The skin of her thigh was lightly tanned and clearly toned. "An apartment that I love has opened up, and if I want to secure it, I need to wire the money tonight. So, thank you for seeing me at the last minute. I appreciate it."

Why was she buying an apartment? "I treat my clients like family. I'm happy to help you." I turned back to my computer. "How much money are we wiring for the transaction?" I found it odd that her husband wasn't here and that she didn't mention him, but my clients came here because of our discretion.

"Fifty thousand euros."

I wanted to raise an eyebrow, but I kept my expression stoic. "Alright." I looked through her various accounts. "Which account are we using today?" I picked the one with the highest amount of funds, which totaled over a hundred million euros.

"Those accounts aren't mine." She spoke in a calm manner, her voice subdued and slightly quiet.

"I see Liam De Luca and Annabella De Luca. That's you and your husband, correct?"

It was the first time she didn't seem as in control. She fidgeted slightly and broke eye contact. "No. That's my ex-husband. I've asked him to remove me from the account, and he still hasn't done it."

I was never interested in the drama of my clients' lives, but I was curious about this. And I was a bit intrigued that she was single.

"If you bring me the settlement from your divorce, I can separate the funds into different accounts and get you off this one."

"I don't want his money." Her tone was suddenly stern, like a button had been pressed with a fat thumb.

I tried to remain indifferent, but it was getting harder as the conversation continued. "According to law, you're entitled to a fair percentage of your joint assets. If you—"

"I'm fully aware of what I'm entitled to." Without raising her voice, she somehow commanded the room by simply changing her tone. It was obvious she was passionate about the subject. "I didn't want his money when I married him, and I certainly don't want it now. Please remove me from the account."

I tried not to stare at her, tried not to be transfixed by the sternness of her gaze. "As you wish. Do you have another account?"

"Yes. Annabella Lazio. Your assistant must've used my married last name."

I typed in her name and saw her funds.

She was broke.

She had enough money to complete the transaction she was asking for, but very little on top of that. I never reacted to my clients' incomes because they were all multimillionaires and billionaires. Honestly, she shouldn't even have been a client of mine because she had no need for my services. She didn't need money laundering or government assistance. But I wasn't going to be an ass to this gorgeous woman. "Where am I sending the funds?"

She pulled out a document from her purse and set it in front of me. It contained the wiring directions to send the funds to the escrow company. There was usually a fee to do this kind of transaction, but I decided to waive it because if I didn't, she might not be able to eat. I worked on the computer in silence.

Minutes passed, and she didn't make small talk. She didn't talk shit about her husband or gossip about the details of her divorce. People were usually so bitter, they aired their dirty laundry to anyone who would listen.

But she was tight-lipped.

I finished the task then printed out the confirmation code. "Done." I set the paper on the desk.

She grabbed it with her painted fingernails and read the details before she folded it up and placed it in her purse. "Thank you." She rose to her feet and extended her hand to shake mine.

I took it and felt my fingers automatically squeeze her wrist. I looked into her blue eyes and felt compelled to give her some kind of advice, to help her when I didn't even know her. She'd only been in my office for ten minutes, but I felt some sort of connection to her. "I understand you are angry and stubborn right now. But his money was your money, and you are fairly entitled to half of it." I didn't want this beautiful woman to stress about money every single day, to take the hard way just because she was stubborn. After a few months, she would regret that decision.

Her blue eyes slightly narrowed in offense. "I don't need your pity." She dropped her hand and stepped away from my desk. "I'll be just fine." She flipped her hair over her shoulder then strutted out of my office like she was still a billionaire.

I ARRIVED at the lab and got to work. When I told Hades I didn't need him, it was a lie. I was working a hell of a lot more now than I used to. That meant more hours for me, but since I didn't have anything else to do, it wasn't the end of the world.

When I was home, I just drank.

One of my four men came up to me before I went to the office. "Damien."

I didn't bother to look at him. "What?"

"We've got trouble."

I stopped in my tracks and turned around to face him. Maddox had only been dead for a few months, and I wasn't ready for more drama. With him out of the way, I was at the top of the food chain, so I shouldn't be afraid of anybody. I just didn't want a pain in the ass. "What?"

He looked hesitant, as if telling me this news would result in his neck being snapped. "The Skull King stopped by...said he wants to talk to you."

Hades and I had managed to escape the clutches of the Skull Kings because they had so many other projects to worry about, including a war on Lucian and something about a woman. They were too busy to care about us. But now that Balto was gone and his twin Heath replaced him, it looked like things had changed. "God-Fuck-ing-Dammit."

I WAS WORKING in my office when my curiosity got the best of me.

I went into Annabella's account to snoop.

I had no idea why; I would never see her again. She was newly divorced, so why would I want to get involved in something like that? There was just something about her that intrigued me, the way she started over with nothing so fearlessly.

The way I had to start over.

I looked at her recent paychecks to see where she worked.

She was a waitress.

That only made me feel worse. How was she supposed to support herself in Florence on a salary like that? Maybe she had a side hustle that was paid under the table. If she really got desperate for money, it would be easy for her to be a stripper...with a body like that.

"How are you?"

I nearly jumped out of my chair because I got caught red-handed doing something I shouldn't. "Shit."

Sofia walked inside in leggings and a loose sweater and approached my desk. "What? Looking at porn or something?"

I shut my laptop. "What do you want?"

"Someone's in a bad mood..."

I cast her a cold gaze.

She continued to stand there and stare at me expectantly, like she wanted me to say something. "Everything alright?"

I considered telling her about Heath, the new Skull King who wanted me to pay my business taxes. I knew that conversation wouldn't go well, and there would probably be stab wounds as a consequence. But then I realized my problems weren't her problems. They weren't Hades's problems. I was on my own now. "Just a long day..." I ran my fingers through my hair and relaxed in the chair.

She was quiet for a while before she kept talking. "Well, I have some good news to share."

My temper flared because of my bottled-up frustration and my deep depression. "Look, Hades and I don't speak. And if we don't speak, why the fuck do *we* have to speak?"

Her eyes immediately dilated in offense.

"Our only connection was Hades, and now he's just a piece-of-shit bastard, so there's no point in us continuing whatever the fuck this is." It was cold, harsh. No, it was cruel. But seeing her only reminded me of the person I never wanted to think about again. I wanted to move on with my life and forget he ever existed.

She gave me a pained look of disappointment as she stood with her hands on her hips. She stared me down a long time before she took a step back. "You don't want to be my friend? Fine. But I'll always be yours."

2

ANNABELLA

I GOT LUCKY THAT DAMIEN HELPED ME AT 4:59 PM BECAUSE IF HE hadn't, I would've been on the street for the night. My lease had ended at my other place, and I was going to get kicked out unless I got this apartment.

I also needed this apartment because it was the only decent place I could afford. The owner had been relocated for work and needed to sell it as quickly as possible to use the money as a down payment on his new place.

So I got a deal.

I needed as many deals as I could get...

I spent the evening with the TV on in the background while I unloaded and unpacked all the boxes that comprised of my life. It was all my clothes and personal possessions, and when I saw it all packaged up, I realized my life was just a small accumulation of junk.

I spent my best years with my ex-husband, filling my life with memories that made me feel rich. Losing him made me realize I'd lost everything else too. I lost my friends, social acquaintances, relationships...everything. He was the rich and powerful one, so even though our divorce was entirely his fault, they chose him over me.

What a fairy tale.

I tried not to feel bad for myself because I knew I would pick up the pieces and come out stronger in the end. I could start over. I'd done it before. I'd do it again. Getting married, though...not sure if I could ever do that again.

It'd been six months since we signed the divorce papers, so it was still raw but there had been a good amount of time for us to move on.

But he continued to call me.

As if he could read my thoughts, my phone lit up with a call from him.

I watched it ring on the table, the light filling my dark apartment. I was never enticed to answer. Damage was done. I'd already moved on.

It went to voice mail.

I kept unpacking.

A minute later, my screen lit up with a text message.

It was Liam. *Talk to me.*

I ignored him.

Anna.

I had gotten a new phone and changed my number, but he still tracked me down. I blocked his number, but that only made him show up on my doorstep instead. He hadn't moved on, and he had this ridiculous notion in his head that he might be able to win me back.

Never.

When his text messages kept coming in, I turned off my phone so I wouldn't have to see or hear it.

———

I WORKED at a bistro in the city, a casual place with a couple tables in a small restaurant. It wasn't a fine-dining experience, mainly a common place for lunch. The menu mostly consisted of sandwiches and salads, and our very delicious tiramisu.

I knew it was delicious because I ate it all the time.

I'd just finished delivering food to a table when a previously empty table was taken by a new customer. I pulled out my notepad and pencil and smoothed down my apron before I approached the stranger.

When I was almost there, I lifted my gaze and looked into the eyes of someone I already knew.

Masculine features, intense eyes, and a rough jaw all made up the man looking at me. With his Omega watch on his wrist, his arms out on the table, and his shiny shoes noticeable next to his chair, he made the restaurant stink of cash. He looked at me with fearless eyes, ready for whatever reaction I was about to have.

It took me a few seconds to process what had just happened. It was the suit from the bank, the guy who helped my transaction go through. He pitied me, which was obnoxious. He probably thought I was some poor, weak girl who would be impressed by his fat wallet.

I was only impressed by a fat dick.

I held the pencil to the notepad. "What can I get you?"

He glanced at the menu for a second before he turned back to me. "Coffee. Black." He handed the menu to me. "And the seasonal salad."

I tucked the menu under my arm and walked away.

"I know you recognize me."

I should keep walking and not give in to his comment, but I was a temperamental woman who became irrational quickly. I turned back around and approached him with one hand on my hip. "No, I don't."

He smiled in an amused way. "Come on, I'm a handsome guy."

"It's nice that you think so." I turned around and walked away again. I tended to my other tables and pretended he didn't exist. Even though he'd caught me off guard, I managed to appear indifferent to his visit.

When his coffee was ready, I grabbed it from the barista and carried it to his table. I leaned down as I set it in front of him. "Here you are, sir. Your lunch will be ready soon." I straightened next to the table and continued to pretend to be unaffected by his surprise visit. After I'd walked out of his office, I hadn't thought about him again. Yes, he was a good-looking man, but it took more than that to catch my attention.

He spoke before I walked away. "It's Damien. You can drop that sir bullshit."

"I call all my customers sir."

He smiled. "Even the chicks?"

I perfected my posture and held myself rigidly as I looked down at this arrogant man. He was witty and smart, like being good-looking wasn't enough. The man had everything...which was annoying. "Do you stalk all your clients?"

"Having lunch constitutes stalking?" He grabbed the mug by the handle and took a quick drink, the steam rising past his face before he licked his lips and returned it to the saucer. When he moved his arm, his fancy cuff links were noticeable, looking more expensive than all my jewelry combined. He was another rich pretty boy, the kind that thought he could get away with anything...just like my ex-husband.

"If you aren't here to see me, I'll get back to work." Before he could say another word, I walked off and took care of the rest of my tables as if he didn't exist.

———

I HOOKED my apron on the back wall and clocked out. My hair was pulled out of my ponytail so my strands could be free. One of the things I hated about working with food was having to keep my hair back. Most of the time, the restraint was too hard, and it gave me a headache. So, the second I could, I let my hair go free...even if there was a crease in it.

I left the room with my purse over my shoulder and headed to the door.

Damien was still there. His eyes followed my movements, and when he saw me focused on the door, he rose to his feet and got to the entryway first. He opened the door wide, acting like a gentleman. When he was out of the chair, it was clear how tall he was. I'd never noticed because he was sitting behind the desk during our first interaction. With one hand on the door, he stared at me as he waited for me to cross the threshold.

In defiance, I stopped and stared at him, annoyed by the chivalrous act.

My annoyance seemed to amuse him because he gave a slight smile that reached his eyes. He had very strong, masculine features, eyes full of warning and a jawline so sharp it could cut glass, but when he smiled like that, he had a boyish innocence.

I stepped outside and joined him on the sidewalk. "Thank you." I forced out the sentiment because it would be unacceptable to be impolite. I was annoyed that he was following me around, but at least he was being a nice guy.

Damien moved beside me and joined me on my walk to my apartment. He slid his hands into the pockets of his slacks, sticking out compared to all the casual people on the sidewalk. He looked like a man who didn't walk anywhere because he had a private driver at his beck and call. "Want a ride home?"

I stopped in my tracks and stared at him. "Damien, how can I help you?" I had only had one interaction with him that was strictly professional, and now he was trying to take me home. "I used your services at the bank under the assumption you would respect my privacy. Instead, you come to my place of work, and now you're walking with me as if we know each other. It's inappropriate." Maybe I was being harsh, but he'd abused his power.

With his hands still in his pockets, his body pivoted toward me, and he stared at me with a cold expression. His boyish charm was gone, and now there was a terrifying coldness about him. His eyes didn't blink as they looked into mine, and he held the silence like he thrived in it. "I've never done this before."

"Why don't I believe you?"

He slowly raised an eyebrow, and that serious expression deepened into a terrifying one. "I can get a woman anywhere, anytime. I don't need to follow a client like this to get a date."

"So, I'm supposed to be flattered?" I asked sarcastically.

"A little."

I rolled my eyes before I started to walk again.

Instead of that being the end of our conversation, he caught up with me. "Annabella." My name rolled off his tongue so well, so elegant when spoken in his masculine tone.

The sound got me to stop walking, but I didn't know why. "It's Anna."

He faced me again. "I prefer Annabella. Why would you want to shorten such a beautiful name?"

My mother had been the only one who liked to use my full name. Everyone else preferred the nickname. "I should get going. I'm already late."

His eyes darkened like he knew I was lying. "I know what you're going to say, but I'm going to ask anyway."

When he'd dropped by the restaurant, I was annoyed because Liam had done that so many times. He assumed if he pestered me enough times, I might change my mind. Seeing another guy do the same thing brought back all those feelings of frustration. I had to remind myself that Damien wasn't my ex-husband, that he couldn't possibly understand where I was coming from.

He paused as he stared at me, taking in my features for a full minute before he continued speaking. "Let me take you out."

I probably should have been flattered that a handsome, tall, muscular, rich guy came all the way down to my waitress job just to ask me out, but I wasn't in the headspace to be flattered. I was still a mess from my divorce and particularly bitter about it. I was in my midtwenties and already divorced—my life wasn't going well. "I'm not interested in dating right now." I thought about giving him more of an explanation, but that shouldn't be necessary. He knew I was divorced.

"Are you interested in fucking?" He asked the question with such confidence, it was obvious he had asked the same question before. With his straight shoulders thick and powerful, he held his body like a strong man who was nothing but muscle underneath that suit. He didn't even blink as he asked something so blunt, like he had said worse things in his life.

"You just said you have no problem getting women, so you don't need me for that."

He took a step closer to me, bringing our bodies just inches from each other. His green eyes slightly shifted back and forth as he looked into mine. "True. But you're the woman I wanna get."

I'd been with other men since Liam, casual rendezvous that were just about physical satisfaction. The first few were awkward because I was getting used to being with someone else besides my husband. The others were fine, but not great. The best I'd ever had was Liam, and I was disappointed I couldn't find anyone to replace him. Damien would probably be the same. "I'm not in the right place right now."

His eyes dimmed in disappointment. "I'm not asking anything from you. No expectations, no commitments, no explanations. I am kinda going through something myself...and I'm in a pretty dark place. I understand how you feel."

That was the first thing he'd said that actually intrigued me. I'd felt alone in this because I lost everyone close to me. I didn't have any friends, relatives... I was on my own. It would be nice to have someone...a friend. "You're divorced?"

"Pretty much."

"You're either divorced, or you're not."

"I said no explanations."

Now, I was more intrigued. "I may be bitter about my divorce, but I won't be with a man who's made a commitment to someone else. I won't be the other woman. That's nonnegotiable."

"Then we have no problem. I have no commitments."

I stared at him with slight confusion because I wasn't sure what I'd just agreed to. One moment I was walking away from him, and now

I was talking about a physical relationship I had somehow entered into.

"So, I can call you some time, Annabella?" He spoke in that same deep voice, looked at me with those same deep eyes. When he was serious, he was so potent I could feel his energy in my blood.

"Yeah...I guess. Let me give you my number."

"I already have it." He turned and walked away.

3

DAMIEN

I'd never chased down a woman.

Not once.

Most of the time, women came to me. Maybe they just wanted good sex. Maybe they wanted to be taken out to a place they could never afford on their own. Maybe they just wanted to make their ex jealous. Whatever the reason, they came to me.

Annabella was different. Cash and suits didn't impress her. She wasn't afraid to start over and get her hands dirty. So, I really had nothing to offer her, nothing that would catch her attention.

Until I told her I had my own problems.

It wasn't a lie, but it wasn't the full truth either. But if our relationship was just physical, I guess it didn't make a difference. Ever since she'd stepped into my office, I hadn't been able to stop thinking about her. A part of me wanted to help her. A part of me wanted to know all the details of her divorce. And another part of me just wanted to fuck her.

With Hades gone, I felt isolated. Sofia was my only other friend... but I'd burned that bridge. Every time I looked at her, I had to think about the asshole I despised. I already had to deal with him at work, so I didn't want to think about him a second longer than I had to.

It really did feel like a divorce.

We hated each other because there had been feelings there once...a long time ago.

I waited a few days before I called her because I had shit to do. The Skull King stopped by and wanted to have a conversation, but I wasn't going to crawl to him like some obedient servant. So, I was working a lot, preparing for that unexpected visit. With Maddox gone, I was running the city and the entire country. It was a lot of territory for one person, and I lost a lot of sleep because I was too busy making money. The bank was hectic too. It made me wonder if Hades could really handle it if I did step away.

I doubted it.

I sat in my office at the end of the day, leaning back in my chair. I dialed the number into the phone and stared at the screen before I finally had the courage to connect the call. I'd never been a nervous guy, even with a gun pointed at my head, but this woman made me nervous. She was different from the others, smart and independent. She was even different from Sofia.

It rang a couple times before she answered. With a deep voice that was soft as a rose petal, she answered. "Hello?" She possessed an innate level of professionalism, like a secretary. But there was always a hint of unmistakable sass. She didn't take shit, and she subtly gave off that vibe.

"Get a drink with me." I refused to state who I was because my voice did it for me. I wanted to see her tonight, to see her sit across from me with her beautiful long hair and a short dress. I wanted the night to conclude in my bed, but I was also fine if it didn't. My loneliness made me crave things that had never been on my palate before. My closeness with Hades gave me intimacy

I'd never needed from someone else. He was family to me, and even though he'd been gone a long time, the wound was still fresh.

"Depends. Who is this?"

"Annabella, you know who this is." I liked the way she could hold herself in a conversation without making a nervous giggle or saying random shit just to fill the silence. She was confident, and that was sexy. I imagined she was hit on all the time at work, that I wasn't the only one who'd waited for her to clock out and leave.

"Arrogant and demanding...I think I know someone who fits that description."

"And tall and sexy. You forgot those."

A quiet chuckle came over the line. "I can't hear those things."

"Trust me, you can." I could definitely hear her long sexy legs. I could hear her silky hair. I could hear her smooth skin under my soft lips. "You want me to pick you up? Or do you want to meet there?"

"Presumptuous..."

"No. Presumptuous would be me telling you to come over right now." It would be ideal if she came over and we got straight to the point, but I didn't mind a night of conversation. She was so pretty, it would be foreplay.

"I'll meet you there."

I'd rather her not walk there alone, but I knew I couldn't be suffocating like that. If this was casual, I had to act casual. "Alright. I'll see you soon." I gave her the name of the bar, hung up the phone, and left my desk. When I stepped into the hallway, I wished I had picked a better time because Hades and Sofia were about to pass by.

Hades had her hand in his as he guided her along, tall and proud and always protective. He knew I was standing there, but his eyes remained forward as if he didn't know I existed.

Sofia was the only one who looked at me, and she gave me a sad smile like she didn't know what else to do. I'd been an asshole to her last time we spoke, so she wasn't very warm to me. She looked at me in acknowledgment but didn't actually say anything.

I stared back and watched them walk away.

WE SAT TOGETHER at the bar, side by side on the stools.

She had elegant posture and held her back perfectly straight with her legs crossed. Black heels were on her feet, and she wore a short black cocktail dress. Her hair wasn't constricted in a ponytail. It was big, luscious, and all over the place. It was in curls like the first time I saw her. She possessed a lot of features that were beautiful and intoxicating, but something about her hair really turned me on. It wasn't just the length or the shine, it was something else altogether. Or maybe it was everything combined.

She ordered a gin and tonic when she'd first arrived, which surprised me. She seemed like a woman who would order red wine or some shit like that. But she ordered a stronger drink, something I might order depending on my mood.

I wasn't much of a talker, so I spent my time staring at her, mesmerized by all the perfect features of her face. I tried to remember the last time I'd seen a woman this beautiful, but I couldn't recall. Maybe that occasion never existed.

She tilted her head back and took a drink before she set down the glass again. "You stare a lot."

"You're easy to stare at." I grabbed my scotch and pulled it closer to me but didn't take a drink. I'd been drinking too much these last few months, and I constantly kept canceling my doctors' appointments because I didn't want to be told that my liver was dying.

She turned her attention back to me and stared at me with the same intensity. "See how it feels?"

"I think it's hot."

She smiled slightly before she turned back to her drink.

Since I didn't want to interrogate her about her divorce, I didn't have much to ask her. Her walking into my office and demanding to be removed from his accounts was the only shared experience that we had. I'd be lying if I said I wasn't interested in the details. If they were divorced and he still wanted her to have his money, that could only mean he'd fucked up. He probably cheated, but that didn't make sense because why would a man cheat on a woman like that? "How do you like your new apartment?"

"I like it a lot." She rested her hand over the top of her glass, as if she were afraid someone would spike it if she looked away for a few seconds. "I got a good deal on it, and it's close to work. It's not in the best neighborhood and it's a little small, but it has everything I need."

I didn't like imagining her in a dangerous area, so my initial impulse was to buy her a beautiful place. But that would offend her, and it would be totally inappropriate on my end. I didn't even know this woman. It didn't matter how many billions I had; I shouldn't spend any of it on someone I hardly knew. "What are your plans for the future?" I assumed she didn't intend to be a waitress forever, but I didn't want to ask her what other skills she had because that would make me sound like an ass.

"What kind of question is that?" She turned back to me. "What are your plans for the future, Damien?"

I took a drink before I answered. "The same shit I always do. Work." I didn't have much of a life, but that had never bothered me until recently. I used to work, fuck, and then do it all over again. It was satisfying...until Hades left. Now, I was alone all the time, tortured by my guilt and regret. "To be honest, I don't have a lot in my life. I don't have a lot of friends or family. I'm a slave to my job."

Instead of judging me, her eyes softened. "I don't have anyone either."

My other hand rested on my thigh, and there were times when I wanted to reach out and rest my fingers against her knee. I wanted to touch her like she was mine, but she was different from other women, so I couldn't do those things. "I find that hard to believe. You're a lovely person."

"Even if that's true, it doesn't matter. After my divorce, people took sides. And of course, they sided with him."

Why would they do that if he was in the wrong? Maybe she was the one at fault after all. "Why did they choose him?"

"He's the one with the money." She rolled her eyes and took a drink.

Since she didn't elaborate, I didn't pry.

"The bank closes at five, so I'm surprised you have to work so much. Don't you own it?"

"True. But I have a second job." If her husband used our services at the bank, he wasn't a clean-cut guy. He must break the law in many ways. She was either aware of that or completely in the dark. The fact that she didn't want his money made me wonder if his criminal activities were the reason she was opposed to it. If she knew I was a drug dealer, would she walk out right now? I didn't want to lie, but I didn't want to ruin this before we even had a chance.

Thankfully, she didn't ask. "I might have to get a second job too, but I'm sure my reasons are different from yours."

"What did you have in mind?" I could get her a good job somewhere with a nice salary, but I suspected she would reject my offer.

Maybe after we got to know each other a little better, she'd be more receptive to it. I could tell this woman was too proud to take a handout. I admired her for it even though I didn't like it. But the thing that surprised me the most was myself. Why did I want to help her at all? Why did I care?

"Maybe bartending." She turned on her stool, and her knee gently grazed mine. She had beautiful tanned skin that didn't possess a single flaw. Her body was toned like she did weights or some other form of exercise. "Maybe stripping."

Both of my eyebrows rose up my face. "You'd be a damn good stripper."

She chuckled slightly at my reaction.

"I'd be in the front row every night."

She chuckled again. "I'm kidding. My ex-husband would march in there and drag me out by the hair."

I wasn't sure how long they'd been divorced, but I was surprised he still felt involved in her life. "You don't seem like the kind of woman that would let that stop you."

Her smile faded away, but her eyes had a new look. They softened like warm butter. She took me in with an expression she hadn't given me before. "I could use the money...but not the headache."

"You could strip for me...privately." I smiled so she knew I was kidding...even though I wasn't kidding.

That pretty smile was back, and her shoulders relaxed now that she was growing more comfortable around me. She ran her fingers through her hair and pulled it from her face. I noticed the way her fingertips glided through the curls so easily.

I wanted to do the same thing.

"Truth is, I don't have a lot of work experience. I got married too young and didn't work for years. I'm basically starting over."

"You're still young and have plenty of time to do anything you want. Question is, what do you want to do?"

She considered the question in silence, swirling her drink as she tried to find an answer. "I really don't know. Right now, I'm just looking for a stable job that pays the bills."

"I always have positions at the bank...if you'd be interested in that."

Thankfully, she wasn't offended by the offer. "That's sweet, but no thank you."

"You could be my secretary...or sex-retary."

"You already have a secretary."

"But you're way sexier." I winked at her.

Even when she laughed, she was beautiful. Her lips parted, and all her beautiful teeth were visible. Her eyes crinkled in the cutest way. "I don't think that's a very good qualification."

"Depends on what you're trying to get done. Having a beautiful woman in my lap is far more important to me than expense reports, meetings, all that boring bullshit." I could visualize it now, her dress riding up and exposing her slender thighs as she straddled my hips.

"Sounds like you wouldn't be in business long."

I shrugged. "I do have my other job, so..."

She grabbed her glass and took another drink, this time finishing it off. She didn't ask me about my other occupation, and this time, it seemed purposeful.

"You want another?"

She pushed the empty glass away. "No. I've already had two. That's my limit. Any more than that and I lose my mind and think I'm a wizard."

I chuckled. "I'd like to see that. I have a wand for you to use."

She smiled slightly at my joke. "Thank you for not asking a million questions about my divorce." Maybe the alcohol had suddenly hit her hard and made her vulnerable. When I'd shown up at her restaurant, she had been a spitfire of anger and sass, but now she was calm and interesting...the way she was at the bank. "Every time I go out with a guy, they fixate on that. They ask me a million questions, and it feels like an interrogation."

"You can tell me as little or as much as you want." I had to admit I was curious, but I was glad I hadn't asked. It seemed to make her more comfortable around me. I hadn't looked into her husband's account to figure out what he did or what he was like. I thought it might make me jealous, so I refrained. "I would like to know how long you've been divorced, but you don't have to tell me that." It seemed like it was fresh because she was still on his account and she'd just bought her own place, but she talked about other men, so some time must have passed.

"It's been six months."

I could barely control my reaction. That was a long time, and I was surprised she wasn't able to get herself off his account until recently. Why hadn't she gotten her own place before now? A million questions came into my mind, but I didn't ask any of them.

"What about you?"

It'd been a long time since Hades said he wanted nothing to do with me, at least eight months. I'd expected him to come around at some point, but he was just as cold as ever. Every time I saw him, it seemed to get worse. His hatred only grew, and my resentment matched. "About eight months."

She nodded slowly. "It's rough."

Hades wasn't a lover or a spouse, but he was my closest friend. He was family. When he couldn't forgive me, part of me died and never came back. My regret turned to rage, and I became so cold that I felt like I had ice in my veins. I understood how she felt when she said she didn't want to talk about her divorce, because I didn't want to talk about him.

She studied my face. "I can see it in your eyes."

I stopped trying to control my expression and realized how black my heart had just turned. I focused on her face and felt my fingers grip my glass. "See what?"

"Everything."

4

ANNABELLA

HE PAID THE TAB, AND WE LEFT THE BAR.

I tried to pay for my drinks, but he threw down a wad of cash and wouldn't let me go near my clutch.

I didn't fight the money dance for long because I knew Damien would win, and I really didn't have that much money to spare—not that I would tell him that. I had way too much pride to act broke. He probably would never have known if he hadn't seen my bank account. I guess it was a bit flattering that he knew I had nothing, but he still wanted to be with me. He wasn't afraid I would only be interested in him for his money.

We stepped outside onto the deserted sidewalk. It was late, far later than I usually stayed out, but the drinks and good conversation made me lose track of time.

"I just live a few blocks from here. I can walk."

He stood in front of me with his hands in the pockets of his pants. He was dressed casually in jeans and a t-shirt, but the outfit was far sexier than the suit. In the short sleeves, his strong arms were visible, the muscles and the veins under the skin. He also had a beautiful tan, as if he ran outside in the mornings. His strong chest was also noticeable under the fabric because it stretched the shirt in perfect ways. His pants were low on his hips but tight on his muscled thighs. It was obvious he had a perfect body with an eight-pack and an enormous chest without even taking off his shirt. "We both know how this is gonna end."

I raised an eyebrow at his assumption. "Meaning?"

"I'm gonna walk you home or drive you home. Or, and this is my preference, I take you to my place. I can interview you to be my new secretary. What do you say?" He tilted his chin down slightly to look at me because of our height difference. His facial features were just as hard as the rest of his body, with sharp cheekbones, a jawline with a shadow of hair, and kissable lips. He was handsome enough to pull off lines like that.

I'd be lying to myself if I said he wasn't hot.

He was super hot.

He was the perfect amount of serious and playful. And while he invaded my space sometimes, he also respected my privacy and my boundaries. He could make me laugh too...which was really sexy. I was curious to see what would happen if I did go to his place, if the sex would be as good as I hoped it would be. I missed satisfying nights, when I would go to bed and know it would end well. I suspected he was good in bed, which was exactly what I was looking for right now.

But it also felt too soon.

I'd had one-night stands before, slept with a guy I'd just met, but since I actually liked Damien, I didn't want to mess it up. "You can walk me home." I looked at his face to see if he was disappointed.

He wasn't. "I have one condition."

I crossed my arms over my chest. "I'm not going to be your secretary."

A boyish smile came over his face. "I get to kiss you."

A gentle thrill moved up my spine.

"I'm talking about when a man kisses a woman...a real fucking kiss." He maintained his confidence as he stared at me, building up the kiss without fear of it being a letdown. "You're gonna ask me to come inside, but I'm gonna say no. Like, that good of a kiss."

"You sound awfully sure of yourself."

"Because I know what I'm doing."

"Then why don't you want to come inside?"

"Because that wouldn't be fair. I know I can change your mind, but I don't want to change it that way. It's like spiking your drink, you have no chance."

The more I got to know Damien, the more I liked him. His confidence was a turn-on because it wasn't arrogance. He danced on that fine line and never swayed. "Alright. I accept your condition."

"Good. Let's go."

———

HE LEFT HIS CAR BEHIND, and we walked the few blocks to my apartment. He kept his hands in his pockets and didn't wrap his arm around my waist or try to hold my hand. He didn't make small talk either, letting the silence linger between us.

The closer we got to my apartment, the more my heart began to race. I imagined how this kiss would be, if it'd make my toes curl and my skin bubble with bumps. I wondered if it would be a slow, deep kiss, or would it be a kiss of urgency, where he would take me from zero to sixty in one second. Where would his hands be? In my hair? On my waist? Would he push me into the door and pin me there? Would he really get me to beg him to come inside?

I would know soon.

My apartment was on the second floor, so we took the stairs then approached the front door. My clutch was tucked under my arm, and I didn't reach for my keys because I knew I wouldn't need them for a while.

I got there first then turned around to look at him.

He was just as self-assured as before, no hesitation in his gaze. He slowly moved into me as he pulled his hands out of his pockets. His gaze dropped and looked at my lips, the target of his desire. Without moving his gaze, he grabbed my clutch and slipped it into the back of his jeans so I wouldn't have to hold it.

My heart began to race inside my chest, and my fingertips immediately went numb. I could feel my nipples harden against the fabric of my dress because I wasn't wearing a bra. My breathing became uneven, shaky and unpredictable.

He moved closer into me, bringing his face nearer to mine without actually kissing me, without actually touching me. He held his position and stared at my lips, the world silent around us.

He actually made me nervous.

His hand moved to my cheek, and his thumb rested against my jaw. He gently tilted my face up so my lips were accessible to his. There was a long pause before he did anything, a buildup before the fall.

He finally inched closer and rested his lips against mine. It was a gentle landing, a combination of our soft mouths aligning. It was a handshake of our lips, a sensual meeting of our bodies.

He held our lips together as his fingers gently stroked my cheek. He breathed into my mouth as he felt the same spark of electricity burst between us. He opened his eyes and looked at me before he kissed me again, this time his embrace more purposeful than the last. He really felt my lips this time, felt the shape of my upper lip, felt the softness and the fullness.

Then he moaned quietly.

It was the sexiest sound.

The kiss had barely begun, and I was already weak.

His kiss continued, slow and deliberate, moving up and down, exchanging lips and breaths. He eventually gave me his tongue, and that was an erotic surprise. He was just as good with that as he was with his lips, never giving me too much or too little.

His fingers slid into my hair, and he fisted it like he wanted to control me, to get a grip so I could never get away. He slowly backed me up into my door, so I was cushioned between his hard body and the wooden surface.

I could taste the scotch on his tongue, feel the desire of his hungry lips. I stopped thinking about my life, how little I knew him, and just gave in to the feelings he incited within me.

My hands went to his chest first because that was the part of his body I desired the most. I liked a strong man, a man who had a brick wall for a chest. My fingertips could feel just how solid he was. He was bulletproof.

I kissed him harder as I got swept away by desire. My hands became excited and slid underneath his shirt so I could feel his solid abs. At first, I didn't know what I was feeling because he was so hard. It was warm skin with mounds and rivers of muscle.

Now, it was my turn to moan.

My hand glided up his back, feeling the powerful muscles that made his body so strong. I moved to his shoulder then dug my nails into his skin, slicing and cutting because I was so excited.

He pressed me harder into the door and kissed me with more ferocity. His tongue was more aggressive, as if he'd lost control of the most sensual part of his body. He wanted to reach the inferno burning in my soul, to let the sparks catch him on fire and consume him until he was ash.

Damn, this was one hell of a man.

His fingers latched on to my hair like a cowboy gripping the reins of an obedient horse, and he overtook me with more power. He angled my chin exactly where he wanted, gave himself full access to everything he desired. He cherished my bottom lip, moved to my top, and then gave me his eager tongue.

If he fucked as good as he kissed...I was a lucky lady.

He pulled his delicious lips away from mine and looked at me in the shadow of the hallway as if somehow we weren't in public where a neighbor could pass by. Our surroundings changed like a mirage, and we were in my bedroom, the glow from the bedside lamp the only light to highlight that strong jawline, those dark eyes.

Time stopped, and all I did was stare, lips slightly parted with anticipation. My nails loosened against his back, apologetic for their previous aggression. I could stare at this man all night, fascinated by the perfect features of his face. I was in the presence of flooding testosterone. The scent filled my nose, the presence permeated the hallway, the taste was sugar on my lips.

I held my breath.

Without taking his eyes off mine, he grabbed the back of my knee and raised my thigh. He positioned me harder against the door so it would support me as he wrapped it over his hip. His confidence never wavered, and the silence before the boom didn't make him uneasy. I was one of a hundred, maybe a thousand, but he somehow made me feel like the only one who counted.

He cocked his head slightly as his eyes dragged over my face, appreciating my looks like he found me as beautiful as I found him. His fingers dug into the skin of my thigh before he leaned in again.

And took my breath away.

His kiss was slow and seductive once more, as if he wanted to slow the speed of this racing train. He wanted to appreciate every caress, every sound of breath that escaped our lips.

My fingers slid into his short hair, and my body turned into loose rubber bands. All the tension left my body, and I stopped thinking entirely. I just felt every touch, every heated breath, every single thing this man gave me.

He pressed his body farther into me, and I felt it...

His fat dick.

It was thick, long, fucking perfect.

"Oh wow..." I spoke into his lips as I felt his proud package, felt how hard he was for me, imagined all the things he could do with that special gift.

He smiled slightly against my lips as he continued to kiss me, his hand tugging on my hair in a seductive caress. His hips started to move, and he ground against me, pressing the thick shaft of his dick against the area that ached to feel it the most.

Yes.

He fucked me in the hallway through our clothes. He made love to my lips with his. He brought me to my knees without letting me fall. He made good on his promises, unleashed his solid threats.

Now, I wanted to take him to bed. Not let him leave until sunrise.

My dress rose to my waist, and I ground back against him, huffing and puffing like a horny teenager. My fingers tugged on his hair, and I rolled my hips to feel his dick at the perfect pressure.

Our heated moment lasted fifteen minutes. It felt like a lifetime but also a nanosecond at the same time.

He was the first one to pull away.

Good. Because I probably never would have.

His gaze was intense like burning coals. He watched me with hesitation, like he didn't want to leave but forced himself to step back. Now, he was even sexier, thoughts of the two of us clearly written on that hard expression. He fixed his jeans discreetly.

I glanced down so I could get a glimpse of that monster cock.

There was a noticeable stain on the front...from yours truly.

When he raised his gaze, there wasn't a smile on his lips, but there was definitely a pleased look in his gaze. This evening had played out exactly how he'd imagined, from the first kiss to the dry hump against the apartment door.

When I'd walked into the bank that afternoon, I had been too stressed to really notice his appearance. I knew he was attractive, but he was also just another suit. When he showed up at the restaurant, he annoyed me even more, because he behaved just like another entitled suit. But after tonight, I saw him in a different light, appreciated every inch of his height, every soft curve of his lips, every drop of confidence. "I guess you keep your promises..."

He stilled in front of me, those pretty green eyes shifting back and forth between mine. His countenance was stern and he was motionless like a mountain, but he could convey so much with the subtle shifts of his face, from the way his jaw tightened to the way his eyes dropped to look at my lips. "Always." He pulled the clutch out of his back pocket and handed it to me. "Goodnight, Annabella."

My weak fingers took the purse without watching what I was doing. My eyes were obsessed with his masculine features, with every perfection he possessed. Silence stretched between us, and I suddenly imagined that t-shirt on my body tomorrow morning.

He continued to linger.

I didn't know what he wanted, so I continued to wait.

The corner of his mouth rose in a slight smile, and he reached for my clutch. He fished for my keys inside before he grabbed my wrist and placed them inside my open palm.

My fingers slowly closed around them when I realized what he was waiting for.

He nodded to the door.

Disappointed that he hadn't changed his mind, I stuffed the clutch under my arm and shoved the key into the door. After working the lock, I got the door open and stepped inside. I tossed the clutch on the table in the entryway before I turned around.

He was gone.

5

DAMIEN

"When can you take care of it?" Vince sat across from me in the booth in the bar, dressed in a dark blazer over a V-neck. Every few minutes, a woman in a tight skirt would walk by, and he would grow too distracted to carry on the conversation. After a blonde passed, he turned back to me.

"Depends. When can you get me the money?"

He rolled his eyes before he took a drink. "My partner is stubborn."

"He's gonna be more stubborn if you make this deal behind his back." I'd learned that from personal experience with Hades. I'd made a lot of stupid mistakes, mistakes that no apology could erase. "If this is gonna work, we need transparency."

"It's hard for him to trust people."

I extended my hand and glanced at the drinks. "We're having a clandestine meeting at one in the morning. Those trust issues could be legitimate." I didn't want to do business with someone when I had to spoon-feed their partner at the same time. I didn't have time for that shit. "Let's meet again. Bring him this time."

After a few more words, he excused himself and left the booth.

My drink was still half full, so I wasn't going anywhere until every drop was gone. The second I was alone, I got lost in the loud bass from the speakers, and my mind drifted to the beautiful brunette who stole my soul right from my lips. She tasted as sweet as she looked...and now I wanted to explore the warmth of her neck, the hollow of her throat. I hadn't called in days because I'd gotten busy. But I also knew she wasn't interested in a clingy pussy either.

I could see a man approach my table out of the corner of my eye, his massive size casting shadows in the already dark club. His large hand placed a glass of booze on the table before he slid into the leather booth.

I kept my expression neutral and didn't seem surprised by his unexpected visit. It was my fault for letting my guard down by wondering about Annabella's perfect curves, fantasizing about those full, red lips.

Now, I paid the price.

Deep blue eyes pierced mine. Full of warning, unmistakable threat, a horde of demons, he was the man of nightmares. He relaxed in the seat with his fingers loosely gripping the glass in front of him. He cocked his head slightly as he examined me, full of indifference but also intrigue.

The Skull King.

I'd evaded his grasp for years because of our mutual interest in avoidance, but I knew my time was up.

"We haven't officially met." He shook his glass so the cubes tapped against the sides. He glanced at the glass without taking a drink then lifted his eyes to mine once more. He was identical to his twin brother, carrying the same muscularity, possessing the strength of a Clydesdale. "Heath."

"I can already tell I prefer Balto."

A slow smile crept onto his lips. "Not the first time I've heard that. Must be doing something right." He finally took a drink, his thick throat shifting as he got the fire into his belly. His eyes stayed on me as he dropped the glass back onto the table.

"Or something wrong." I wasn't easily intimidated. Maybe that would be my downfall someday.

He shrugged. "Time will tell."

I kept up my relaxed posture and held his gaze with a bored expression. "Something I can help you with?"

"You know why I'm here, Damien." He placed one arm over the back of the booth, his fingers slightly curling into a fist.

The Skull Kings were the gatekeepers, keeping the various factions of the underworld in line. He collected royalties as payment, a percentage of the total profit of the business. He expected me to pay my due, but that wasn't gonna happen. "And you know you aren't getting a dime from me."

Like this was funny, he smiled. "I disagree. You and Hades are past due."

"Hades is out. It's just me."

"That's too bad. Give him my best."

I took a drink to moisten my mouth.

"I like you, Damien. Don't make me torture you until you cave. Don't make me kill you if you choose to be stubborn."

"You don't know me. If you did, you wouldn't like me."

He continued to smile. "You're right. I'm starting to like you less..."

"It's not gonna happen, Heath. You expect to be paid for a service— and I've received no such service."

"You have no idea what goes on behind the scenes."

"But I do know that Maddox destroyed my business before he destroyed my life. Where were you?"

His smile disappeared.

"I asked you a question."

After a long pause, he answered. "We were in transition…"

"I don't care about your excuses. You weren't there, so I'm not paying for a fictional service."

He gently tapped his fingers against the glass. "I'll cut you a deal. I'll consider your overdue balance a wash. We'll start fresh now."

I smiled because it was ridiculous. "There was no overdue balance. I didn't owe you shit, so you weren't going to get paid anyway. And asshole, I'm not gonna pay you now. Maybe you can push around your smaller clients, but you can't push me around. I've absorbed Maddox's business and his men. I'm unstoppable—we both know it."

That sinister smile was back. "That's a bit arrogant."

"Heath." My tone darkened. "I'm not paying you. Not now. Not ever. So, get the fuck out of my face."

His smile faded, and his blue eyes darkened like the deepest part of the ocean. He straightened in his seat then leaned forward, bringing an intimacy that was sharp as a knife. "You just won a war. But now you're tired and weak. You don't have the strength to fight again. The money is nothing to you, so take the easy way out."

"You could ask for a euro, and I'd still give you the same answer."

He relaxed into the booth again. "You're proud. I respect that. But it's not worth your life, Damien."

"You're right. It's not worth my life—and it won't be worth my life."

His expression didn't change. "I'll give you some time to think about what I said." He grabbed his glass and finished it off before he slid out of the booth. "But trust me, our next conversation won't be so civil."

I STEPPED into Hades's office first thing in the morning.

He was sitting at his desk, a large piece of mahogany wood with a picture frame on the corner. It was Sofia kissing Andrew, her face glowing with motherhood. A vase of flowers was on the coffee table, his wife's touch, obviously. She'd added a few pieces to the room to make it cozier.

In a black suit, he was reading a document in his hand, probably studying the investment performance from the day before. When he finally noticed my frame in the doorway, his gaze lifted to meet mine. Indifference and annoyance mixed together to form the customized expression he made just for me. "What?"

I felt like a bug on the bottom of his shoe, a disobedient child he didn't know how to punish. It cut me to the bone—every time. "There's a new Skull King." I shut the door behind me and walked to his desk.

He wore the same bored look. "Alright."

"Balto has a twin, apparently."

He set the document down and leaned back in the chair.

"Said we owed back taxes. When I refused, he—"

"We?" The derision was heavy in his tone. "No." He straightened in his chair then pointed his index finger at me. "*You*. You owe him back taxes. This is your problem, not mine. You have to solve it on your own."

I could never accept his coldness. It seemed to get worse and worse, like his hatred festered into resentment. "I thought you should know. Because I can tell he's not gonna go away."

"Did you tell him I'm no longer part of the business?"

I nodded.

"Not my problem." He grabbed the document again and started to read.

I continued to stand there. "What an ass I am, warning you."

He looked at me again. "There's nothing to warn me about. You're the one who's in charge of that bill."

"And you were the one who refused to pay it years ago," I snapped. "It seems like you conveniently forgot."

He put the paper down again. "Then pay him, Damien."

"No."

He sighed loudly. "What the fuck do you want from me? I don't give a shit what you do with him. If you go head-to-head, I won't have your back. If he comes to me and asks me to hand you over, I'll do it in a heartbeat." He rose to his feet and pushed his chair back. "So what the fuck do you want from me?"

My chest rose and fell with the heavy breaths I took. The adrenaline was in my veins, and I was eager to reach for the knife inside my jacket. I wanted to stab him right in the neck and watch him bleed and die. I hated this man, hated him so fucking much. "Nothing. Not a damn thing." I headed out the door.

"Asshole."

I had no idea why the fuck I turned around.

"Talk to my wife like you did again, and I really will hand you over on a fucking silver platter."

I LIVED in a three-story place in Florence. It had its own parking lot and a private gate. I was just one man so I didn't need the space, but I did need the privacy and protection. I never used the other rooms in the house, sticking to the bedroom and my private gym. I had a maid who handled the kitchen, so I never set foot in there.

Now I sat in my living room with a glass in my hand. My dinner tray was on the table, only partially eaten because Hades had demolished my appetite that afternoon. *Scarface* was on the TV, and all I could think about was shooting that asshole with a tommy gun until his guts spilled out.

Piece of shit.

My phone sat on the armrest of the couch, and it started to ring.

Annabella.

I hadn't spoken to her in a week, not intentionally. Life got busy, and I barely had time to sleep, let alone invite her over. Not to mention, I just wasn't in the mood. I watched it ring and kept my hand steady.

If I answered, I would just be an ass.

I was in a dark place, and I was drunk. Bad combo.

It went to voice mail.

I watched the TV again.

My phone lit up with a text message. *Did that stain come out of your jeans?*

I read the message three times because I couldn't believe what she'd just asked. Brazen, unexpected, shocking…it was fucking hot. When I'd gotten home, I noticed the circular stain on the front of my jeans, the arousal that soaked through her panties and transferred to me. I'd taken them off and smelled the spot before I jerked off.

I grabbed the phone and wrote back. *Why would I wash them?*

You're going to walk around with that stain forever?

Damn right.

She sent an eye-rolling emoji.

I knew I should call her because it looked like I was hiding behind my text messages. After her candid message, I was in a better mood, but I was still bitter as hell. But I'd rather look like an asshole instead of a coward. I called her.

She answered after a few rings. "Took you long enough."

Her bluntness was refreshing. Never had to wonder what she was thinking. "You caught me at a bad time." I reached for my drink and held it in my grasp.

"Are you busy right now?"

"No. Just had a rough day." I put the movie on mute but watched the action sequences anyway. The bloodshed was just as potent without the sound.

"Oh." When she realized I wasn't in the greatest mood, she turned quiet. "Want to talk about it?"

"Not really." I didn't want to dump my personal bullshit on her. I hardly knew her.

"Alright..."

It became silent. Awkward. Now I regretted making this phone call. "I'll talk to you later, alright?"

"Um, okay." She faltered for a moment before she spoke again. "Bye, Damien." She hung up without waiting for me to say goodbye.

I cringed as I lowered the phone. She'd called at the worst possible time, and I should have just ignored her. Or I should have called her sooner instead of waiting for an entire week to go by.

Goddammit.

6

ANNABELLA

DAMIEN BLEW ME OFF.

I didn't know what happened. He was so hot for me, and now he was ice-cold. Did he meet someone else? A woman who slept with him right away? Maybe I was too much work and he lost interest.

I shouldn't care...but I did.

I'd started to really like him.

But he was a jerk like the rest.

I needed to forget about him, to pretend like he hadn't hurt me, to pretend I wasn't devastated that our kiss would never turn into something more. I'd been fantasizing about him all week, imagining him between my legs, while I took orders at the restaurant. I couldn't get him off my mind at all. It was the first time I was actually excited about a man since my husband.

But I'd been wrong.

Whatever.

I was home in my pajamas when there was a knock on the door. I was enjoying a bottle of wine in front of the TV when the hard knuckles echoed against the wood. I knew the sound belonged to a man, so I assumed it was Damien.

Maybe he'd had a change of heart.

I jumped to my feet and checked myself in the mirror.

Ugh, I looked like shit.

I fixed my hair as much as possible, but there was nothing I could really do. My makeup was off, and my shirt had a wine stain on the front. It was my worst look.

He knocked again.

"Ugh," I whispered under my breath.

I headed to the door and pulled it open, in a sour mood that Damien had picked the worst time to show up at my door. I wasn't in the mood to hit the sheets when I looked like trash. I opened the door and gave my best smile.

When Liam watched me smile at him, his eyebrows furrowed. "I'm surprised you answered the door."

Liam was the last thing on my mind even though he was the most logical person to show up on my doorstep. "I wasn't expecting you." I pushed the door closed.

He stuck his boot in the crack so I couldn't shut him out.

Dammit.

He pushed the door back open and helped himself inside. He was muscular and over six feet in height, so he forced me to back up with his enormous presence. He stared at me with intense blue eyes as he invaded my apartment. "Then who were you expecting at this time of night?"

A beautiful man with lips from heaven. "Not you." I turned around and moved farther into the apartment. Now I was glad I looked like shit so he would lose interest and leave, even though he'd seen me without makeup thousands of times.

He stopped in the entryway and surveyed the area. He glanced at the wine bottle and the bowl of popcorn. His hands slid into the pockets of his jeans, and he turned his gaze back on me. Heartbeats passed, and he said nothing. In dark jeans and a tight t-shirt, he looked just as fit as ever.

"Please leave." I stood near the door to my balcony with my arms crossed over my chest. "I'm tired of repeating myself."

He tilted his head down slightly and continued to stare. "I'm tired too."

I waited for him to walk out.

"I'm tired of living without you."

I couldn't stop myself from rolling my eyes. "It didn't seem like you were thinking about me much when your dick was in someone else." Like a snake, venom was in my mouth. I wanted to bite him and let the poison sink into his flesh. It'd been a long time since our relationship had fallen apart, but I hadn't let go of my bitterness yet because he kept showing up everywhere. He wouldn't let me go, and that forced me to deal with the past over and over again.

He cringed slightly at the insult. "It was a lapse in judgment."

"Lapse in judgment?" I hissed. "The situation is black-and-white. You either cheat on your wife, or you don't. Doesn't need much judgment."

He sighed. "She meant nothing to me."

"Yet she was worth ruining your marriage."

He bowed his head. "I'm sorry. And I'll be sorry for the rest of my life. I made such a stupid fucking mistake, and I would do anything to take it back. You know I mean that." He stepped toward me.

"Come near me, and I'll smash that bottle of wine into your nuts."

He stilled. "Anna..."

"I'm done talking about this. I divorced you because we're never getting back together. Let me go."

He dropped his gaze then scanned the apartment, as if he was looking for a way out of the mess he created. "I love you... I will always love me."

"That's not good enough, Liam. You were disloyal, disrespectful, and dishonest."

He shook his head slightly. "You never would have known if I hadn't told you."

"Doesn't fucking matter." I raised my hand and pointed to the door. "Get out. Now."

He stayed rooted to the spot.

"Liam."

"Give me another chance—"

"Never."

He took a deep breath before he kept talking. "I can provide for you. You like living in a shithole like this?"

"Wow...fuck you."

He didn't apologize. "I can take care of you. I can provide for you. I can protect you. There's no other man out there who can give you what I can."

Damien popped into my head even though there was no reason for him to. "That's not what I'm looking for in a man."

"Anna, I love you," he whispered. "And I'll spend the rest of my life earning your forgiveness. I would never do that shit again. I know how shitty it feels to lose you, and I never want to go through that again. Please."

Sometimes I believed he was truly sorry. It'd been months since I'd left, but he was still trying to get me back. He was a sexy, rich man. He could have anyone he wanted, so if he was still trying, I must be the only thing he wanted. Being single was rough because it was impossible to find a man who made me feel something...and wasn't a jerk or bad in bed. Sometimes I wanted to cave just so my life could be easy again.

But I didn't want to settle. "Please leave." This time, I turned my back on him and stared out the back window. Sometimes when I looked at his face, I pictured him with that mysterious woman, pumping into her the way he used to pump into me. It still made me sick to my stomach.

Instead of arguing, he did as I asked. The last thing I heard was the gentle click of the door when he walked out. Then he was gone.

7

DAMIEN

After I finished at the bank, I went home and walked into my bedroom. My jacket was stripped off my shoulders and tossed onto the bed before I grabbed my phone and called Annabella.

Went to voice mail.

I tried not to assume she was blowing me off. I was a jackass to her last time we spoke, and she seemed like the kind of woman that wouldn't put up with nonsense. So maybe she did ditch me.

Or maybe she was just at work or something.

I hoped she was at work.

By the end of the night, she still hadn't called me back. So I caved and texted her. *Still haven't washed my jeans.*

Nothing.

I was just about to leave the office when a guy in a suit stepped inside. With a tight face coupled with rage, he seemed pissed. He was a big guy, my size and height, so a fight could easily turn into a brawl.

I opened my top drawer and quickly grabbed my loaded gun.

"This is the guy?" The stranger stopped in front of my desk, flashing a fancy watch and a ten-thousand-euro suit.

Hades emerged behind him. "Yes, this is my business partner, Damien—"

"Leave us." He barked orders like he owned the place.

Hades glanced between the two of us before he walked out, shutting the door behind him.

I kept the gun concealed under the desk. "Something I can help you with?"

He continued to stand. "You took my wife off my account?"

Both of my eyebrows rose because I had no idea what he was talking about. "How about you sit the fuck down and start over? Because I have no idea what you're talking about."

His fingers quickly snapped open the button of his coat, and he lowered himself into the chair, calmer but filled with restrained rage.

"Good." I held up the gun. "Now, I don't have to shoot you." I returned it to the top drawer.

He glanced at the gun but didn't react.

I leaned back in the chair and opened my arms. "You were saying..."

He had brown eyes the color of hot espresso, and his muscular frame indicated he had a private weight room in the convenience of his home. If he was a client, then he must be worth billions, but I had no idea who he was. "You took my wife off my account, and I'm not happy about it."

"Who's your wife?" I asked, pulling out my keyboard.

"Annabella De Luca."

I froze at the mention of the name, recognizing it instantly. It was the name of the woman who was constantly on my mind, the name of the woman who dumped me the second I stepped out of line. It'd been two days, and she never responded to my message. She didn't deal with bullshit, which was sexy, but I wished she understood it was just a misunderstanding.

He noticed the way I flinched. "Now, you know exactly what I'm talking about."

I pushed the keyboard back because I didn't need it. I turned my chair forward again and faced him head on. "She's a client. When a client asks me to do something, I do it." Jealousy filled my veins when it was unfounded. I'd ground her into a door and gave her a kiss that left a permanent scar on my lips. It wasn't enough to feel possessive or entitled. But that made me hate this guy anyway. Hated the fact that he wasn't some fat, old guy. He was handsome, fit, and had a spine.

"Good. I'm your client, and I'm telling you to put her back on."

I held his gaze and felt my heart race.

He continued to stare at me, his eyes colder than mine.

Now I knew why I didn't recognize him. He was a client who had belonged to Hades. The only reason he'd stormed in here was because he realized I'd cut the last chain that bound him to Annabella.

"You deaf?" His tone darkened, containing a thinly veiled threat.

"She's just gonna come back in here and ask me to take her off again."

"Then I'll put her back on again."

This asshole wasn't gonna let her go. They'd been divorced for six months, and he was still possessive over her. "That doesn't sound like an effective use of your time."

He cocked his head slightly. "Don't concern yourself with my time. Just do as I say."

I still didn't turn to the keyboard.

His eyes narrowed. "You've got a little crush on my wife?"

More than a crush. I wanted to be a dick and tell him I made her pussy soak onto my jeans, that she wanted me to come inside and fuck her, but I held my ground. That would turn into a gunfight, and it would also jeopardize my relationship with Annabella. She wouldn't respect me if I didn't respect her privacy. "She's not your wife."

That was his undoing. He rose to his feet and buttoned his jacket again. "What the fuck did you say to me?"

"She's. Not. Your. Wife." I got to my feet too, leaving my gun in the drawer because I didn't need it.

This man wasn't used to being challenged; that was clear. He probably got whatever he wanted at a snap of a finger.

Well, so did I. "I'm not putting her back on the account. I have better things to do than deal with an asshole who tries to control a woman who doesn't want him anymore. She dumped you. Get the fuck over it."

His eyes narrowed with a spark of fire. "You're brave."

"Bravery implies I have something to be scared of." I looked him up and down. "I'm not scared of you."

He stepped closer to the desk. "Keep talking, and I'll walk. I'll take my money elsewhere."

"Good. I don't need your money, bitch."

His face turned red at the disrespect. His eyes shifted back and forth with hostility, his mind deciding if he wanted to stab me or walk out the door. He processed his rage in silence, his nostrils flaring.

I didn't blink.

His fingers reached for his jacket, and he unbuttoned it so it opened once again. Then he turned around and walked out. "You'll regret this, motherfucker."

I watched him go. "I doubt it."

I CALLED ANNABELLA AGAIN.

Went to voice mail.

Her feelings toward me were very clear.

She was blowing me off.

God-fucking-dammit.

I could throw in the towel and move on. Women were never in short supply, and I had the charm and money to get anyone I wanted. A trip to the bar would end with a woman on my arm. Then in my bed.

But that wasn't what I wanted.

I wanted Annabella.

I went to her apartment and knocked on the door, a bottle of gin tucked under my arm. I tapped my knuckles against the door and hoped she was home and not out with some other guy. She'd probably been hit on three times in the last week. There was nothing to stop her from saying yes.

No answer.

I knocked again. "Annabella." The sound of my voice wouldn't encourage her in the least. If anything, it probably annoyed her that I'd shown up on her doorstep after she'd made her disinterest perfectly clear.

I hoped an explanation would fix that.

To my surprise, footsteps sounded against the hardwood inside as she approached the door. After the audible sound of turning locks, the door cracked open and she showed her face. There was no beautiful smile. No joy in her eyes. She was like the Great Wall—a slab of concrete. "Can I help you?"

I wasn't going to get inside unless I charmed my way in. I held up the bottle of gin. "Thirsty?"

She glanced at it, a bit intrigued.

I shook the bottle. "It's the good stuff."

She stared at the bottle for a second before she shut the door and unlocked the chain.

Yes.

She opened the door, grabbed the bottle from my hand, and then shut the door in my face.

Damn. I knocked on the door again. "You can't drink that all by yourself."

Her voice sounded through the door. "Bet your ass, I can."

"No one likes to drink alone."

"I disagree."

"Annabella, come on." I knocked again. "I wanna talk."

Silence.

"I'll stand out here all night."

She opened the door and handed me a glass of gin before she shut the door again.

I stared at the glass and chuckled. "Sexy and funny...I like it."

Flattery worked, and she opened the door. With one hand on her hip, she nodded for me to come inside.

I followed her and set the glass of gin on the counter. She was in lounge clothes, wearing pajama shorts and a black spaghetti strap top. Her hair was in curls around her face, and her makeup highlighted her beautiful features. She stood leaning her hip against the counter and took a drink. She was more beautiful than I remembered, so I couldn't help but stare. Her long, tanned legs were the most hypnotizing of all her features. Lean, toned, and a sexy golden color, they were flawless.

"You wanted to talk?" She took another drink.

I got lost in her features and didn't realize how long I'd been staring. "Yeah..." Now I wished I'd taken a drink to cool my nerves. I wasn't easily intimidated, even when a big-ass guy was telling me off, but her beauty, humor, and intelligence made me quiet. "Don't blow me off."

She set her drink down before she crossed her arms over her chest. "I'm not. I just don't like to waste my time."

"I'm not a waste of time." I blurted out the words without thinking, desperate to change her mind. I left my drink behind and came closer to her, reaching the empty space between the kitchen and the living room. "You caught me on a bad night."

Her eyes were glued to mine, forbidding towers blocking her entire perimeter. "You didn't call all week, and when I did call you, you seemed annoyed. If you aren't into me, that's fine. If you think I'm a bad kisser or a bad lay, that's fine. I really don't care about your opinion because another man would be happy to take your place."

So sexy. If only more women were that confident. She made her statement without breaking eye contact with me, not the least bit intimidated. "Trust me, I know." There had been one in my office that afternoon, gripping her as tightly as possible so she wouldn't slip away for good. "I was swamped that week, and then shit hit the fan. I'm not playing games."

Her arms loosened on her chest as her defenses came down. She must have seen the sincerity in my eyes, must have felt it in the energy in the room. "I'll give you the benefit of the doubt. But that's only because I like you."

I couldn't stop the smile from spreading across my face. "I know. My jeans told me."

She smacked my arm playfully, a suppressed smile on her face. "Jerk."

I chuckled then circled my arms around her waist. The affection was instinct, like my hands knew what they wanted to do before my brain realized it. My hand flattened against her lower back, and I tugged her to me, bringing our faces close together.

Once I could feel her warmth, smell her perfume, all playfulness evaporated. I could see the beautiful color of her blue eyes, the way they sparkled like sapphires in the sunlight. There were a couple freckles on her cheeks, but so small they were hardly noticeable. With a perfect complexion and the sexiest set of lips, she was like a collectible doll.

Her back arched at my touch, and her hands immediately went to my chest, her body reacting to mine in the same instantaneous way. Her breath halted in her chest, and she stared at my lips like she wanted to rekindle that heated night in her hallway.

I wanted to kiss her, but I was paralyzed by the intensity of the moment. There was so much electricity in the simple touch, so much ecstasy as our lungs held our breath. The air burned with chemistry like two chemicals that exploded the moment they came into contact. I was the fire, and she was the gasoline. A quick splash and I was an inferno.

Her hands slowly slid down my chest as her chin dipped to the floor. She stared at my body while her fingers mapped out my pecs and abs. Her fingers pressed harder into me, wanting to feel every groove that my large muscles created. As if I wasn't even there, she explored me through my clothes.

It was hot...watching her touch me like I belonged to her.

She lifted her gaze once again, her lips slightly parted as if she was anxious for a kiss. Her fingers moved to the hem of my shirt, and she grasped the material with anxious fingers before she slowly pulled it up.

I read her desires and pulled it over my head. It fell to the tile of her kitchen floor.

Her eyes moved back to my physique, admiring the strength of my muscles as they swelled against the skin. Her fingers moved back to my sternum, feeling my chest and then my beating heart.

I watched her want me, watched her fantasize about me. I'd seen that look in a stranger's eyes before, but it never meant anything until now. It was never so flattering, never so powerful.

She moved into me and pressed a kiss to my chest, right below my left nipple. She looked up at me as she did it, displaying the most seductive stare. Her tongue made light contact with my skin, moist and warm.

Jesus.

That was all it took. I was hard in my jeans and already imagining those little shorts on top of my shirt. I wouldn't hit the brakes on the heat tonight. If she wanted me, she could have me as much as she wanted.

She could have all of me.

My hand slid under the fall of her hair, and I tilted her face to create the perfect landing for my lips. I commanded the attention of her gaze, and when I had it, I pulled her in tighter and kissed her.

Kissed her hard.

My lips consumed her at first touch, picking up exactly where we'd left off. My fingers tightened on her dark hair, and my hand fisted the fabric of her t-shirt. Our mouths were motionless as we felt each other, feeling the fire rekindle deep in our bellies. I inhaled her breath before I kissed her again.

Her hands planted against my stomach, and she felt my bare skin. She dug into me, holding on to my muscles like they were ridges on a cliff face. Her lips were as hungry as mine, eager for lips and tongue. She whispered through our kiss, showing an innate vulnerability that was so sexy. "You're so hot…" Her eyes opened to look into mine, but they closed again once they were filled with a dreamy gloss.

My mouth devoured her top lip with purposeful heat, feeling the silky softness before I gave her my tongue.

She took it like she wanted it more than anything.

I wondered if she would take my dick with the same enthusiasm.

I gripped her shirt then pulled it over her head, loving the way it caught her hair and pulled it high above her head. When it fell down again, the strands scattered along her shoulders in the perfect way, like fresh powder on the front lawn at Christmas.

She was naked underneath.

And damn.

Small, perky tits were the targets of my gaze, rosy nipples that were pointed straight ahead. They were firm, perfect in their roundness. I liked all shapes and sizes when it came to tits, but there was something especially appealing about these. My hand immediately cupped one, my thumb flicking over the hard nipple.

She moaned quietly as she closed her eyes.

I backed her up to the kitchen island then lifted her onto the surface so her height was comparable to mine. My hand cupped the back of her neck, and I leaned into her to kiss those perfect tits, to kiss that beautiful skin that ached to be sucked.

She leaned her head back and gripped me as she enjoyed the kiss. Her legs wrapped around my waist, and she dug her fingers into my hair, moaning and groaning like she was living out her ultimate fantasy.

I was her fantasy. She was mine.

I lowered her back to the surface of the island then tugged on her shorts as I kissed her flat stomach. My tongue dived into her belly button as my hands got the shorts to her knees. They fell the rest of the way on their own.

Logic was gone. All that was left was emotion, lust, desire...

I grabbed her sexy pink thong and pulled it down her long legs.

Her pussy was ready for company even if she wasn't. Perfectly groomed and glistening with arousal, she was prepared for me, and she hadn't even seen my dick yet. A nice nub sat above a pink slit, the most perfect pussy I'd ever seen.

My arms scooped her legs apart, and I bent down to taste that slit, to properly introduce myself before my dick slid inside. I cherished her sweetness, every drop of arousal that dripped from her entrance to get ready for me. Unlike most guys, I didn't mind going down on a woman, especially when they looked like Annabella. My testosterone made me eager for every inch of a woman, from the back of her neck to the tips of her toes. In sex, I gave it my all, a hundred percent.

But I was giving a hundred and ten percent for her.

She moaned loudly in the kitchen and jerked at my unexpected touch. Her fingers dug into my scalp, and her hips vibrated at my intimate touch. She inhaled a deep breath, her high voice full of pleasurable surprise. "Oh..."

I kissed her cunt with the same passion as I kissed her mouth. Every embrace was purposeful, feeling each of her lips and then her little clit. When I slid my tongue inside her, I could feel how tight she was.

I could tell the sex would be good.

She had the enthusiasm of a virgin but the experience of a woman.

When I righted myself, she sat up quickly and grasped my belt. She yanked it loose then popped open the button. Her fingers pushed down the zipper before her hands clutched the denim. Then she shoved them off with the same aggression.

They fell to the floor, and my boxers followed immediately afterward.

She halted at the sight of my dick, like an innocent woman who had never seen a man in his purest form. She stared for several seconds, the hollow of her throat shifting at the sight of me. "Wow..." Her voice escaped as a whisper, and without a hint of shame, she lifted her gaze to meet mine.

She didn't play games. She was easy to read, her eyes like words on a page. She'd loved and lost before, so she had nothing to lose now. She'd been married and had her heart broken, so there was no need to play it cool. She liked what she saw and told me that.

If only her husband could see me now.

He might actually kill me.

We moved past the kitchen to her small bedroom. It held a queen-sized bed and a single dresser. The entire apartment was about a thousand square feet, a modest place compared to the palace she'd probably lived in before.

We got to the bed, her lithe body underneath mine. When her head hit the pillow, she looked up at me as she licked her lips, her hands caressing my chest with soft fingertips. She opened her thighs on her own then pulled me close to her, telling me exactly what she wanted, how she wanted me to fuck her.

Jesus, I liked this. A lot.

My condoms were in the pocket of my jeans in the other room, and now that my fat shaft was sliding against her wet pussy, I couldn't move. This gorgeous woman was completely open to me, her tits firm and ready to bounce, her lips anxious for my kiss.

She saved me from the painful experience of leaving. "I have some in my nightstand."

I wondered how many men had been here before me, if she enjoyed her newfound single status by fucking as many guys as she wanted. She wouldn't have a stash of condoms for any other reason. But I reminded myself that I shouldn't care. If she weren't looking for hot sex, I wouldn't be there right now.

I grabbed one and rolled it on before I positioned myself on top of her once more.

I was so eager to fuck her, I didn't even know where to begin.

Had I ever been with a woman so beautiful?

If I had to think about it, the answer was no.

My fingers pressed against the base of my dick and pointed it downward so I could slide into her wetness. It was tight but so easy to get inside because our foreplay had thoroughly prepared her. I sank slowly, pushing against her walls as I made my way deep inside, groaning like a horny teenager the entire way.

She did the same. When she had all of me, she looked at me with a heated gaze as if I were a god.

Her god.

Both of her hands gripped my ass and pulled me a little harder, getting the last inch I didn't think she'd be able to handle. She winced slightly in pain, but it was clear she wouldn't want it any other way.

Jesus.

She started to rock on me first, telling me she was perfectly fine with the pain from my size.

This woman would be the death of me...one way or another.

My arms were pinned behind her knees, and I thrust my hips as I pushed and pulled my dick in and out. Even with the muffling sensation of the condom, hers was the best pussy I'd ever had. I could feel the tightness of her channel, feel the lack of friction because of her juice. My eyes watched her expression as my gentle thrusts became more forceful, as her headboard started a gentle tap against the wall.

"That's so good..." Her tits shook with my motions, her nipples still hard from desire. She bit her bottom lip, her eyes squinting closed when the pleasure pulled her under. Her nails started to sink into my flesh, like knives carving flesh.

She'd better not expect me to fuck her long if she was gonna act like that.

Like the sexiest thing in the fucking world.

I wanted to kiss her, but I was working too hard to steady my breath. Minutes passed, and my skin turned slick from the sweat. I could feel it form on my chest, feel the way her hand would slip as she tried to hold on to me.

When she was about to come, she grabbed my ass with one hand and guided me at the speed she wanted. She wanted it fast, but she wanted it deep. She wouldn't let me pull out because she wanted each inch inside her while my body ground against her clit. "Yes... I'm gonna come." Emotion escaped in her broken voice, as if she couldn't believe this miracle had arrived. She didn't want anything to interrupt it, so she told me what was coming so nothing would sabotage it.

As if I'd ever leave her hanging.

Not that kind of man.

"Annabella." I loved saying her name, letting all those vowels roll off my tongue. It was a profound name, fitting for a woman with her sass. "Take your time. I'm not going anywhere." My dick was in check, and my mind was focused on the race, not the finish line.

Her hands slid up my chest to my neck, and she cupped my face as she breathed hard in pleasure. Her hips rocked with mine, and she kissed me with trembling lips. Her pants were filled with moans. Her nails were filled with flesh and sweat. She breathed into my mouth, each breath growing farther and farther apart.

And then she came.

Her lips stopped kissing mine so she could scream instead. Her pleasured moans hit me right in the face, her warm breath washing over me. Her head tilted back onto the pillow as her hips bucked uncontrollably. Her hand smacked down onto the bed beside her, and she clutched the sheets until they nearly tore. "Yes...yes." Tears formed in the corners of her eyes and streaked down the sides of her face until they vanished into the pillow. It was a powerful performance, enough to really make me feel like a god.

My ego exploded.

When her high started to dwindle, she came back to me, her arms hooking around my neck so she could kiss me in gratitude.

As if she owed me anything.

Baby, it was a pleasure.

She kissed me as she continued to rock her hips, her channel softening now that the sensation had passed. "God..." Her nails dragged down my back, tracing the muscles on either side of my spine.

Fuck, I wasn't gonna last long. Not after that.

"Now, you." She grabbed my shoulder and rolled me onto my back.

I wanted to tell her I had no problem coming missionary, but if she wanted to bounce on my dick, I sure as hell wasn't going to discourage that.

She straddled my hips then sank down my length, sliding to my balls in one quick motion.

I closed my eyes and moaned. My back was on the sheets, and one foot hung off the edge of the bed. My eyes took in the sight of the beautiful woman on top of me, her legs spread to take my dick, her back arched so she could grind her clit against me. Her small belly extended slightly, but I liked the curve.

Then she rode my dick like she was the queen of my cock.

She planted her hands against my hard stomach for balance and rolled her hips over and over.

Jesus-fucking-Christ.

I propped myself up on one elbow and grabbed her hip with the other, wanting to feel her body move as she worked to please me. I saw the way her skin gleamed from my sweat that had transferred to her body. Her tits bounced in the most erotic way, up and down with her thrusts. My fingers spread apart, and my thumb moved over her stomach, feeling the muscle tighten before it released.

She pressed her hand against my chest and leaned over me,

trusting that I was strong enough to support her. Her eyes locked on to mine, her hair fell down, the ends landing on my chest and shoulder, and her lips parted like she was about to moan in her own ecstasy. "Come with me."

I closed my eyes as my body instantly shuddered. My cock obeyed her command like he was his own man. He twitched before release.

And then erupted.

She moaned with me, like she was coming at the same time, her pussy squeezing my cock as it thickened in release. Her forehead rested against mine as she felt the high, as she was exploding with the same euphoria that set our nerves on fire. "Yes..." She ground her clit hard against me until her high started to dissipate.

I moaned so loud I didn't recognize my own voice. It was so good, the kind of orgasm that made me see the stars. Sex wasn't even this good when I paid for it and stated exactly what I wanted. It was the kind of pleasure that made me breathless. The kind of pleasure that humbled me...because I'd lived over thirty years without experiencing it before.

Damn...where had this woman been all my life?

8

ANNABELLA

I LAY IN BED BESIDE HIM, THE SHEETS WRAPPED AROUND MY BODY UP to my chest. My bedside lamp was on, and the bed was a mess from our rendezvous. Instead of hightailing it out of there right away, he lay beside me, his muscled chest peeking out from underneath the sheets. We were both tired, both immersed in the endorphins our bodies released after all the orgasms.

I studied his perfection. Even when he was relaxed, his stomach was so tight, the muscles strong at every hour of the day. His wide chest was made of two enormous bricks. There were scars on his skin, long scratches that looked like knife wounds, but the blemishes added to his sex appeal.

The man was so damn hot.

And sooo good in bed.

There were so many times I had been left hanging in the past. Men would satisfy themselves and wouldn't even bother trying to make up for their quick climax. They would leave and I would take care of myself, but that wasn't nearly as satisfying.

Damien wasn't like those jerks.

When I turned to look at him, his eyes were already on me.

Green eyes were set in a handsome face, deeper than a well and full of mystery. His masculine features were always hard, as if he could turn angry at any moment. But when he was calm like this, he was just intense...manly.

I was annoyed with his previous behavior because I was sick of men acting like boys. I didn't want to be misled. I didn't want to be lied to. I just wanted a man who was straight with me. Damien seemed to be playing games. But I'd given him another chance because he was so hot and made me laugh.

I was glad I did.

Didn't know men could fuck like that.

He held my gaze without blinking, as if an entire conversation were passing between us. His hand reached out to me and slid into my hair, his fingertips gliding past my soft cheek. They moved to the back of my neck, where he gently massaged me. The touch was so simple and easy but so sexy at the same time.

I closed my eyes because it felt so right.

His fingers continued to touch me, continued to explore me. He was all muscle and testosterone, but he could touch a woman with a caress as soft as a rose petal. His hand was enormous compared to my cheek, large enough to crush my face if he lost his temper. But that intimidating strength somehow made me feel safer.

His fingers trailed to my chin, and his thumb gently tugged on my bottom lip before he pulled his touch away.

A man had never made me so hot with so little.

He moved his hand behind his head and continued to watch me.

I slipped out of bed and grabbed a t-shirt from my drawer along with a fresh pair of underwear. Then I walked into the kitchen and made two gin and tonics. I returned to the bedroom and handed one to him.

He smiled slightly, one side of his mouth rising above the other as he stared at my offering. He accepted it with his large hand and took a drink. When he finished, he licked his lips. He gave me a slight nod in appreciation.

I sat up against the pillows at the headboard with my body pivoted toward him. My knees were bent, and my feet were tucked close to my ass. My glass returned to my lips, and I let the alcohol numb my tongue before it moved down my throat.

He scooted back against the headboard, sitting up with the sheets still around his waist. He didn't get dressed, as if he had no intention of leaving.

Good. Because I didn't want him to go anywhere. "You're a really good lay."

He stared into his glass like he was about to take a drink. That soft smile returned to his lips again, but he never got the gin in his mouth. He raised his chin and looked at me. "A man is only as good as his woman."

"His woman?"

"Yeah." He took a drink then set the glass on his thigh. "If a woman is beautiful, sexy, enthusiastic...he's gonna work pretty hard if he wants to fuck her again."

"You want to fuck me again?" I asked bluntly.

He held my gaze without flinching. "I did a good job, right?" His deep voice was like an ocean tide across my ears.

It'd been so long since there'd been a real man in my life, and Damien's masculine presence was exactly what I craved. My ex-husband had his faults, but he was a good man...for the most part. Damien was the first man who'd brought that excitement back into my life. It was probably just a mixture of attraction and lust, but it was exactly what I was looking for. "Five stars."

Even when he chuckled, it was sexy. "Did you just review me like an Amazon product?"

I shrugged. "At least you got a perfect score."

"True." He drank from his glass before he set it on the nightstand. "Does that mean you'd recommend this product to other customers?"

"No." I spoke my answer candidly.

He raised an eyebrow.

"Because I want you to myself."

His gaze hardened into that intense expression that was inherently sexy. He didn't flinch at my bluntness because he knew I wasn't looking for a serious relationship, just a good dick between my legs. "You can have me whenever you want."

"Good." I scooted closer to him on the bed so our skin came into contact. "The other guys I've been with act like hot shit, but they have no idea what a clit is."

He kept up his stare without saying anything for a while. "The guys you've been with since your divorce?"

I nodded. "They are either clueless or selfish. They get off and then walk out like they're God's gift to women." I rolled my eyes. "And then I finish when they're gone..." My hand moved to his arm and felt the large muscles underneath the skin. "But that's not you." I didn't want to let this guy go. I wanted him on my speed dial, the guy I called for all my physical needs. Why search for someone else when I already had the perfect man?

He continued to watch me with that same intense stare, his thoughts a mystery behind his masculine veneer. He hardly needed to blink, never flinched at the intimacy between our locked eyes. "You're right." His hand slid to my knee, and his callused fingers gently caressed the skin. "That's not me."

When he'd ambushed me at the restaurant, I was annoyed with his forwardness. Now I considered that day to be the most magical one in recent history. A sexy man chased me until he got the answer he wanted. Now I was beside him, the loneliness and frustration replaced by joy and satisfaction.

"Your husband wasn't good either?"

I flinched slightly at the personal question.

"You don't have to answer."

I was fiercely private about my life, but if Damien was the man in my bed, it was unrealistic to keep everything a secret. Besides, I had nothing to hide. "No, he was. No complaints. That was what made being single so hard."

His fingers continued to stroke me. "Then why did you leave him?"

"Why do you assume that?"

His eyes looked me over. "There's no way a man would walk away from you—unless he's gay."

Liam hadn't walked away, but he'd done something worse...he'd betrayed me. "He slept with someone else." The truth still left a bitterness in my mouth. I'd always worked hard to be a good partner. I watched my diet, stayed fit in the gym, and showered him with constant affection. I was spontaneous in the bedroom, surprising him with lingerie and handcuffs. I wasn't perfect...but I put our marriage first.

Damien didn't react in any way, as if he'd been expecting that response.

"Picturing him with someone else is painful on so many levels. But the disrespect is what bothers me the most. The betrayal is so insulting…his lack of loyalty." I stared at his hand on my knee as the flashbacks played across my eyes.

He nodded slightly. "You're partners. He should always put you first. That means honesty, integrity, loyalty…all of the above." His fingers continued to touch me. "But he's probably not smart enough to understand all of that. Otherwise, he wouldn't have messed around in the first place. If he comes home to you every day and still wants someone else…something is wrong with him." His hand moved to my neck, and he brushed the hair from my shoulder. "Look at you."

I wasn't shy, but that statement made me blush. The gentle touch of his fingers made bumps form on my arms. My heart raced a little faster when I felt his heat transfer to me.

"Don't take him back." His thumb brushed across my bottom lip. "He doesn't deserve you."

My eyes lifted to his. "What makes you think he wants me back?"

His eyes stayed focused on mine, his hard cheekbones making his expression naturally sinister. "Just a hunch…"

———

I KICKED off the sheets at three in the morning.

I was warm, sweat on the back of my neck. My eyes opened, and I saw Damien beside me, lying there with his hand on his hard chest. When he was deep asleep, his chiseled jawline was relaxed, and he didn't seem so intense. The shadow on his jawline seemed more noticeable, even though only a few hours had passed.

I should just go back to sleep, but now I couldn't.

How could I sleep when a beautiful man like that was beside me?

The heat of my body mixed with the desire between my legs, and before I knew it, I was moving onto his chest. My legs straddled his hips, and I kissed his immobile lips. I was purposely disturbing his sleep for my own selfish reasons, but I couldn't get enough of him, couldn't get enough of the fire he ignited across my entire body.

He inhaled a deep breath when he felt me, his hands moving to my hips before he squeezed me. His eyes opened, and he watched me kiss him, the realization quickly coming into his gaze. His mouth started to move, and he kissed me like he was wide awake, his hand moving into my hair as he rolled me onto my back. "Annabella..." He spoke my name with the sexiest tone, so much affection and desire packed into the name I'd had my entire life. He gave it a whole new meaning, made me feel sexy with just the sound of his voice.

I held on to him like we hadn't spent the evening screwing in this bed. I wasn't just hungry, but starving. I wasn't just lustful, but desperate. Damien brought my body to life, thawed the ice around my heart, and made me hot like summer sun.

He kissed my neck as he pressed me into the bed with his large size. He grabbed me savagely, holding on to me like he was insane with longing. He pushed my shirt up my body so my tits could be free and then yanked my panties off like he couldn't get me naked fast enough.

I couldn't get him inside fast enough. "Hurry," I whispered between our kisses, my fingers clawing his back.

He got the condom out of the nightstand, rolled it on, and slid inside me with a sharp thrust.

I moaned against his mouth as I locked my ankles together around his waist. "Oh yes..." My nails clawed at his back, and I felt my pussy clench around him, rejoicing at his return. "Fuck me, Damien." I started to tug on his body, showing him how I wanted it. I didn't hesitate to tell him exactly what I wanted, didn't feel insecure issuing orders like a drill sergeant.

He seemed to like it. "Yes, Annabella..."

THE NEXT MORNING, I woke up alone.

He'd slipped out before my eyes opened. He didn't say goodbye, walking away like a cliché. I preferred my dates to leave once the fun was over, but I didn't mind Damien sticking around. That was probably why I was disappointed.

I got out of bed and headed to the kitchen.

Damien sat at the small dining table with a hot cup of coffee in front of him. He was dressed in the outfit he'd worn the night before, a dark t-shirt with his denim jeans. His hair was less messy, like he'd fixed it with his fingertips in the bathroom. He was absorbed in his phone, his thumbs quickly typing a message.

I felt the smile creep onto my lips as I grabbed the coffeepot and poured myself a mug.

When he heard me, he set his phone down and looked up. The shadow on his jawline was more prominent in the natural light flooding through the open window. Steam evaporated from his mug and drifted to the ceiling. He stared at me with a controlled expression, taking in my features as if it were the first time he'd really looked at me.

I sat across from him. "You're still here."

"Disappointed?"

"No. The opposite."

He smiled slightly before he took a sip of his coffee.

"You seem like the kind of guy to slip out first thing in the morning."

His eyes remained trained on me. "I am."

"Then why are you still here?"

He held up his mug. "The coffee."

I rolled my eyes even though I knew he was just teasing me.

"And the company." He rested his elbows on the table and leaned forward slightly, like we were talking over the loud noises in a restaurant.

"You aren't late for work?"

He shrugged. "I work when I feel like it."

"Must be nice." I showed up to my shifts right on the dot, and I still barely made enough to get by. I couldn't afford to ditch work just because I'd had a long night.

He didn't respond.

It was nice to sit with him without the pressure of a conversation. There was a natural comfort there, like we were friends. My mind wandered to our night together, focusing on the instant when I woke him up just to screw. He hadn't seemed to mind, at least.

"What are your plans today?"

"I work in the afternoon. You?"

"I'm working all day and all night."

I knew he had his hands in several businesses, but I never asked him personal questions about it. My ex-husband had always been possessive of his money and how he earned it. He didn't keep secrets from me, but he didn't talk about it much. I knew Damien's bank laundered a lot of his money, so I assumed Damien wasn't a clean-cut guy either. "You seem to work a lot."

"Wasn't always that way. I lost my partner recently."

"Oh...I'm sorry."

"He didn't die," he said quietly. "He decided it was time to walk away."

My curiosity was getting the best of me. I wanted to know more about him, especially since I'd become infatuated with his performance in the bedroom. It was only natural that I wanted to know more about him. But I also reminded myself his career choice didn't matter much. I wasn't looking for anything serious, so I didn't have to worry about getting mixed up in trouble. "What kind of business is this?"

He stared at his coffee as he considered his answer. It was hard to read him, but it seemed like he didn't want to respond. Seconds passed before he lifted his gaze to give me his full attention. "Drugs."

I stared at him blankly because I didn't know what response to give. I didn't live a sheltered life full of rainbows and unicorns. I knew the underworld was full of horrors, and on the spectrum, Damien's business was on the tame side. He made a product and sold it, and that product wasn't a person. And it really didn't matter anyway, because I wasn't looking for a new husband.

He watched my reaction. "I was hoping you wouldn't ask."

"Why?"

"Because I don't want you to run away. And I can't lie."

"You can't lie?"

He shrugged. "Not who I am."

His drug operation was slightly disappointing, but he quickly made up for it with that response. He could have made up something, and I would have had no idea if he was telling the truth. But he gave the real answer, even if that meant I kicked him out the door. That was an unusual quality in a man...and a sexy one. "I respect that."

Relief moved into his gaze. "This last week was hectic. I had a lot of shit to deal with. That's why you didn't hear from me. But trust me, I was thinking about you." He leaned back in the chair, his heavy shoulders relaxing.

"If you're stretched so thin, why don't you sell one of your businesses?"

He considered the question for a long time. "I've put too much into each one just to walk away."

Liam was just as ambitious. There were many nights when he never came home. Now I wondered if he had really been working in all those instances. Trust had been incinerated, and I wasn't sure what was real and what wasn't. "Why were you in such a bad mood when I called?"

He paused again, as if this question were even more difficult than the first one.

"You don't have to answer that."

"It's fine," he said quietly. "I got into a fight with someone."

I knew he had recently left a relationship, so I wondered if his ex was the person who pissed him off. Did he see her a lot? Was she involved in his business at the bank?

He elaborated when I hadn't expected him to. "I fucked up pretty badly and lost someone. Anytime we're together, it's like another world war. I apologized a million times, but it didn't make a difference. Now I'm bitter...angry."

Now I wondered if he'd been married too. "Did you cheat?"

His eyes glossed over as he recalled a distant memory. When the question registered in his brain, he shifted his gaze back to me. "No. I've never been committed to someone before."

Instead of asking him to clarify the instance he referred to, I fixated on the statement he'd just made. "You've never been in a serious relationship?"

The glaze left his eyes, and he looked at me again. "No."

I wanted to interrogate him about that, but I thought it was inappropriate. We were sleeping together, but it was causal, and I really didn't know him that well. If I didn't want him to ask me a million questions about my divorce, I couldn't pry either. So I sipped my coffee and didn't say anything.

He stared at me expectantly, as if he was waiting for a dozen questions. When it didn't happen, he grabbed his phone and checked the time. "I need to get—"

Someone knocked on the door.

You've got to be kidding me.

Damien stilled then looked at me.

I knew who it was. I'd gamble my life on it.

"Anna." Liam pounded his fist into the door. "Open the fucking door, or I will."

I'd gotten lucky in the past, and Liam had never visited when I had dates over. Most of the time, I went to their place, so that erased the problem altogether.

Damien stared at me with the same fixed expression, his look hard and unreadable.

I couldn't let Liam see Damien. He'd beat him to death... I wasn't exaggerating.

Damien didn't seem concerned about the man pounding on my door. "I can handle it." He rose from his seat.

I threw myself over the table and pushed him back down. "Oh my god, no."

He fell back into the chair, visibly disappointed.

I had nothing to hide and I wasn't ashamed of Damien, but I knew

Liam would lose his shit if he saw him there. "I'm so sorry to ask this...but could you wait in my bedroom?"

Both of his eyes narrowed. "I'm not afraid of him."

"That's not why I'm asking."

Liam pounded on the door again. "Anna!"

Damien's eyes darkened as he listened to my ex-husband practically rip my door off the hinges. "Let me handle this for you."

"No." I kept my voice at a whisper. "I appreciate it, but it'll just make bigger problems for me."

He clenched his jaw tightly. His hand rested on the table, and his fingers tightened into a noticeable ball.

"I'm not ashamed of you. I'm not trying to hide you."

"Seems that way."

"He's just... Please."

He stared at the desperation in my eyes and finally released a sigh. He slammed his hand onto the table then dismissed himself to my bedroom. He shut the door quietly, but he obviously didn't want to.

I felt terrible.

I went to the front door and twisted all the locks so I could open it.

He barreled inside with rage in his eyes. "You took yourself off the account?"

I knew he was going to figure it out eventually. His next statement would show he was the sole holder of the account. He might have even gotten a notification that I'd left. "Yes."

"What the fuck, Anna—"

"We aren't married anymore." I was sick of having this same conversation over and over. I wanted to move on, start over, but he refused to let that happen. "We're divorced. Do you understand that?"

His lips were pressed tightly together, and his eyes burned with dark fire.

"I'm moving on with my life, Liam. That means I don't want your money. I can take care of myself."

Liam looked around. "You live in a dump, Anna. You're a waitress who barely makes a living—"

"Still better than being married to you."

His jaw slackened, but his eyes looked devastated.

"It's over, Liam. You need to move on."

His chest rose and fell at an increased speed as his hurt eyes took me in. "It's still my responsibility to take care of you. Together or apart."

"It's not..." Sometimes I got so angry with him, but I had to remember he was a good man...despite what he did. This was just hard for him, even though he'd had plenty of time to get used to the change.

"You didn't take any of my assets in the divorce. You didn't take alimony—"

"Because I don't want it, Liam. All I ever wanted was you."

He closed his eyes as if that comeback stabbed him through the heart.

"You need to stop showing up like this. It's inappropriate."

He opened his eyes again. "You don't take my calls."

"Because you shouldn't be calling me, Liam. And that's my right."

He stepped back and ran his fingers through the back of his hair.

The vein in his forehead was popping because he was so livid. He was used to getting whatever he wanted, and if he couldn't, he physically fought for it.

"I'm seeing other people." I'd never directly told him before because I assumed he already knew.

He closed his eyes once more, this time, his jaw clenching in agony. He dragged his hand down his face and took a step back, so furious that he didn't know how to bottle the rage.

I said it because it was true. I didn't want to hurt Liam, but he needed that push to finally move on. And I also wanted Damien to know I wasn't keeping secrets either.

When Liam righted himself again, his eyes moved to my closed bedroom door.

Shit.

After a heartbeat, he started to move.

I grabbed him by the bicep, gripping the enormous muscle before I tugged him back. "No."

He twisted out of my grasp.

"Liam." I didn't raise my voice, but my tone was full of promise.

He came back to me, but his eyes kept glancing at the door. He was livid when he had no right to be.

"You're seeing other people too."

"I haven't." His eyes darted back to me, his tone barking. He challenged me with his gaze, as if he dared me to accuse him of lying. "And I'm not going to. We can make this work. I believe we can—"

"Liam." I pressed both palms against his chest. "It. Is. Over." He was the one who'd thrown us away, the one who'd broken my heart, the one who made me cry every night. But I still felt like shit doing this to him, being so cold and heartless. "Move on. I already have." My features wanted to slacken because it was so painful to say that to him, to hurt him when I knew he genuinely loved me. But I had to be cold, fierce. Otherwise, he would be stuck living on hope.

He took a deep breath as he held my gaze, devastated by the knife I'd just stabbed into his heart. His gaze dropped for an instant, searching desperately for something to say, but when he couldn't find the words, he stepped back. My hands slid down his chest as he headed to the door. He didn't look at me again before he walked out.

I stared at the closed door for several heartbeats, feeling guilty when I was the one who hadn't committed the crime. It'd been six months since I'd signed those papers, so he had enough time to come to terms with the finality of our divorce. He couldn't keep showing up on my doorstep like he had the right. He needed that devastating blow to finally move on, to know there was a man in my bedroom who had slept over the night before.

If I saw him with someone else, it would bother me. Of course it would. But I would bottle my feelings and accept the inevitable.

The bedroom door opened a moment later, and Damien slowly walked into the room. With his hands in the front pockets of his jeans, he approached me with empty eyes. He glanced at the door as if he expected Liam to return before he looked at me. He was the strong and silent type, so he didn't say much in general. He didn't say a lot now. "You alright?"

I nodded. "Yeah...I'm sorry about that."

He shook his head. "No need to apologize. I don't blame the guy, honestly."

I crossed my arms over my chest.

"If I lost you, I'd be devastated too."

9

DAMIEN

HADES MUST HAVE ASKED THE FRONT DESK TO CALL HIM WHEN I stepped into the building because he barreled down the hallway like a bullet—with me as his target. His arms swung hard with his movements, and the murderous expression on his face told me exactly what he was pissed about.

I stopped in front of my door and slid my hands into my pockets. "Bad day, huh?"

That only pissed him off more. "What the fuck, Damien?" He stopped just inches from me, his red face covered in rivers of veins. There were two on his forehead, forming a noticeable V shape. He was sweating like he had just gone for a run, even though the AC was always set to 68.

"How do I look so good?" I glanced down at my suit. "Jessica. She picks out all my clothes—"

He held his fist and closed it, his knuckles turning white. He shut his eyes hard, trying to control himself from pulling out his knife and shanking me between the ribs. "I swear to fucking god…"

"I thought we only prayed on Sundays—"

He slammed his closed fist into my face.

I jerked back with the hit, but it didn't hurt so bad because I knew it was coming. I felt the blood drool from the corner of my mouth and wiped it away with my thumb. His fist didn't hurt my face, but the action did. For as long as we'd known each other, we'd never struck each other...for over ten years.

I straightened my spine and faced Hades. "Nice shot." I wiped away the blood on the sleeve of my suit—even though it cost me ten thousand euros. Maybe the blood would wash out and I could donate it.

"De Luca was one of our biggest clients. What the fuck did you do?"

"The guy was a dick."

His eyes were wide. "Answer the goddamn question."

I'd finally stopped bleeding, so I didn't need to keep wiping away the blood that had dripped down my chin. "Asked me to put his ex-wife back on his account."

His eyes shifted back and forth at supersonic speed because he was completely bewildered. "Why is that a problem?"

"Because she came in a few weeks ago and asked to be removed."

"So?" I hissed. "Just do what the fuck he says."

"She's just gonna come in and ask me to do it again."

He threw down his arms. "So? Their marital bullshit is their problem. Let them deal with it."

"She's our client too, asshole."

He stopped narrowing his eyes so he could see my full expression, take in my complete reaction. Seconds passed as his intuition kicked in. He was a smart guy, could read people with little stimuli. "You better not be fucking her."

"What does it matter if I am?"

He lost his temper again and dragged his palms down the front of his face. "Jesus fucking Christ…"

"They've been divorced six months. It's not like it happened yesterday."

He threw out his arms. "Doesn't fucking matter."

"She's a single woman. I'm a single guy."

"Does he know?"

"No." If he stopped pestering Annabella, he would probably never know.

"Thank fucking god."

"I couldn't care less if he knew."

Hades crossed his arms over his chest, his eyes narrowed on my face. "Know how he earns his money?"

Never cared enough to check. I shook my head.

"Death fighting."

There were lots of underground fighting rings. People put down their bets and made millions. But death fighting was rare.

"And he's undefeated."

Okay…that was a little impressive.

"Fix this, Damien." He stepped back and prepared to turn away.

"No." I had way too much pride to ask him to return.

"What the fuck did you say?" He turned back to me, his head cocked. "He was my client until you screwed it up. If you don't do it, I will. And you owe me, asshole. You owe me for a lot of shit."

He was going to throw it in my face forever. "Doesn't matter what I owe you. We aren't friends, so what does it matter?"

His eyes narrowed. "You were never really sorry, were you?"

I was...from the bottom of my heart. But I refused to say it.

"If you don't fix this, I will. And when I do, I'll tell him you're fucking his wife."

I didn't give a shit if he knew, but I knew that would make Annabella's life difficult. She was still trying to shake him. "Ex-wife."

He shook his head slightly. "We both know he'll kill you."

"Not if I kill him first."

When I got home, Sofia texted me.

When are you going to apologize to me?

She had always been good to me, fought for me when Hades couldn't see straight. Through the good and bad, she'd always been a friend. When I'd snapped at her a month ago, I was in a bad place. I'd lashed out without thinking, the bitterness getting the best of me. It was wrong to only associate her with Hades, because she'd been there for me, no matter what.

But before I texted her back, Annabella texted me. *I was gonna call, but I wanna make sure you aren't in a bad mood first.*

I was in a bad mood, but I grinned anyway. *I'm always in a bad mood. But I feel a little better talking to you.*

A little? Her teasing tone was audible in the words.

A lot better.

Good. So...have plans tonight?

I should probably go down to the lab, but I'd rather forget my troubles with her.

Unless my ex made you lose interest...

The ape did complicate my life, professionally and privately, but I didn't want to lose her yet. This would end eventually since I wasn't in the right place for a relationship and neither was she. But I wanted to enjoy her for as long as I could. *I don't scare easily, Annabella.*

Good. Neither do I.

Come over. At least we didn't have to worry about Liam on my territory. There would be no interruptions.

That sounds nice. Where do you live?

I'll pick you up. She didn't have a car, so she would walk. I'd rather her be alone in public as seldom as possible.

Not sure if that's a good idea...

Why?

I doubt we'll make it back to your place. Does your car have a back seat?

This woman was spontaneous and adventurous, and her obvious attraction to me was a turn-on. She stared at me like she'd never seen a sexier man. She moaned for me like I was better at making her come than her vibrator. Why the fuck did Liam cheat on her? She was the perfect woman. *No. But how does an alley sound?*

———

SHE GAVE a few compliments about my place but also didn't seem surprised by it. If her ex was a billionaire, then she'd probably lived in a fabulous mansion just like this. Or maybe dick was on her mind so she didn't give a damn about the place.

My bedroom was a private apartment in itself. With a large walk-in closet the size of a full kitchen, and a bedroom that had a full living room, it was a spacious and exclusive. My favorite part was the enormous hearth that took up most of the wall. When I had a fire going in the winter, it was basically an inferno that could burn the whole place down if it got out of control.

She stopped and stared at it, as if that was something that genuinely impressed her.

I stripped off my shirt and jeans behind her then made a drink.

She continued to stare at the fire.

I moved in front of her in my boxers with the glass. "Want a drink?"

"Sure."

I pushed my boxers down my front so my hard cock came free. She'd teased me in that text message, and I'd been turned on ever since. The car ride was silent because my heated thoughts made me fantasize about the things we would do when we got to my place. An obnoxious ex-husband wouldn't interrupt us. She was mine...all mine.

Her eyes dropped to my length, the desire burning a little brighter.

I poured the scotch on my chest, letting the liquid drip down the rivers between my abs until it reached my length and balls. It dripped to the hardwood afterward, the drops making gentle taps against the surface.

Her eyes dropped down and stared at my soaked skin.

I lowered myself into the armchair near the fire and planted my knees apart. "Drink." My arms stretched over the armrests, and I gripped the rounded edge with anxious fingertips. I wanted this beautiful woman on her knees, the skin reddening from the contact with the hard wood. I wanted her to devour me the way I devoured her, to watch her attempt to shove every inch of my dick in that pretty mouth.

She approached me until her knees touched mine. The look of desire was in her eyes, the same one I saw when I was on top of her, pounding her into the mattress and erasing the memory of the losers who came before me.

I didn't blink. "Undress."

She had a sassy ferocity to her, quick to reject any demands she wasn't obligated to obey. She respected herself, valued herself as her own powerhouse. But in this instance, she didn't mind obeying whatsoever.

Piece by piece, her clothes fell around my chair.

I gripped the armrests a little tighter, my knuckles starting to ache from the exertion. My cock twitched like it'd just been electrocuted with high voltage. I wasn't sure which was sexier, her obedience or her skin.

When she was in just her thong, her thumbs tucked into the straps over her hips, and she prepared to push them over her perky ass.

I snapped my fingers then motioned for her to turn around.

She stood still with her fingers in place, her flat stomach defined with her visible, slender abs. Her skin was tanned everywhere, a beautiful inheritance from her Italian genetics. Her tits were firm because she was a bit cold—or horny. Her hard nipples were pointed right at me. With her long hair stretching down her chest to her breasts, she regarded me with a hard gaze.

Then she turned around—and bent over.

Damn.

She slid the black lacy thong over her ass and then down her thighs, her perfect pussy staring right at me. She pushed the material to her knees then let them fall the rest of the way. When she righted herself, she ran her fingers through her hair and arched her back, posing for me like a stripper about to hit the pole.

I didn't even notice that my mouth was hanging open.

She slowly turned back around and gave a slight smile, like she could read my expression because I didn't have the strength to hide it anymore. I was the one in charge, but now she had the upper hand.

I shut my mouth and turned rigid, but my dick would always be an indicator of my deepest feelings. I was somehow harder than I'd been before…even though I was at full mast. More blood drained from my brain and was stuffed inside my length. "Kneel."

When she heard my command, that knowing smile disappeared. She held on to my knees as she lowered herself to the ground, not issuing a grimace when her bony knees hit the wood.

Her hands slowly migrated up my thighs, and she leaned forward so her tits were on top of my body. She looked at my hard physique and stared at the drops of liquor that were still sprinkled across my skin. After a swipe across her lips with her tongue, she looked at me.

Jesus.

She got to work.

She pushed my knees apart to get herself closer to me, then placed that warm tongue against my balls.

My entire body flinched at the initial contact because it felt like a pleasurable shock. The grooves of her tongue were noticeable, the warmth and wetness of her mouth heaven. I closed my eyes involuntarily and let out a groan I couldn't control.

Something told me she gave good head.

Her gentle kisses turned to forceful sucks, and she adored my balls even though they weren't the best part. She closed her eyes and dragged that tongue over every sensitive inch of my sac, making all my nerve ending fire off in pleasurable waves.

I was paralyzed by this woman.

Once she got every drop of scotch, she moved farther up until she kissed my hard shaft. Gentle kisses were placed up the prominent vein, giving it her delectable touch as she moved to my head. When she got there, her tongue flicked across the top, tasting more of the booze I had poured all over myself. "You're gonna make me drunk..."

I was already drunk...and high...watching this.

She opened her mouth wide and started to take me in, a slow descent so she could get used to my dimensions. When she sank as far as she could go, she quickly pulled back to take a deep breath. Her eyes watered at the pain then she tried again.

I liked watching a woman choke.

She slowly moved up and down, her flat tongue cushioning my dick as I slid deep inside. She kept her teeth far away and never sliced me, even though there wasn't much room in that little mouth. Her nails dug into my thighs as she kept moving, her mouth filling with saliva that she had to pull away to swallow.

The booze was long gone so I expected her to stop, but she kept going for it.

I wanted to roll on a condom and fuck her, but I was paralyzed by the things she did to me. One hand left the armrest and slid into her hair, pulling it away from her face so she could keep up her excellent work. "Look at me."

Her eyes lifted to meet mine as she kept sucking my dick, giving me long strokes that started at my head and moved all the way down to my balls. She could fit most of me, but sometimes when she tried to go too far, she had to pull away and suffer the consequences of her gag reflex. Her eyes watered further until beautiful tears formed and cascaded down her cheeks, sparkling like diamonds. One hand remained wrapped around my dick, holding it for support as she got the air back into her lungs. "I'm sorry...you're just big."

"Don't be." I guided her face back to my dick. "I like it." My fingers rested on her neck as I guided her down my length the way I wanted. I wanted to come inside her throat, fill her with enough come to make her choke again.

She kept going, and now that I was so deep in the moment, I couldn't stop for anything. My neck tilted back toward the chair, and I inhaled a deep breath as I prepared for the explosion. The pleasure started in every part of my body before it moved down, slowly approaching my fat dick as it slid inside her. I moaned even before I came, my fingers digging into her neck. I closed my eyes at the moment of release, feeling the explosion as it entered her small throat. "Fuck." I opened my eyes again and watched her take it all, not gagging even though it had to be uncomfortable, having her airway clogged like that.

It lasted an eternity, pleasure reaching new heights I'd never experienced. Time and space seemed to disappear, and I could feel every sensation to the micro levels. My dick had been sucked hundreds of times...but not like that.

She pulled my dick out of her mouth then moved into my lap. Her palms planted against my chest, and she straddled my hips with her knees. Her back arched as she leaned into me, her hair falling around my shoulders. Her hand slid into my hair, and she kissed me intensely, her tits pressing against my body as she leaned into it. "Now me."

MY FISTS WERE PLANTED FIRMLY into the mattress behind her knees as my hips thrust into her body at a rhythmic pace. It was an instance where the sex was so good that speed wasn't a priority. It felt amazing, no matter what we did. Just being together was enough to make us both writhe in pleasure.

Eyes filled with fire looked up at me, perfect tits shaking with my thrusts, and the sexiest woman I'd ever seen stared at me like I was a god. Like I was the only man in the world who could make her feel this way.

She was flexible, so bending her into the perfect position was easy. I could get my entire length inside her while doing the least work possible. We moved together, our wet bodies sheathing each other in an orgasmic marathon.

I lost track of the number of times she came. Ever since she'd walked in the door, we'd been at it like two rabbits in spring. The furniture in my bedroom had been blessed with her naked body, and now I would never be able to look at my couch or dining table without thinking about her fine ass.

It didn't matter how long we screwed; she was always wet.

That was such a turn-on.

Her hands slid up the back of my neck and into my hair, and she brought my lips to hers for a slow kiss. She breathed into my mouth as she ground against me, little moans escaping her lips and combining with mine. "Damien..."

My hips started to thrust harder as my instincts kicked in. My dick wanted to come, and it couldn't resist the sexy moans of a woman like that.

"Yes..." Her lips stopped caressing mine altogether because she got swept away by the heat. She was a passionate lover, a woman unafraid to hide her high in the most obvious way possible. Her fingers dug deep into my hair as she started to buck against me.

I ground against her clit harder and got consumed by her performance. My body lost control, and I filled the condom as she released at the same time. We both lost our minds, surrendering to the euphoria created by our bodies. "Annabella…" I'd never enjoyed saying a woman's name in bed as much as hers. It was such a sexy name, sexy enough to match the woman it belonged to.

We finished together, sweat on sweat, breath on breath.

I rested my forehead against hers as my breathing returned to normal. I was hot from the exertion but also so comfortable. I normally wanted to roll off in pursuit of space as quickly as possible, but I didn't mind being this close with her.

She continued to breathe hard as she looked at me, her claws slowly withdrawing and releasing my skin. Her eyes looked deeply into mine, seeing something no one else ever saw. Then she gave me a kiss in conclusion, a final embrace that was still filled with longing.

How could I continue to want a woman so much?

I finally moved off her and cleaned up in the bathroom. The condom was disposed of in the trash for my maid to clean out, and I washed my face in the sink because the sweat made my skin shiny. Normally, I'd be in the shower, but I was eager to get back to her… for whatever reason.

When I returned to the bedroom, she was wrapped up in my white sheets, turned on her side with her eyes closed like she was ready to fall straight to sleep. I watched her for a second before I poured two glasses of water. I set one on the nightstand for her before I moved to the other side of the bed.

She opened her eyes and looked at me, a slight smile on her lips in satisfaction but also a look of exhaustion in her pretty eyes. Then she pushed the sheets aside, inviting me back into my bed.

I put on my boxers then moved beside her.

She clearly had no intention of going home tonight.

But I didn't mind.

Once I was comfortable beside her, she took it a step further and cuddled into my side, hooking her leg over my waist. Her face rested beside mine on the pillow, her fingertips feeling my warm chest. She was affectionate with me, wanting to touch me at all times. She said she wasn't ready to move on to a new relationship, but she treated me like she never wanted to lose me.

"Can I get you anything?" I'd slept at her place because everything was new. I'd wanted more sex, as much as I could get it, and she woke me in the middle of the night just to have it. We were perfect for each other.

Her hand glided over her stomach. "I'm hungry…"

I'd been too busy fucking to think about dinner. Now that she mentioned it, I was hungry too. "Yeah? What do you want?"

She shrugged. "I'm not a picky eater."

Patricia knew me well enough not to bother me when I came home with a woman. Normally, she would knock on my door with a tray of dinner or leave it on the dining table. I grabbed my phone and texted her.

"That's all you have to do?" she asked. "I thought we'd order a pizza or something."

"I can have Patricia make you a pizza."

"No," she said with a laugh. "Anything is fine. I'm just impressed it's that simple."

I was surprised it impressed her at all. "You didn't have a maid before?"

"Well, yes," she said. "But I cooked dinner most of the time."

"You can cook?"

She nodded. "And I'm pretty good...not to be braggy."

"Let me get this straight. You can fuck and cook?"

She chuckled. "I'm a woman of many trades, I guess..."

"The two trades that matter the most."

"I don't know about that." She stared at her fingers as she caressed my chest. "I'm not good at making money, and that's pretty important."

"For now." She seemed bright, resourceful, and possessed a good amount of pride. I could imagine her being perfectly independent on her own. "You're starting over, and that's rough for everyone."

"True. But I don't have any skills or a university degree. I suspect it'll take a while for me to find my footing."

"Nothing to be ashamed of."

"I'm not," she said quickly. "It's just scary. Pretty much everyone told me to stay with Liam because with him, I had more money than I knew what to do with, and I had a strong man who could protect me against everything. But I just...couldn't look at him the same. I didn't want to settle if I wasn't happy."

Anyone else would have taken the easy way out, especially since he seemed sincere in his regret. But I admired her for refusing to settle for less than what she deserved, for knowing that he shouldn't have cheated on her in the first place. The fact that she was perfect in every way imaginable just made his infidelity worse.

What was the asshole thinking?

"I think you made the right decision, but I'm incredibly biased."

She chuckled. "I guess you are."

We never talked about the time when I hid in the bedroom. Once he was gone, I left because I needed to get to work. There wasn't much to say anyway. The guy was still in love with her and couldn't face the harsh reality of losing her. I never told her that he and I had butted heads at the bank when he was in my office. She might stop seeing me if she knew we'd crossed paths.

Patricia knocked on the door moments later, and I answered it half naked to take the tray from her. She didn't blink an eye over it because she'd seen me in just a towel many times. She was in her late forties, moving here from Greece after her husband passed away. She didn't have any children, so she enjoyed making a home for me. I was nearly half her age, so she probably looked at me like a son.

"Thanks, Patricia." I set the tray on the table and listened to her shut the door behind me.

Annabella got out of bed and helped herself to the dresser against the wall. She found a t-shirt of mine and put it on. "Do you mind?"

A beautiful woman in my t-shirt? Fuck no, I didn't mind. "Help yourself."

She ran her fingers through her hair, her long legs sexy underneath the t-shirt. She'd picked a white cotton shirt, a perfect contrast to her sun-kissed skin. With no panties underneath, she stopped at the dining table and looked at the meal. "Wow...that looks delicious."

It was two steaks, mashed potatoes, and asparagus. "Not to be braggy, but Patricia is a good cook." I uncorked the bottle of red wine and poured two glasses. I wasn't a big fan of red wine, but Patricia probably included it in the meal since I was entertaining.

"I can tell just by smelling it." She took a seat and moved the glass of wine toward her. After a sip, she nodded appreciatively. "Good wine. Barsetti vineyards?"

"You know your wine."

She shrugged. "I drink a lot."

I sat across from her, and we started to eat.

She took her time eating, choosing to pause several times so she could enjoy the wine Patricia had paired with it. She subtly licked her lips, just the way she did after she devoured my cock. Even something as basic as eating was sexy when she did it. "How long have you been here?"

"About ten years."

"It's nice. But it's pretty big for just one person."

I cut into my steak and took a bite, appreciating the fact that there was no judgment in her tone. "I like my space."

"You have a nice perimeter too. Would be difficult to get in here."

Being married to Liam clearly made her think about these things, about safety and protection. Maybe that was why she didn't blink an eye when I told her I was a drug dealer. "Helps me sleep at night."

She continued to eat again, running out of questions. She didn't ask for personal details about my life, probably because she didn't want me to pry in return. There seemed to be a thin wall around her body.

If we weren't fucking, we didn't have much to say to each other.

But it was kinda nice...to say nothing at all.

"Have family in Florence?" She dragged her steak through the creamy mashed potatoes, combining the two flavors before she placed the bite into her mouth.

"Yes. My father lives a few blocks away. My sister is also in town."

"Oh, that's nice. Are you close with your sister?"

I shrugged. "We don't have gossip hour, but I would kill anyone that crossed her."

She smiled slightly. "Protective brother...got it. How old is she?"

"A few years younger than me. What about you?"

She shook her head. "I'm alone. My parents passed away years ago, and I'm an only child."

"I'm sorry to hear that."

She returned her gaze to her food. "It is what it is..."

We spent the rest of the meal in silence, and she used most of her time to look out the main window to the city beyond. She was a slow eater, so she didn't eat much. By the time she was done, her plate was still half full.

I'd eat it tomorrow for lunch. "Has Liam stopped by for any more visits?"

She stilled at the question, her mouth slowly chewing her food until her throat swallowed it. "How did you know that was his name?"

I kept a stoic expression and told her the truth. "You said it last time I was there." That was true; she'd said his name a couple times, so I was off the hook.

She believed me. "No. Haven't heard from him."

"That must be nice."

"Yes...and no. I was pretty harsh with him, and I feel guilty about that." She set down her fork and pushed her food away. "But since he wasn't backing off, I had to hurt him to help him, you know? I don't want him to waste his time when there's no hope. It's just torture for his heart."

I could tell how much she still cared about him. Another woman wouldn't be so sympathetic. After all, he'd cheated and she didn't. "He doesn't deserve you. Not then and not now."

"In his defense, he was a good husband before all that happened. He was always good to me. Kind, affectionate, thoughtful... I don't think his entire reputation should be shattered by one mistake."

She really was kind.

"But it's too hard for me to forgive him. It's more than just the cheating...how it happened."

I didn't ask for details, but I had to admit I was curious. I drank my wine then leaned back in my chair.

She answered on her own, opened up to me for the first time. "We were trying to start a family...and I got pregnant. But...I lost the baby." She looked out the window, reliving the painful moment. "It was hard for both of us, and he didn't handle it the right way. He got drunk at a bar...and met someone."

I tried to control my anger, but that was pretty damn hard. "Fucking asshole."

Her eyes shifted back to me.

"Who the fuck does that?" After Sofia was raped and stopped sleeping with Hades, he didn't go out and find someone else in the meantime. There were offers, but he rejected every single one. That's what a real husband did—a real man. "Is that supposed to be an excuse? How could he possibly justify that behavior? He should have stayed home—with you." Good thing she didn't take his sorry ass back. The guy was worthless.

Her eyes dropped to her wine, and she took a drink. "My feelings afterward were complicated. Obviously, I was angry at him because of what he did, but I also know it never would have happened if we hadn't had a miscarriage."

"So?" My eyebrows shot up. "It doesn't matter what happened. Tragedy is normal. Shit happens. What if you were in an accident and couldn't walk again? Would he just get his fix every night on the town? It's easy to love someone when things are good, but loving a woman when things are bad is what defines a man. He failed. He fucking failed." I didn't know Annabella very well, but my passion told me I cared about her. That affection happened quickly, and it wasn't just based on good sex. "He should have been home with you every night, getting through it as husband and wife."

Her fingers rested on the rim of the glass as she regarded me. "You sure you've never been married?"

"No." I'd watched a womanizer love one woman exclusively, sacrifice everything just to see her smile. I knew what love was—because I'd seen it with my own eyes. Despite my bad blood toward Hades, I respected him for the way he treated Sofia. "But I know how a man should treat a woman."

I SAT at my desk with a steaming cup of coffee. It was almost noon, but I'd never really woken up. I was up late last night...with Annabella. We finished dinner then got to dessert...but it took us a long time to finish. Insulting her ex-husband seemed to make her want me more, which was fun.

Hades stepped into my office, eyebrows furrowed and his jawline hard.

I lifted my chin and met his look. "Do you fuck Sofia with that expression? Not a good look..."

His stare hardened in threat.

"Just trying to help." I drank from my mug and set it down. "What do you want?"

"Did you get De Luca back?"

I hadn't even bothered to try. After Annabella told me what he did, I didn't want his money. "No."

His eyebrow rose. "Because he refused? Or because you didn't try?"

He knew me so well. "We have plenty of other clients. We don't need him."

"Don't need him?" His voice came out cold. "We don't need an extra billion dollars?"

"We're both rich motherfuckers. We'll be fine."

He slammed his fist onto my desk. "He was my client, asshole. I want him back."

"Then get him back," I snapped. "You have two legs and vocal cords."

He closed his eyes for a second, seething. "I swear to fucking god..."

"The guy is a dick. Why would we want to help him anyway?"

"All of our clients are dicks, Damien. We're dicks. We're thieves, murderers, liars. Are you kidding me right now?"

I got out of my chair. "What if I replace him with a better client? Is that fair?"

"I don't want another client. I want him."

"You got a crush on him or something?" He was a good-looking guy with a strong physique. I could understand how he'd landed Annabella in the first place.

His hand tightened into a fist. "Get him back, or I'll tell him, Damien. This is your final warning."

He would never throw me to the wolves when we were close, but I knew he was telling the truth now. "Fine."

His nostrils flared before he turned around and walked out.

The moment I sat down, Sofia texted me again. *That's how it's going to be? You're just going to ignore me?*

10

ANNABELLA

In the beginning, Damien was just a pretty face, a nice body.

But now, he was more.

Hearing him talk about commitment like that, with so much passion and respect, made me see him with new eyes. He was a man who understood loyalty, who talked about men like he knew exactly how to be one.

It was hot.

Liam was the definition of testosterone. He was powerful, muscular, rich, and knew how to fuck a woman. But all that went out the window when he turned disloyal. That was the piece he was missing, that he'd never really had. He said it only happened one time, but now I wondered if there had been other instances he never told me about. His betrayal made me wonder if any man could be trustworthy, monogamous.

But now I believed they could.

Maybe Liam was just a mistake. Maybe I got lost in everything else he offered and missed all the signs. My infatuation misled me, made me turn a blind eye to his obvious flaws.

Damien seemed different, even though I didn't know him that well.

We never had serious conversations because we constantly danced around our mutual need for space. But maybe it was time for that to change. I hadn't slept with anyone else since I'd met him a month ago, and I wondered if he had either. If I asked him, he would probably tell me.

I texted him. *I'd like to make an appointment, please.*

He responded right away. *Sorry?*

A dick appointment. Is your dick available tonight?

The three dots never popped up, and a moment later, he called. His tone was playful when he spoke. "He's available whenever you want, Annabella."

"Ooh…it's like a warehouse club membership."

Now he actually laughed, deep and sexy. "Without the annual fee."

"Even better. So?"

"I actually do have plans tonight. But I'm yours the rest of the night."

I wanted to know what his plans were, but I refused to ask. "What time?"

"Probably ten. I can come to your place on my way home."

"You wouldn't rather go to your house?" My apartment was little, and let's be real, it was a dump. He practically lived in a mansion.

"Why would I?"

"Well…my place kinda sucks."

"It has a bed, doesn't it?"

I liked that he didn't care, that he wasn't pretentious and judgmental. Liam didn't refrain from calling my place a shithole. "Where are you going this evening?" I was tired of all this incognito bullshit. If we were going to continue seeing each other, I didn't want to be mysterious all the time.

He answered right away, like he had nothing to hide. "The ballet."

"Really? You don't seem like you'd be a fan." The second I said that, I realized he might have a date. Perhaps he was taking a woman there. It was odd that he made plans with me immediately afterward, and it was even odder that he might intend to sleep with both of us.

"I'm not," he said with a laugh. "I'm just going to watch my sister."

"She's a dancer?"

"Yes."

"Aww...that's so cute."

"I'm not cute. It's an obligation."

"Sure."

"You wanna get laid or not?"

"Now I wanna get laid even more."

11

DAMIEN

MY FATHER OPENED HIS PROGRAM AND SQUINTED HIS EYES. WHEN HE couldn't read a single word, he fished his glasses out of his jacket pocket. "They make the writing on these things so damn small..." The glasses were placed on his nose, and he could decipher the page. "Catalina is in nearly the entire production."

My sister was quite talented, not that I would ever tell her that. "That means this will suck."

"Damien." He continued to scold me like a child because he seemed to lose track of reality sometimes. I was in my thirties, but sometimes he thought I was still a dumb teenager, sneaking girls into the house.

"I'm teasing, Father."

He shut the program and gripped it in both hands, as if he intended to put it on the fridge when he got home. My mother had been gone ten years, and he'd been alone ever since. I offered to let him live with me, but he refused. Catalina offered the same thing. He was just too proud.

But age claimed his body more with every year, and since he was older when they had me, he was now in his midseventies. He couldn't live alone much longer, and I knew he would prefer to live in a home than burden me with his presence.

But Annabella was right. My place was awfully big for one person.

"What's new with you, son?" He turned his gaze on me, crinkles around his eyes and the loose skin on his face. He'd aged pretty well, but for the last few years, his appearance had taken a steep dive.

"I've been working a lot." He knew I owned the bank, but he had no idea about my side hustle.

"You should be working toward finding a wife. The bank won't always be there for you—but a good woman will."

I let my father say whatever he wanted because, you know, he was my dad. "True."

"And you need children. You're getting old, Damien."

"You're one to talk," I teased.

He raised his finger at me. "But I have you and your darling sister. When your mother was gone, I still had you. I'd have no reason to live otherwise."

Conversations always turned to discussions about mortality. Death seemed to be the number one thing on his mind. "I'll work on that."

"You better." He lowered his hand.

I would work on it tonight, actually.

The lights dimmed and the curtains opened. The sound of piano filled the theater, and the first dancer to hit the stage was my sister. Lean and toned, she moved across the stage on her tiptoes, her arms raised in the air with perfect posture. When she stilled, there was a pause in the music, but once it returned, she started to spin, to jump, to command the hearts of every person in that audience.

Including mine.

AFTER THE SHOW, I gave my father my arm and helped him up the stairs and to the back of the stage. Dancers were still in their leotards and were pulling the clips from their hair. Spouses and lovers handed over arrangements of roses and issued kisses of congratulations.

We moved to the rear, where my sister stood at her dressing table. Her hair was already pulled free from its constraints, so it flowed freely down her chest. Her green eyes were identical to mine, a gift from our mother.

Before we reached her station, I noticed there was already a bunch of roses on the surface.

When she saw our father, her eyes lit up in joy. "Daddy!" She wrapped her arms around him and hugged him hard. "I didn't know you were coming."

"Wouldn't miss it for anything." Despite his weakness, he managed to pull strength from nowhere and hug her hard. He held her like he didn't want to let her go, like she was a little girl reading in her bedroom. "You were wonderful, sweetheart." He pulled away and watched her with affectionate eyes. "The best dancer on that stage."

She smiled but rolled her eyes. "Of course you think that."

"And I mean it." He took her hand and kissed the top.

Emotion entered her gaze.

Father took the flowers he'd picked out from my hand and gave them to her. "For you."

"They're beautiful. Daisies...my favorite." She brought them to her nose and smelled them. "Thank you, Father." She turned to me next. "Hey. Hope you didn't fall asleep."

I gave her a one-armed hug. "Father is right. You really were the best on that stage."

"Really?" she asked in surprise. "You usually say I look like a troll in my tights."

"You do. Doesn't mean you aren't a good dancer."

She elbowed me in the gut. "Jerk."

I chuckled then let her go. "Can we take you to dinner?"

She glanced at the flowers on the vanity discreetly. "Actually, I already have plans. What if we get together tomorrow night instead?"

I connected the dots quickly and realized she was seeing someone. Irrational-older-brother-syndrome kicked in, and I wanted to tie him up and give him the interrogation of a lifetime. But I had to remind myself not every man was a drug dealer who visited whorehouses. "That's fine with me."

We said our goodbyes then made our way out of the theater. On the way, my father needed to take a detour to the bathroom. I opened the door for him and let him inside then waited in the hallway.

Most of the people had filed out of the building and got into their cars, so the place was mostly empty. I leaned against the wall and pulled out my phone. Instead of texting Annabella, I opened Sofia's message box.

I should say something.

I knew I was in the wrong. I knew she deserved better.

But it was late and I couldn't think of anything to write, so I slid the phone back into my pocket. I lifted my gaze and looked across the hall.

And made contact with bright-blue eyes.

Tall and muscular, he leaned against the opposite wall, his suit fitting his large frame like it'd been tailored for the event. His hands rested in his pockets, and he stared at me with a slight smile, enjoying the fact that he'd caught me off guard.

I didn't react—but my heart did pick up in speed.

I thought of my father, who was about to exit the bathroom and right into the line of fire.

Heath was still, letting the eye contact last a full minute without blinking.

I didn't blink either.

He finally pushed off the wall and came toward me.

I didn't have my gun—but I had my knife in my coat pocket.

He stopped in front of me, his smile stretching wider. "Taking your father to the theater—that's cute."

"You really want to die outside a bathroom?"

"Whoa." He chuckled as he raised both hands. "Are you always this aggressive?"

I kept the same expression. "Yes."

"I just want my money, Damien. Then I'll go away."

"I don't owe you a damn thing—"

He moved too quickly for me to see, and he slugged me hard in the stomach.

I lost my breath with the gasp and felt my back slam into the wall, but I controlled the groan from escaping my throat.

He grabbed both of my shoulders and pinned me against the wall. "I told you I wouldn't be so civil at our next meeting. It's just going to get worse and worse. And if I can't get what I want...I'll kill you."

12

ANNABELLA

It was past ten, and I still hadn't heard from Damien.

I wanted to play it cool, but I lost my patience. *My dick appointment hasn't been rescheduled, right?*

Nothing.

An hour passed, and I didn't hear anything.

Now, it was eleven, and there was no way he was still at the theater. And if he took his family out to dinner, they would be finished by now. Or he would have texted me back and said otherwise.

Unless that was a lie...and he was out with another woman.

Would Damien do something like that?

Liam promised to be faithful to me forever...and he broke that promise the second I couldn't give him what he wanted.

Was Damien just putting on an act?

We weren't exclusive and he could see other people, so why lie?

But then why else was he blowing me off?

13

DAMIEN

"Tell him to get his ass out here." I stood at the gate, looking into the dark eyes of the security guard who had a gun pointed at me. "That motherfucker owes me, and he knows it. Open the doors, and let me in. Or I'll keep showing up until that asshole shows his face."

"Or maybe I'll just shoot you right now."

My hand moved with the speed of a viper, and I reached through the bars and pointed his gun to the ground. At the same time, I pulled the knife out of my jacket and pushed it right toward his jugular. "Maybe I'll butcher you like a pig."

The guard was stuck, because if he even breathed too hard, I'd pierce his skin.

A guard from the rear yelled to the front. "Open the gate."

I let him go. "That's right, bitch."

The gate rolled open, and I stepped onto the property. The brown truck was parked to the left, and the high walls kept unwanted foes far away. I approached the front doors but was blocked by two men with guns.

I sighed and waited.

A moment later, he stepped out of the double doors and walked toward me in his black sweatpants without a shirt. His shoulders rolled with his movements, and his blue eyes were trained on me like a riflescope. He stopped in front of me, his cold expression showing his paramount annoyance.

The skull diamond sat on his left hand.

One of the three.

"What's so fucking important, Damien?" He didn't raise his voice because he didn't need to. He was deadlier when he was quiet.

"Heath."

The mention of his twin brother softened his features slightly. "What about him?"

"That asshole needs to be holstered. Get him under control."

Balto processed what I'd said. "Elaborate."

"He demands I pay my royalties."

"And?"

"You failed to provide a service, so I don't owe the Skull Kings shit. Explain that to him so he gets off my tail."

He still hadn't blinked. "He's the Skull King now. I'm nobody."

"You're his brother. You'll never be nobody."

"How he chooses to run that organization is his business, not mine. I'm retired. I have no power to influence his decisions."

"Bullshit."

His eyes narrowed. "I made a clean break when I parted from the Skull Kings. I traded in my power for peace. I won't risk that because you refuse to pay your dues."

"Pay my dues?" I snapped. "When Maddox was raping Hades's wife and monopolizing the business, where were you?"

He was quiet.

"Nowhere. Fucking nowhere."

He crossed his arms over his chest. "I can't help you, Damien. Nothing I say will change Heath's mind. If he lets you slide, then he has to let everyone else slide. That will cause a lot more problems. Want my advice?"

No, but he would give it to me anyway.

"Pay him. Or retire."

Neither one of those was an option.

"Unless you can wipe out the Skull Kings, which I doubt, you're starting a war you'll never win."

I stared at him coldly.

"Just pay him, Damien." He turned around to walk back inside.

"I saved your life, asshole."

He halted in place for seconds before he turned back around. He came back to me. "And I will repay that debt if you ever ask me to."

"That's what I'm doing now."

"No. You're asking me to coddle your pride." He squared his shoulders and stared at me with an irritated gaze. "When your life is on the line, I will walk over fire for you. But that's not now. Call me when it is."

IT WASN'T until I woke up the next morning that I realized what I'd forgotten.

Annabella.

Once Heath had punched me in the stomach, all thoughts of her ceased. I'd dropped off my father at his house and got to work.

I saw her missed call and text message. *My dick appointment hasn't been rescheduled, right?*

Ah, fuck.

I put the phone to my ear and called her as I walked into the bathroom. I listened to it ring as I stared at myself in the mirror, seeing the discoloration on my stomach where Heath had slammed his fist.

No answer.

I had a crazy night last night. Talk to me.

Nothing.

Did I just fuck this up again?

Annabella.

I skipped the office and went straight to her apartment. I knew she didn't work until lunchtime or the dinner shift, so she had to be home. I knocked loudly.

No response.

I knocked again. "Annabella, please."

Nothing.

I slammed my fist into the wood. "Want to watch me break it down?"

Finally, the locks turned, and she opened the door.

Looking pissed.

"It's annoying when Liam shows up like he owns the place." With one hand on her hip, she stared at me in irritation. "It's even more annoying when you do it. At least I was married to the guy. I hardly know you."

I pretended that didn't hurt. "If you hardly know me, why are you upset?"

Her eyes narrowed because she knew I had her. "I'm not upset. I've just lost interest."

"Bullshit." I pushed myself inside, forcing her to back up, and I shut the door behind me. "Don't ignore me."

"Don't ignore *me*," she snapped. "You said you were coming by, and you ghosted me."

"I didn't ghost you."

"You sure as hell as ignored me." She crossed her arms over her chest. "Then tell me what happened...this time."

I didn't want to dump the intimate details of my business life on her, didn't want to scare her off, but if I didn't give her a reasonable explanation, she had every right to think I was a dick. "Work stuff... I had to take care of it."

She narrowed her eyes like she didn't believe me at all. "We aren't exclusive, so if you were out with someone else, you're perfectly entitled to it. But to lie...that's so damn hypocritical."

That was what she thought? "I wasn't out with someone else. I told you I went to the ballet to see my sister."

"But maybe you didn't go alone."

"You caught me," I said sarcastically. "I took my father..."

"You don't get to be an asshole. You completely ditched me—twice now. Shit happens and I get that, but the fact that you aren't giving me an explanation tells me you were doing something you don't want me to know about."

"Exactly." I moved closer to her. "My personal shit is personal. I don't have to tell you a damn thing."

She was still as the words washed over her, not showing any anger at the stupid thing I'd just said. "That's fair, Damien. You don't owe me anything. But I don't have to put up with a man who flakes without explanation. So, get out."

I'd lost my temper because I wasn't getting my way, and now I'd put myself in a situation I didn't want to be in. I could walk out that door and find another woman to warm my bed tonight, but I didn't want that. Annabella was the only woman I wanted to be with right now. "This is what happened..."

"Forget it." She walked to the door. "Just go." She held it open.

I pushed it closed again. "Annabella."

"You told me you didn't lie." She turned around to face me. "You said my ex was an asshole because he didn't know how to treat me. Well, you're all talk because you're just another fuckup."

Ouch.

"Whatever you were doing, you could have texted me back and said you couldn't make it. That's it. I wouldn't have cared. But you completely ignored me."

Because I got punched in the stomach, was threatened, and tried to take care of it through back channels.

"And that's fine," she said. "But I don't want to do this anymore. I didn't put up with my husband cheating on me, and I sure as hell won't put up with a guy who drops me like that, even if this is just a fling."

"Let me explain."

She crossed her arms over her chest, sticking her tongue in the side of her cheek in annoyance, as if she expected me to say something stupid.

"I'm not seeing anyone else, and I'm aware that I can. If I were, I would answer you straight. I've got nothing to hide. But since I met you, I haven't had any time to hook up with anyone else. I've been working around the clock, and all my free time has been spent with you—minus last night."

She stayed silent and didn't argue, which was a good sign.

"I don't talk about the details of my life because I don't want to scare you off."

That snagged her interest. She stopped playing with her inner cheek. "You already told me you're a drug dealer."

"And I have to deal with shit every day because of it. Like last night."

She stared and waited for an explanation.

"There's a guy who's demanding money from me, says I owe him for city services...which is bullshit. I basically told him to fuck off, and he said there would be consequences. So he accosted me last night while my father was in the bathroom." I lifted up my shirt and showed the bruises on my stomach.

Her eyes widened. "Oh my god..."

"I dropped off my father and headed to a friend's house...who is this guy's twin. He owes me a favor, so I asked him to get the asshole off my tail. But that didn't work. By the time I was done, it was midnight, and all I could think about was painkillers, so I went straight home and totally forgot about you." I dropped my shirt.

Her eyes lingered on my injury even though she couldn't see it. "You're talking about the Skull King, right?"

Maybe I should give her more credit. "You know him?"

"Not personally. But Liam has mentioned him."

Maybe I didn't need to censor my life at all. With other women, I pretended the bank was my only source of income because there was no point in sharing the whole truth. But I wanted Annabella to know...for reasons I couldn't explain.

She moved into me and lifted my shirt again. "Maybe we should go to the ER..."

"Don't be ridiculous." I shoved the shirt down. "I've been through worse." Like being tortured by Maddox until Hades traded for my freedom. A simple punch to the stomach wasn't a big deal.

"Is that supposed to make me feel better?" She righted herself again, a look of concern in her eyes.

"A little." Her wrath seemed to disappear, so it felt like we were back to normal. A slight smile formed on my lips. "Can we move past this now?" This fling really made no sense. I'd never continued to see the same woman for an extended period of time, but once I'd met her, the impulse to go to a bar disappeared. She was the person I wanted to call. She was the person I wanted to know more about.

"Yeah...I guess." She glanced at my stomach again but didn't say anything about it.

I wanted to take her into the bedroom so we could break the tension further, but I still had a long day ahead of me. "I need to get to work. If I call you later, will you answer?"

She rolled her eyes.

"Fifty percent of the time, you don't."

"Because fifty percent of the time, you're an asshole," she said playfully. "But yes, I'll answer. I'm working the dinner shift tonight, but maybe you could come over later." Now that her rage was gone, she was the beautiful and soft woman I liked. Perfect in every way imaginable, flawless to the bone. She was really something.

"So you're willing to reschedule that dick appointment?"

She laughed loudly, her cheeks turning red in embarrassment. "God, I wish I hadn't said that now."

"Why? I liked it."

"Kinda slutty..."

"Why do you think I liked it?" I grinned wider.

She hit me in the arm playfully. "Shut up."

"I'm kidding, Annabella." My arms moved around her petite frame, and I pulled her close, getting that same feeling that I always had when she was near. My mouth came close to hers, and I immediately became engrossed in our potent chemistry. I wanted her, and she wanted me...and that was never more obvious than when we were close like this.

She turned quiet as her arms rested on mine, her lips slightly parted like she expected a kiss. She looked up at me through her thick eyelashes, so spectacularly beautiful it was hard to believe she wasn't wearing a drop of makeup.

"I like it because it's the sexiest thing in the world, you wanting me." My hand slid to the area between her shoulder blades, and I brought our foreheads together. My dick was hard because I wanted to take her to bed, to get lost in that lustful dream that made me forget about everything else. But knowing me, once I stayed, I would never leave. We would lie in bed all day, order a pizza, and keep at it.

Judging by the way she looked at me, she wanted the same thing. She was so pissed at me minutes ago, but now she was melted butter. She claimed she lost interest every time I was a jerk, but clearly, that wasn't true. She still wanted me, which was why she was so angry.

I didn't even kiss her because I knew where that would go. "I'll see you later." My arms slid from her body, and I turned away, telling my dick to wait until tonight.

She grabbed me by the arm and pulled me back. "You think I'm gonna let you walk away like that?" She rose on her tiptoes and planted her soft lips against my mouth. Her kiss was demanding, like she owned me with an invisible leash.

I smiled against her lips and kissed her back. "Doesn't seem like you've lost interest..."

She pulled away for a second, trying to look angry when she only looked cute. "Shut up and kiss me."

HADES KNEW I'd stepped into the building, because he was standing in the hallway when I made it to our floor. He was in a midnight-black suit with his muscled arms by his sides, and his eyes were wide and demonic, like he might kill me if I took a step closer.

I slid my hands into my pockets as I stopped near the window.

"Talk to Liam?"

Geez, he wasn't gonna let this go.

"Don't show your face until you get it done." He warned me with his gaze before he turned away and walked off.

I rolled my eyes and turned on my heel. "Pain in my ass..."

AFTER A BIT of detective work and calling in some favors, I located Liam at a gym in the city. He probably had a private weight room in the convenience of his home, but he met his trainer at a local spot a few blocks from his home.

I was dreading this.

After the beef we'd had, he would never come to the bank...unless I got on my knees and begged.

Fuck that shit.

I walked inside and found him in the center of a boxing ring. His trainer held up padded boards for him to slam his fists into. He was shirtless, all of his cut muscles and tattoos visible. He really was a beefy guy.

A few pretty girls hung their arms on the ropes outside the ring, dressed in sports bras and little gym shorts. They watched Liam like he was the next man they each wanted to conquer.

He was working so hard to get his ex-wife back, so I wondered if he was screwing any pretty woman who checked him out. He did cheat on her the second they lost their baby, so I didn't have high expectations for the guy.

With sweat dripping down his face and flushed cheeks, he finished the set then stepped back. He hopped in place and shook out the tension in his biceps and triceps. He paced the ring before he pulled off his gloves and grabbed his jug of water from the ground.

I stood opposite the girls, my arms resting on the ropes.

He chugged the water as his eyes moved to me. It took him two heartbeats to recognize me, and when he did, he stopped drinking, so the liquid splashed all over him. He pulled it away from his face then marched toward me. "Got a death wish, motherfucker?" He threw his bottle on the ground, the water spilling all over the place.

The entire gym went quiet, the sound of bars and weights suddenly going silent.

He opened an access point through the ropes and slipped through.

I backed up and returned my hands to my pockets, responding to his hostility with indifference.

He marched toward me, his muscled mass covered in sweat and tattoos. He stopped in front of me and stared at me with wide eyes, as if he was waiting for the right moment to give me an uppercut that would knock me out.

Maybe visiting him during his workout was a bad idea. He was pumped full of adrenaline, testosterone, and protein. He was trained in the art of killing, and he probably wanted to turn me into his next carcass.

"Caught you at a bad time?" I asked like a smartass.

His eyes narrowed. "I just need one reason to bash your skull in..."

"That wasn't it?"

He lunged at me.

I didn't move. I didn't blink.

It was a fake-out, and he stilled after his failed attempt. "I'm not coming back, if that's what this is about. I warned you."

"We both know no one can help you like we can. If you don't launder your money right, you're gonna have a lot more problems later. We know all the right people to get the bad people off our backs. And the biggest reason of all...you're leaving a lot of money on the table. You love money, right?" I pointed at my chest. "Because I love money, and I'm not leaving a single euro on the table."

He continued to breathe hard, his shoulders moving up and down like he was still exhausted after beating the shit out of the pads his trainer held. "I don't want to work with a jackass like you."

"Good news, you won't have to. You're Hades's client."

He continued his hard stare.

"Come on, let's cut the shit, Liam. You need us, and we need you."

"Why are you here instead of him?"

I rolled my eyes. "Said I fucked it up, so I should fix it...whatever that means."

"Alright." He stepped closer to me. "But on one condition."

Fuck.

"Apologize. Bitch."

No way in hell was I gonna do that. I'd rather Hades shoot me than forsake my pride like that. "I'm not gonna apologize, but before you get all huffy and puffy, just remember you don't want me to."

Both of his hands tightened into fists.

"Your ex-wife is also a client of ours. Wouldn't you want me to execute her wishes? Protect her privacy? Treat her with the same respect I treat you? What if a new guy came along and demanded the same things you are? Wouldn't you want me to have her back?" It was a pretty compelling argument. I could negotiate and manipulate when I wanted to. I had more brains than Hades gave me credit for.

Liam still wore that ticked expression, but the rest of his body softened a bit. "If there is some other jackass, you tell me. I'll take care of him."

Good to know.

"Fine. I'll come back."

"I'll let Hades know."

He turned around and headed back to the ring. "But you better not piss me off again, Damien."

I had a feeling that might happen. "Can't promise anything..."

I LET myself into Hades's office. "I fixed it."

His hand was on the mouse, and his eyes were focused on the computer. After he clicked on something, he turned his head toward me, that restrained hatred still in his gaze...constantly. "Congratulations. You did your job."

This never-ending hostility was getting the best of me, feeding the flames of my temper with oxygen and gasoline. How could Hades hate me so much after all this time that he sneered at me every chance he got? "I thought you would be different now that you're a father—with another on the way."

His eyes narrowed slightly.

"What kind of example are you setting?"

He was still as he processed my insult. It took him several seconds to absorb every single syllable. "My son will know that years of friendship aren't the equivalent of loyalty. He will recognize a toxic relationship and how to abandon it. He will know how to be a real man, to think about others besides himself. That's what I'll teach him, Damien." The room was frozen like a freezer running on full blast. "What will you teach your son? Arrogance? Selfishness? Or maybe you'll never have a relationship with your son because you'll destroy that too."

14

ANNABELLA

AFTER I FINISHED MY SHIFT, I SHOWERED AND GOT READY TO SEE Damien.

I'd been thinking about that kiss all day.

I was so angry with him, but he quickly changed my feelings with his charm, his smile, and those soft lips. That man could talk me out of anything because he was so suave.

My hair was curled, and my makeup was perfect.

But then I got a disappointing text from Damien. *I have to cancel tonight. I'll see you tomorrow.*

The clipped tone of his message told me he was in a bad mood, so something must have happened after he'd left my apartment. The more I got to know him, the more I recognized his brooding tantrums. *Are you home?*

Why?

Just answer the question.

Yes.

I grabbed my purse and walked out the door.

———

PATRICIA LET ME INSIDE, and I took the long trek to the top floor where his bedroom was located. A bottle of scotch was in my hand because I noticed he drank it when he was home. I reached his bedroom door and tapped my knuckles against the wood.

After a long pause, he answered. "Enter." His tone was dark, like he'd been in a sour mood consistently since he'd texted me.

I stepped inside and saw him sitting on the couch, shirtless and in black sweatpants. A bottle of scotch was already open, and his glass was empty, with the exception of a few drops at the bottom. The TV was on, and a football match played on the screen. The enormous fire in the hearth burned with powerful flames. He looked like Dracula sitting at the top of his castle. "I thought you could use a drink, but it looks like you're covered…"

He turned his head at the sound of my voice, his eyes narrowed in annoyance rather than pleasant surprise. He was still as he stared at me, as if it took him some time to understand the situation that had just developed.

Maybe stopping by was a mistake.

I shut the door behind me then approached his living room. The fans on the TV yelled when a shot was missed, and that sound filled the room around us.

His eyes continued to follow me. "What part of 'see you tomorrow' didn't you understand?"

I did come over uninvited, but I wouldn't feel guilty about it. "You've never done the same?" If I didn't take his phone calls because I didn't want to talk, he just came over anyway. And when I didn't answer the door, he threatened to break it down.

He sighed, acknowledging the hypocrisy.

"I thought you could use a friend. Someone to talk to." I set down the bottle. "It's better than sitting here alone in the dark, right?" I poured myself a glass then sat in the armchair across from him.

He leaned back into the couch, his stomach still tight and hard even though he wasn't trying to flex his abdominals. He ran his fingers through his slightly unkempt hair then looked at the TV, a defeated sag to his frame.

"Or we can just sit here and not talk…"

He propped his chin on his closed fist and stared at me.

"I can leave if you really want me to." If he was closed off like this, then maybe it was pointless.

He closed his eyes for a second and dragged his fingers down his face. "Have you had dinner?"

I shook my head.

He grabbed his phone and texted Patricia. Then he left his phone on the table beside him. "You didn't need to bring this." He grabbed the bottle and filled his glass. "I buy you things, alright?"

"Who said it was for you?" I took a drink.

He smiled slightly, but it only lasted a few seconds before it disappeared again. He took a drink then set it on the table.

"So…you want to talk about it?"

He shrugged.

"It seems like you have more bad days than good."

His words came out sarcastic. "You're very observant."

"Talk to me, Damien." When Liam betrayed me, I had friends to talk it through with. I lost them in the divorce, but they were there at the time. "We're friends. That's what friends do."

"I don't have a lot of friends, but I know you don't fall into that category."

"I could."

He shook his head. "I don't want you to. I like what we have...whatever it is."

"Then let's make it our own. Talk to me."

He stared at me for a while before he grabbed the remote and turned down the volume. "My partner at the bank and I don't get along."

"Why does that bother you?"

"Because he used to be my best friend..." His eyes filled with noticeable sadness when he said the words, showing his heart for the first time. The pain was obvious, the burden of the regret he felt.

"That's the person you lost..." It wasn't an old lover. Now it made sense, because he said he'd never committed to someone before, but he talked about this person like they were the love of his life.

He nodded. "I've known him since our years at university...that was over a decade ago. We started our street business and found quick success. We didn't know how to protect all that cash, so we started the bank to launder the money—and launder it for other clients."

It was the most he'd ever revealed about himself. Since we'd met, we protected our privacy like buried treasure, but now we'd stopped doing that because there was more between us than either of us expected. I hadn't known Damien long, but I was quickly drawn to him, feeling vastly different than I did with my other flings. I already felt close to him, felt something special for him.

"We're enemies now...and it fucking sucks."

"What happened?"

He sighed.

"You don't have to talk about it."

"No...I'm just ashamed."

"Oh..."

He was quiet for a long time, his eyes reflecting the height of the flames as he stared into the hearth. "I made stupid choices with the drug business. We had an enemy closing in, and I made a lot of bad decisions, decisions were there irrational and arrogant. As a result... his wife was taken and raped." He closed his eyes as he finished, carrying an invisible burden that was visibly heavy.

I couldn't halt my reaction. "Oh my god..."

"We got her back, and she's okay. They have a son named Andrew and another boy on the way. But Hades could never forgive me for what I did, no matter how many times I apologized. His wife forgave me and wanted us to reconcile, but his grudge is too strong." He continued to stare at the fire. "He left the drug business because of the perils that come with it, but he continues to work at the bank because that's fairly safe. He tried to buy me out, but I refused. But every time we deal with each other...everything goes to shit."

I was speechless because it was such a horrible story to listen to. There were no kind words I could say to make him feel better, nothing that would be fitting.

"The worst part is the way he looks at me...like he wishes I were dead." He ran his hands up his cheek in frustration. "And today he said some tough shit that made me feel lower than dirt. I understand I fucked up, but he's been torturing me ever since." He didn't look at me, as if he were too ashamed to meet my gaze.

"I'm so sorry." What else could I say to that?

His eyes fell to the ground.

Now I understood his inherent melancholy. There always seemed to be something on his mind, a shadow clouding the brightness of his eyes. "How long has it been?"

"About nine months."

That seemed like enough time for Hades to move on...especially if his wife had.

"This is why I don't like to talk." He lifted his gaze and looked at me. "You don't see me the same."

"That's not true," I whispered. "I just...feel for you." I didn't judge him for his mistake because it wasn't intentional. It clearly ate at him every single day because he cared. If he didn't care, he wouldn't have that dead look in his eyes.

A knock sounded on the door.

Damien got to his feet to let Patricia in.

Just as he walked away, a message popped up on his phone.

Talk to me. It was from someone named Sofia.

I shouldn't have looked because it was an invasion of privacy, but it was instinct. A bright light came on, and my eyes darted to it. The message was short, so it was read in a nanosecond. The name was easy to see too.

I felt my heart sink the second I saw it.

He wasn't mine, so I shouldn't care. We agreed this would be casual. I was the one who said I didn't want anything serious, that it was too soon after my divorce. So I had no right to feel jealousy...betrayal.

Until I told him I wanted more.

HE DIDN'T PICK up on my somber mood because the subject of our conversation was already so dark. It was a relief I didn't have to pretend I was fine, to give false answers to his questions.

We had dinner at the table in silence then returned to the living room. The game was still on, but he hadn't seemed interested in it from the instant I'd walked inside. He returned to his spot on the couch, his stomach still flat despite the dinner he'd just had.

This time, I sat beside him on the couch, pulling my knees to my chest to get comfortable.

He grabbed the blanket on his side of the couch and handed it to me.

I pulled it over my body, touched by the gesture.

He stared ahead and looked at the TV. "Let me know when you want me to take you home."

I thought my sour mood would make me want to leave, but knowing there were other women in his life made me want to stay. He said there was no one else, so if Sofia was another fling, he'd lied about it.

But maybe she was an old fling...who still wanted him.

If I left, would she replace me?

I didn't want to vacate my spot so someone else could take it. "I thought I could sleep here." It was almost ten in the evening.

"I'm not in the mood to fuck." The words were callous, rough on the ears.

"Neither am I." I just wanted to be with him. It was nice to sleep in that soft bed with his strong frame beside me. I never did sleepovers after Liam, but now I craved them. It was nice to have a big man beside me again, to feel safe all through the night. My fingers were always in contact with his warm skin, the powerful muscles underneath. It was comfortable...to not worry about anything. I didn't think I'd feel that way for a long time, but it happened so quickly. Damien had to be special to make me feel that way. Really special.

He swallowed the last of his scotch and turned off the TV. "Then let's go to bed." He entered the bedroom and did his nightly rituals like I wasn't there. The sound of the running faucet and the hum of his electric toothbrush escaped the bathroom.

I stripped out of my clothes and found a t-shirt in his top drawer. I pulled back the crisp, soft sheets then slid inside, my skin feeling the gentle friction move past. My phone was left on the nightstand, switched to silent mode, and I waited for him to join me.

He stepped out of the bathroom in just his boxers, his muscled frame so perfect, he seemed to be chiseled from stone. His back was the most impressive, every single muscle prominent to create beautiful lines on either side of his spine. He had narrow hips that led to muscled thighs. He turned off the fireplace so the flames disappeared, then returned the booze to the wet bar.

I stared at him, watching him turn around and walk toward the bed. His strong pecs mixed with his powerful shoulders, and the beautiful abs of his stomach were the topography of a mountain range.

He turned off a couple lights then got into bed beside me. He lay on his back and stared at the ceiling for a moment before he closed his eyes. His final deep breath left his lungs, his body sinking into the mattress.

It was obvious he was miserable.

I welcomed myself to his side of the bed, immediately feeling the warmth that radiated from his body like the sun. My face moved to his shoulder, and my arm hooked around his waist, comfortable instantly.

He didn't ask me to move.

I liked sex...but I liked this better.

I watched his calm expression as he quickly drifted off to sleep. He was perfect at every angle, the shadow on his jawline giving him a rugged look that was irresistible. Soft lips sat in a face of sharp cheekbones and intense eyes. He was beautiful, the definition of perfection.

I didn't want to sleep because I wanted to continue to stare, but he made me so comfortable in his bed, made me forget about all my problems that would still be there when the sun rose.

WHEN I WOKE up the next morning, he was in the shower.

I could hear the water running.

I was so comfortable that I didn't want to move. Even after a full night of rest, I didn't want to get out of his nice bed. I wanted to roll over and go straight back to sleep. The sheets smelled like him, and the imprint of his heavy body was noticeable under my fingertips.

He stepped out of the bedroom with a towel around his waist. His hair was slightly messy from the dampness, and the drops of water that gently dripped down his chest made him look like a cologne model.

He noticed my open eyes. "How'd you sleep?"

"Good. Too good, because I never want to leave." I didn't care about my smeared mascara or the foundation that stained his pillowcase. He'd seen me at my worst, so I couldn't look that different to him.

"That makes a problem for both of us. Because if you stay here, I'll never leave." He was in a much better mood today, just needing to sleep on his misery. The sun peeked out from behind the closed curtains, so it was obvious it was a beautiful day outside.

"That sounds nice to me." I propped my head on one palm and dropped my gaze to the towel around his waist. A thick vein ran down the center of his torso and disappeared under the white cotton. He was so fit that his body couldn't be any tighter. Veins and muscles were plump under his tanned skin.

He grabbed the top of the towel. "Want me to drop it?"

I nodded.

He smiled slightly before he tugged it loose. Underneath was a semi-hard dick, but it was quickly ballooning to its full size. Drops still dripped off his sac, the scent of soap noticeable on my nose.

"Ooh...breakfast."

His smile disappeared, and he pulled back the sheets. "Hungry?"

"Starving." I grabbed his thick bicep and pulled him on top of me, wanting that warm skin to be in contact with mine, to feel his heavy mass press against my chest so I could hardly breathe.

His muscular frame covered me, his thighs parting mine and getting ready to take me. One hand moved into my hair the way I liked, and he gave me a confident stare before he leaned in and kissed me.

Ooh...I liked that.

He went for my bottom lip first, nibbling it between his in a gentle caress. His mouth was warm, minty from brushing his teeth just minutes ago. His jawline was smooth because he'd just shaved the excess hair away. He kissed me again...and again.

That was all it took to make me wet.

He kissed me harder and harder, our mouths moving together in a heated embrace. His tongue moved into my mouth a moment later, making contact with mine in the most intimate way possible. His fingers fisted my hair tightly, wanting to control me like a cowboy with a rambunctious mare.

He made me melt in a way no one else ever had. Not even Liam. It seemed to be more potent, more intimate. It was like Damien had never had another woman like me, like he never wanted to stop, like he could do this every night forever.

My hands explored his body, loving the way his abs were just as strong as his chest. Every inch of his body felt like warm concrete. It was so good, so hard against my impatient fingertips.

I didn't want to share this man.

He broke our kiss long enough to get a condom out of the drawer. He rolled it on while looking me in the eye, like he couldn't wait until he sank inside me, feeling every inch that he was already so familiar with.

His lips moved to mine again as he positioned himself at my eager entrance. Then he gave a hard thrust, pushing his impressive girth inside with an aggressive announcement.

I moaned against his lips, enjoying the size while wincing at the pain.

He seemed to know I could handle it because he thrust instantly, pressing my ass into the sheets as he ground into me.

My ankles locked around his waist, and I pulled him hard against me, demanding all of him. "Damien..." I hadn't said another man's name in bed since I became a single woman. He was the first man to make me writhe hysterically, to point my gaze to the heavens and thank god for making a man like him.

He grabbed my wrists and pinned them above my head even though there was no resistance from me. His fingers dug into my flesh as his hips kept hitting me in just the right spot. He was so strong, he could do everything at once, concentrate and perform at the same time.

He looked me in the eye as he thrust, his eyes dark and clouded with venomous desire. The look was almost one of hatred because it was so intense. His eyes were focused on me like nothing else existed.

Like Sofia didn't exist.

15

DAMIEN

I LEANED AGAINST THE DOORFRAME WITH MY HANDS IN MY POCKETS. I watched her bow her head as she signed the checks for all her employees, her dark hair in a high ponytail that stretched down her back. Her pregnancy was noticeable in the thickness of her cheeks and neck, along with that inexplicable glow that came from within her soul. "This is where you killed him?"

She looked up at the sound of my voice, her expression initially guarded when she stared at me. She dropped her pen and ignored the remaining checks needing her signature. "Yes."

I stared at the spot where the puddle of blood had soaked into the hardwood. Housekeeping did their best to erase the stain, but the subtle evidence was still visible—if you looked hard enough. "You never changed offices?"

"I like knowing he's dead. Gives me satisfaction every day." She leaned back in the chair with her hands on the surface of the desk, her sparkling wedding ring reflecting the light on the ceiling.

I nodded. "Badass."

"Well, I get worked up when people fuck with my husband."

"Then maybe I should go…"

Instead of growing angry at my comment, she had a look of pity. "Took you long enough to come around."

"Who said I've come around?" I crossed my arms over my chest. "You want to get lunch?"

"On one condition."

This should be good.

"I get to pick the place."

WE WENT to her favorite Italian place around the block.

She dove into the basket of bread right away, dipping it in the balsamic vinegar and the extra virgin olive oil. "You don't want any?"

I shook my head. "Not if I want to look like this."

She rolled her eyes. "Well, I'm pregnant. I can eat whatever I want."

"You can always eat whatever you want. Bellies and thighs are sexy on women. It just gives them more curves. But men…I'd look gross with a belly."

"You can't expect to be fit forever."

"I'm gonna try." Annabella had the hots for me. She couldn't get enough of me. She was addicted to my orgasms and constantly demanded more. If I wanted to keep her around, I had to keep everything tight.

"So, what took you so long?" She spoke between bites, her mouth moving as she stared me down.

We already had our iced teas, and we were now waiting for lunch. She didn't waste any time getting to the point. "Just busy."

"Too busy to apologize?"

"I'm especially busy when I have to apologize."

She dabbed her bread into the oil again before she took a bite. "Well?"

"Well, what?"

"I'm waiting for that apology."

I should just get it out of the way...especially since I was a huge dick to her. "I'm sorry."

"And mean it."

"I never apologize unless I mean it."

That must have been enough because she didn't press for more. "Why did it take you so long to respond?"

"I was busy—that's the truth."

"Why are you so busy?"

"I've had some issues on the drug side. The Skull King is expecting me to pay royalties for a bullshit service."

"Who's the Skull King?"

I forgot Hades had hidden most things from her. "An asshole. Then I caused problems with one of our clients at the bank, and Hades threatened me to make it right."

"Did you?"

I nodded.

"Seeing anyone?"

I shrugged. "I'm always seeing people."

"I meant anyone special."

If I were to describe Annabella, I'd probably use that word. "I'm seeing this one woman...she's pretty cool."

"Cool?" she asked. "I don't think that's what men are looking for in a woman."

"You want me to say she's super sexy and a wildling in bed?"

"Yes."

I forgot how down-to-earth Sofia was.

"See it going anywhere?"

I didn't think about it much. We'd had an expiration date the moment I laid eyes on her. "She just got divorced, so I doubt it."

"Would you want it to go somewhere?"

"I don't know... I'm not really in the right headspace for a relationship. I've got so much shit on my plate. Without Hades, everything has fallen to me, and I'm low on time."

"You could hand over the reins."

"No." I dismissed the idea right away.

"You could get a partner."

"The only partner I want is Hades—and he's done with me."

Sofia dropped her gaze. "Why did you snap at me that day?" She stirred her iced tea before she looked at me again.

It wasn't my finest hour, and no excuse would justify treating her that way. "Hades...we just haven't been getting along lately...more than usual. I'm sure he told you about it."

"Actually, no. He hasn't mentioned it at all."

Wow, I was even more worthless than I realized. "He hates me with his gaze every single day, and anytime we speak, his words are loaded with insults. Just yesterday, I told him I fixed a problem, and he said some shit to me...said I would never be an example to my son because I would ruin that relationship too." There was something about that comment that stung so much. I couldn't put my thumb on it.

Both of her eyebrows rose. "He said that?"

"And he's said worse."

"I had no idea. I thought the dust had settled."

"No...it'll never settle."

She stared at me for a long time, sympathy in her gaze. "I'll try talking to him—"

"Don't bother. Please."

Now she pitied me even more.

"Can I say something? Between us?" She was the only friend I had left in the world. Annabella and I talked, but I knew she wouldn't be around forever.

"Of course."

"I thought I would stop caring once enough time had passed. I would hate him as much as he hates me. But I feel like a punching bag...that gets hit over and over. He wants nothing to do with me, but it doesn't change how I feel. I'm so alone...so lonely. A beautiful woman in my bed doesn't erase what I lost. Life without him has only shown me how much he meant to me...that I'm not me without him." It was the lamest, most pathetic thing I'd ever said in my life. I didn't even sound like myself as I said all that bullshit. But I meant it, and that made me feel worse.

She inhaled a deep breath and sighed with sadness, like those words pierced her right in the heart. "I'm so sorry, Damien. I wish

Hades would let go of the past. I think it's just hard for him because I'm involved."

"Yeah. I get it."

"I can tell it bothers him too. We're happy together, but there's a piece of him that's missing. I think you're that piece."

"You must be mistaken...because he loathes me."

"They say hate is another form of love. If you really don't care about someone, you don't think about them. You're indifferent to them. You feel no emotion whatsoever, like anger or bitterness. But hatred is fueled by emotion, a stimulus that continues to linger under the skin. Hades is so aggressive with you because he cares—he still cares."

That shouldn't make me feel better, but it did...just a bit.

My hand was resting on the table, so she leaned forward and placed her hand on mine. "No matter what, you still have me. You'll always have me."

"Why?" My fingers wrapped around hers. "After what I did to you..."

"*You* didn't do anything to me, Damien. You're a good man. I'm not just saying that to make you feel better."

"Hades doesn't agree."

"Because he can't think straight when it comes to me, and instead of facing the truth, he chooses to blame you because it's easier. Easier than blaming the dead person who can't be punished because he's gone."

Even if Hades knew that, I doubt it would change anything.

"I really believe he'll come around...someday. He's just not there."

I could be dead by then. "How's the baby?" I pulled my hand away.

"Which one?"

"The one in there." I nodded to her stomach.

"He's a lot like Andrew—kicking all the time and being very disruptive."

"You mean just like Hades."

She chuckled. "Yeah, that must be where they get it from."

I knew Hades when he was a womanizer, hitting up whorehouses every day after work. Now, he was a devoted husband and father. It was hard to believe he was different in the past because he fit this new role so well.

"He told me the truth...about everything."

I stared at her in confusion.

"About the prophecy...about the woman in Marrakech...that he's cursed to love me forever...and that we're soul mates."

I stared at her in silence because I didn't know what to say. I wasn't sure if Hades would ever tell her the truth because it was impossible to believe. "You believe him."

She nodded. "Of course I do."

I could hear the sincerity in her voice. "I thought he was crazy at first...until the predictions turned into reality. I wasn't sure if he would ever tell you."

"He said he wanted me to know before he asked me to marry him again."

I was invited to the first wedding—but not the second.

"He took me to Marrakech to visit the woman."

My eyebrow raised. "What?"

She chuckled as she nodded. "I wanted to see it for myself...and ask her to read my fortune."

"Seriously? What did she say?" Anything that came out of her mouth was a curse.

"That we would live happily ever after. And when we're old and gray, Hades will die before me. I'll pass away two days later, dying of a broken heart." She continued to smile. "If that's true, I'm very happy."

"I'm sure it is true."

Her phone started to ring beside her, and she eyed it. "Oh no...it's him." She silenced the call.

"Don't ignore it because of me. That will just piss him off more."

"You're right." She picked up before it went to voice mail. "Hey."

His tone was so different from how it was at work that I hardly recognized him. "How's my baby?"

"Which one?"

"You," he said with a chuckle. "But let me know how he's doing, too."

"I'm great," she said as she looked at me. "And he's kicking a lot since I'm eating."

"I was going to ask you to have lunch. Are you in your office?"

"I'm around the corner at the Italian place I like."

"With whom?" he asked, his voice immediately turning suspicious.

I wanted her to lie because he would be ticked if he knew I was there.

"With Damien," she said, refusing to lie to her husband.

After a long pause, he responded. "Why?"

"He apologized and offered to take me to lunch."

Hades was quiet, clearly pissed. It didn't help that he wanted to see his wife and I was hogging her.

"Join us," she said. "We haven't gotten our food yet."

"I'll pass," he said coldly. "I'll see you at home."

She sighed in disappointment. "Alright."

"Love you," he said quickly, wanting to get off the phone.

"Love you too." She barely finished the sentence before he hung up.

She set the phone down and sighed. "Grouch."

"Still have hope?" I asked sarcastically.

"I'll always have hope, Damien." She moved her bread plate to the side when the food arrived.

The entrees were placed in front of us, a lasagna for Sofia and a Caesar salad for me.

She grabbed her fork and sliced into the layers of noodles and marinara. "So...tell me more about this woman you're seeing."

"Not much to say. Like I said, it's not serious."

"What does she do?"

"She's a waitress."

"How old is she?"

"Not sure, but probably a few years younger than me."

"What's she like?"

"You ask a lot of questions."

"Sorry, I'm curious. We don't talk anymore, so I'm interested in everything I've missed."

I hoped we wouldn't have another drought of activity. "Her ex-husband cheated on her, so she left him."

"Good for her. She's strong."

"Yeah. She had a miscarriage, so he got drunk and hooked up with someone else."

"Wow...jackass."

"Yeah, I'm not a fan. The guy was really wealthy and she refused to take his money in the divorce, so she's broke."

"She's proud."

"Very." I admired that about her, even though I wished she would take her cut of the settlement. "She barely makes ends meet, and she lives in a bad neighborhood...so I worry sometimes. Wish she would get a better job."

"Does she have any skills? Education?"

I shook my head. "Other than being smart and beautiful, she's got nothing."

"And good in the sack, apparently."

"That gets her free dinners with me."

She chuckled. "I could find her something at the hotel."

I stared at her blankly because I couldn't believe the offer she'd just put on the table. "What? Are you serious?"

"Why not?"

"She's not my girlfriend or anything. I don't want you bending over backward."

"I'm not. Just want to help. It's hard starting over. It was hard for me, and I had my inheritance and my mother."

It was still really generous. "What positions do you have open?"

"She could work in the office with me. The assistant office manager just transferred to Rome because she's getting married, so that's vacant."

"She doesn't have office experience that I know of. She said she married young and became a housewife."

"It's not that hard. I could train her and get her up to speed."

"Again, I don't want you to do all this work if she's not gonna be around forever."

"It's really not a big deal, Damien."

Knowing Annabella would have a nice salary and work at a good place made me feel relieved. I would bump into her sometimes when I stopped by the hotel, but I ran into old flames all the time, and we either ignored each other or were civil...with the occasional slap or drink in the face. "I'll let her know she's got an interview."

"Great. And since she is gonna be around...maybe you should keep seeing her."

I raised an eyebrow. "You haven't even met her, Sofia. She could be a nightmare."

"I doubt it. I can tell you care about her by the way you talk about her."

"I say nice things about people all the time."

She laughed loudly this time. "No, you don't. Not ever."

I WALKED her back into the lobby of the hotel.

"Thanks for lunch." She rubbed her slightly extended stomach that protruded from her dress. "It was delicious."

"It's the least I could do since I was such an asshole."

She chuckled. "Well, I hope you're an asshole more often."

Both of us stopped when we spotted Hades heading toward us in a deep blue suit with a black tie. His eyes hinted at the underworld.

I slid my hands into my pockets so I wouldn't punch him. "This should be good..."

Hades reached us, and for the first time in his life, he ignored his wife. His wrath was fixated on me. "Leave my wife alone, Damien." He spoke quietly so everyone else in the lobby wouldn't hear the deadly threat. "Get your own damn friends."

Yeah...it really seemed like he still cared.

Sofia stared at her husband like she didn't recognize him. "Hades..."

I thought he couldn't hurt me anymore, but he managed to get that blade right between my ribs. My gaze was hollow, but I was bleeding inside.

He continued that unblinking stare. "Go." He nodded to the door.

Sofia grabbed him by the arm. "Stop acting like this. Now."

Hades listened to his wife but still didn't look at her.

"I'm the one who's been texting him every day because I miss him," Sofia said. "He's my friend, and I don't give a damn if you don't like it."

He finally turned his gaze on her.

"Damien would never hurt me, and you know it." She started to pull him away. "I'll see you later, Damien." She took her husband down the hall so they could talk in private in her office.

I watched them walk away and knew I'd get another earful at the bank.

———

I'D JUST FINISHED with a client at the bar, and now I sat alone with my arms folded on the surface. I stared straight ahead, seeing the mirror behind the shelves stacked with bottles of booze.

My phone lit up with a text message from Annabella. *I know it's after hours, but could I schedule an emergency dick appointment?*

I'd been in a sour mood before I saw those words. Flashbacks of the hotel lobby came back to me, the fiery look in Hades's eyes as he stared at me with cruelty. He marched all the way down there to get Sofia away from me...as if I would actually harm her in some way. I should leave her alone, but to be honest, she really was all I had. When I was beaten and broken, she'd nursed me back to health. I saw Hades as a brother, but I didn't see Sofia as a sister. I saw her as the third person in our group. She was just one of the guys... I grabbed the phone to text back.

A muscular man moved onto the barstool beside me. His tattooed fingers tapped on the surface of the wood, and he quickly got the bartender's attention. "Old fashioned—hold the orange."

Nothing about this was funny, but I smiled anyway. "You think showing up everywhere I go is intimidating?"

"How about I ask your stomach?" He grabbed the glass and took a drink.

I chuckled. "I recover fast."

"But will your father?"

My blood turned cold at the threat. "That's the kind of man you want to be? Threatening elderly people? Real respectable..."

"You're one to talk about respect...going to my brother like that."

I couldn't believe Balto threw me under the bus. If he ever needed me to bail him out of a jam, I'd let him rot.

"You thought that was going to work?"

"I thought he would remind you that you're shitty at your job."

He laughed into his glass before he took a drink. "Now, that's not true. If it were, I wouldn't be here right now. I don't stop until I get my money. You're a banker, you get it."

"I don't go up to strangers and demand money."

"Oh, come on, we aren't strangers. I always thought we were friends...in a weird way." He turned in his stool so he faced me directly. "And just to clarify, Balto didn't sell you out. He actually told me to go easy on you...because you saved his ass a couple years ago."

"Then back off. I'm not paying you." I was so rich that the money meant nothing to me, but it was the principle of the matter. "My friend wouldn't have been raped if you'd done your job. But you didn't, and now I have to live with that for the rest of my life."

"That's rough, but I let the back taxes go."

"Not good enough." I turned my gaze in his direction. "You weren't there then. How can I trust you'll be there later?"

"Because I will. The transition was bad timing."

"Until it's bad timing again." I drank from my glass until it was empty. "I'm not paying you, Heath." I put the glass on the table, upside down.

He turned quiet, his breathing audibly different. "I'm trying to be a nice guy, Damien. But that won't last long."

"I'm not a nice guy either, Heath. Not ever."

He sighed before he finished the rest of his drink. "Your pride isn't worth what's about to happen to you. I encourage you to think it over before it's too late."

16

ANNABELLA

IT TOOK HIM AN HOUR TO TEXT ME BACK. *NOT TONIGHT. TOMORROW.* He wasn't playful at all, telling he was in a bad mood—again.

Was this guy ever happy?

In the back of my mind, I wondered if he was with Sofia. Judging by the content of that message I saw, it wasn't the first time she'd texted him. She was desperate to get his attention—and maybe she'd succeeded.

Bitch.

If it bothered me that much, I should do something about it.

But what?

The next day, I got off work and entered my apartment. I smelled like sandwiches and soup, so I washed that stink away before I did my hair and got dressed. When I grabbed my phone, there was a message from Damien. *Can I come by?*

I hated myself for smiling at his words. *Depends. What are you bringing?*

His response was immediate. *My dick.*

Anything else?

You want me to bring something else?

Guys usually bring a woman flowers...

You want flowers?

No...I'd prefer a pizza.

LOL. You got it.

He arrived at my door twenty minutes later, and instead of knocking, he just walked inside.

"Doorbell doesn't work?" I got off the couch and moved toward him, liking his gray t-shirt and black jeans. In his hand was a pizza box, the smell heavenly.

"You knew I was coming. Why knock?" His eyes roamed over my body, and judging from the intensity of his gaze, he liked the way I looked. A slight smile formed on his handsome lips, enhancing his good looks.

I popped open the top of the box. "Whatcha get?"

He pulled the box out of my grasp. "Whoa, slow down." He bent his neck down. "I don't get a kiss first?"

His charm and playfulness always made me melt, especially when he was so hot too. My hands moved to his chest, and I rose on my tiptoes so I could kiss him. It should be an innocent embrace, a welcoming gesture. But once his lips were on mine, I forgot about the cheesy pizza filling my apartment with its appetizing fragrance.

I focused on the taste of his sexy lips.

My arms slowly slid up his body until they hooked around his neck. I felt his bottom lip and then his top, my tongue delving deep into his mouth right away.

He moaned in my mouth and tightened his arm around my back,

bringing me hard into his chest like my desire had turned him on. He reached and set the pizza box on the entryway table without breaking our embrace. Once his hand was free, it was deep in my hair, his kiss carnal.

He backed me up to my bedroom, his hands sliding up my shirt so it would come free from my body. He cupped the back of my head as he unsnapped my bra with experienced fingers. It came undone instantly with the simple pinch of his fast fingers. He got my jeans unfastened a moment later, the backs of my knees hitting the mattress by the time he was nearly finished.

I yanked his shirt over his head and stared at his chest for a moment, loving his fitness. My nails dug into his skin right away, admiring the hardness underneath that sun-kissed skin.

He watched me praise him as he got his jeans unbuttoned and pushed them down his narrow hips. He did the same to mine, pushing them over my hips along with my panties. His big cock came free, drooling for me when the fun had barely started.

I knew exactly how I wanted him to fuck me, so I crawled on the bed and arched my back. When I didn't feel his knees press into the mattress, I looked at him over my shoulder.

His hand was around his dick, and he stared at my pussy like he couldn't believe what I'd just done. "That's how you want me to fuck you, Annabella?"

"Is this not clear enough for you?" I shook my ass slightly.

A sexy smirk moved across his mouth, and he fished a condom out of his jeans. He took his time rolling it on, staring at my ass as he left himself a generous tip at the end. When his knees hit the mattress, my heart began to race, the excitement giving me the chills. He positioned himself behind me and pushed his head inside me.

Just that was enough to make me moan.

He grabbed my hips and sank all the way inside, pushing through my tightness until he claimed me from front to back.

"Ooh..." I closed my eyes and widened my knees, giving him all the room he needed.

He grabbed my hair in his hand and wrapped it around his fingers, using it as reins to tug my head back slightly. Then his hips worked hard to pump inside me, giving me his entire length with quick speed.

"Damien..." He was the only man I wanted to fuck me. Only man I wanted inside me every night. He made all those other guys look like inexperienced boys. My ex-husband used to satisfy me, but it seemed like Damien was even better. I couldn't even think straight because it was so good.

"Fuck, you're hot when you're getting fucked."

"When I'm getting fucked by you..."

He sat beside me on the couch, wearing his black boxers. His chest was still slightly sticky from the sweat that had poured down his body minutes ago. He opened the cardboard box. "Hope you like cold pizza."

"I'll take hot sex and cold pizza any day."

He grinned as he handed me a slice. "Well said, Annabella." He grabbed himself a piece and took a bite. "Damn, this is good." Even the way he chewed his food was sexy, all the muscles in his jawline shifting under his skin.

"Don't eat pizza often?"

"I can't remember the last time I did."

"What?" I covered my mouth as I chewed my food. "You can't be serious."

"You think I look like this because I eat pizza all the time?" He patted his flat stomach.

"Well, you drink more than would bring down a horse, and you still look like that..."

"I compensate by not eating."

"Then why are you so muscular?"

"I have a super protein shake for lunch."

"Every day?" I asked.

"Except when I showed up at your bistro for lunch."

I couldn't believe I had been so cold to him when he was buried treasure. "Even then, you just ate a salad."

"Yeah, I'm pretty boring."

"Not in bed."

He watched me as he chewed his bite, affection in his eyes. "Have I told you how much I like you, Annabella?"

"No. But I'm listening now."

He chuckled then grabbed another slice. "How was your day?"

"Fine. I worked at the restaurant. Some guy left me a big tip."

"Must be American."

"Yeah. I wish more Americans would come in," I said with a chuckle. "He gave me a hundred euros."

"I'm sure he wanted your number in return."

I shrugged. "He didn't ask for it."

Damien finished his slice of pizza and didn't comment.

Did he care if other men hit on me?

"Speaking of work…" He closed the box and set it to the side of the couch. "A friend of mine owns the Tuscan Rose and said she needs a new office manager. I recommended you, and she wanted to set up an interview."

Friend? Was this an old lover? Would an old lover want to provide his new lover a job opportunity? That seemed unlikely. "That's sweet, but I have no qualifications for the position."

"She said she doesn't mind teaching you."

"Why would she want to waste her time doing that when she could hire someone else?"

He took a while before he answered. "I guess she wants to help me out."

"How would that help you?"

He gave me a long stare. "Because I don't want you to keep waitressing."

"Is there something wrong with it?" I would be hurt if he thought less of me because of the way I paid the bills.

"No. I just want you to make more money. Do you not?"

"Of course I do, but you didn't have to pull any strings—"

"I didn't. She offered."

"But why would she offer unless you brought me up—"

"Because I told her I was seeing you." He continued to stare at me. "I said you were newly divorced and starting over, and that I want you to be financially stable and maybe upgrade to a better neighborhood."

That answered all my questions, so I didn't know what to say.

"I would never ask her to do something like that for me. It was all her."

"That's awfully nice of her…"

"Well, she's a very nice person."

I didn't want to lose an opportunity to make good money and not smell like sandwiches every day. I'd had lunch at the Tuscan Rose, and it was a really nice place. The lobby was always full of flowers, and that was my favorite part. "I don't know what to say… That's really generous."

"Agree to the interview."

"Well, I definitely can't say no."

"Good. I was hoping you wouldn't."

"Besides…my hair always smells like onions after work."

"I noticed but didn't want to say anything…"

I smacked his arm playfully because I knew he was kidding. "That's rude."

"Whether you smell like onions or not, I still want to fuck you, so you're good."

"Good to know," I said sarcastically.

Now that we were done eating, he placed his arm around my shoulders and pulled me close. "Want to watch a movie or something?"

So, he wanted to stay. "Sure."

***

WE ENDED up in bed together again, and this time, it didn't seem like he was going to leave.

My head rested on the same pillow as his while my leg was hooked over his waist. Our bodies were close together, our chests almost touching. My fingers lightly played with his abs, feeling the hardness even when he was perfectly relaxed. "You are going to stay?"

His deep eyes looked into mine. "If that's okay."

"That's always okay." It was getting harder every time he left, especially because I had no idea where he was going, if he would meet a woman better than me. She would make him lose interest in me... and I would never see him again. I wasn't anxious for a commitment; I just didn't want to lose him. "What happened last night?"

"What do you mean?" His hand moved into my hair and pushed it from my face and over my shoulder.

"You didn't want to see me."

"It's not that I didn't want to," he said quietly. "Just another rough night."

"So, you weren't with someone?" I couldn't hold back my question because the jealousy was slowly making me crack. I was such a calm and rational person, but I feared someone would take away this perfect man.

"You mean another woman?"

My fingers stilled against his abs. "Yes."

He stared at me for a long time as he considered the question, his thoughts a mystery because he could hide the darkest secrets inside that hard exterior. "Does that mean you don't want me to?"

He never answered the question, and that made my heart race in dread. Picturing him with someone else made me so sick I wanted to throw up the pizza I'd just eaten. It was nothing like Liam because this was casual, something I specifically asked for, but I couldn't shake the overwhelming disappointment. Seeing Sofia's name on the phone made me so jealous, I had no idea I was this possessive of a man I hardly knew. It wasn't like me...at all. "I'm not looking for anything serious. I'm not looking for a relationship. I'm just—"

"Annabella." He silenced me with his tone. "Just answer the question."

I dropped my gaze.

"And look at me as you give it."

My eyes flicked back to his, so embarrassed that I couldn't feel more ashamed, so I may as well answer. "Yes."

He stared at me in silence, his piercing gaze giving nothing away. His jaw was tight as the answer soaked into his skin. It was unclear if he was annoyed or indifferent to my request. "That's all you had to say."

I'd been holding my breath for a while, and I let it out as I responded. "What does that mean?"

"It means I won't see anyone else." His hand rested against the side of my face, his fingers on my neck and cheek. "If that's what you want."

"When I said I wasn't looking for anything serious, I meant it. It's so soon after my divorce. But I wasn't expecting to meet someone like you. I don't know what I want for the future, but I know it drives me crazy when I imagine you with someone else. I don't want to share you as long as you're in my bed and I'm in yours."

His eyes shifted back and forth as he looked into mine, taking in every word I said. "Alright."

That was it? It was that simple? "Could we stop using condoms, then?" I'd never used them while I was married, and I missed that. Damien felt good covered in latex, but he probably felt amazing when it was just him. "I'm on the pill."

"You want me to come inside you?"

Just the thought turned me on. "Hell yeah."

His eyes darkened in intensity, like he imagined the sensation and it turned him on too. "I'll get you my papers."

"Alright...I will too." I was happy I got what I wanted without chasing him off, but I was disappointed that his feelings weren't clear. Did he want the same thing? Or was he just doing it for me? And he never answered my question.

He seemed to know what I was thinking. "I wasn't with a woman last night. Just a very obnoxious man."

"Do you want this too?" It was still a casual relationship...just one with a few parameters. I wasn't asking anything of substance. I wasn't going back on what I'd said that first night on the sidewalk.

"Do I want to come inside you?" he whispered, his voice deep. "Yes, Annabella. I want to come inside you every night until your pussy breaks."

I GOT to the restaurant first.

I was an innately confident person, but I was nervous for this interview for several reasons.

One, I actually wanted this job.

And two, she was a friend of Damien's, so I wanted to make a good impression. I cared more about that than actually getting the job.

A pregnant woman walked inside, dark hair pulled over one shoulder, with diamond earrings in her lobes. She was in a tight black dress, which made her small stomach more noticeable.

That couldn't be her, so I looked out the window again, my

thoughts returning to the handsome man who had commandeered my thoughts. I used to wonder what Liam was doing throughout the day, who was in his bed at night, but now I rarely thought about him. I hadn't noticed until that moment.

"Annabella?" The pregnant woman approached my table, giving me a genuine smile.

This was the woman. "Yes." I got to my feet and smoothed out my dress. "Such a pleasure to meet you." I shook her hand. "I've always been an admirer of your hotel. I've never actually stayed there, but I've had lunch a few times, and those flowers in the lobby have always been special to me."

That seemed to have significance to her because her eyes softened at the compliment. "Thank you...that means a lot to me." She released her hand and moved to the chair across from me. "I'm Sofia Lombardi, by the way."

Sofia? The same Sofia who was texting Damien that night? "Beautiful name..." Could she be the same person? Why would Damien stop talking to her and then she offer me a job? It couldn't be.

"As is yours. So, tell me about yourself."

"Well, I got divorced a couple months ago. I'm sure Damien mentioned that. It didn't end well, and I had to start over. I got married very young, so I didn't spend that time preparing for a career. I assumed I would be a stay-at-home mom...but that wasn't meant to be. But I'm very bright, I learn quick, and I'm easy to get along with."

"I can tell by the way Damien speaks about you."

"Yeah?" I asked, wondering exactly what he'd said.

"Yes. And Damien doesn't say nice things about anybody." She grinned. "He's kind of a grouchy old man, you know?"

I laughed because her assessment was right on the nose. "Very true. He can be moody."

She got down to business and started talking about the responsibilities of the job, but I wasn't nervous anymore. It seemed as if she'd liked me before she'd even seen my face, that whatever Damien had said about me was good enough for her.

I wondered what he'd said...

17

DAMIEN

THE RECEPTIONIST HANDED ME THE ENVELOPE AS MY PHONE RANG.

"Thanks." I opened the flap as I walked outside. My phone continued to vibrate in my pocket as I stepped onto the sidewalk. I fished it out and looked at the screen. It was Sofia, so I answered as I pulled the report from the envelope. "So, what did you think?" I stopped near my car and read the results.

Clean.

"She's a very cute girl, Damien."

"Why do you think I'm fucking her?" I stuffed the paper back into the envelope and slipped it into my back pocket.

"And she's lovely."

"That isn't really why I'm fucking her, but I'm glad you think so."

"Shut up, Damien," she said with a laugh. "I liked her a lot. I'm going to offer her the job."

They'd met yesterday, and I hadn't spoken to Annabella since. When I was at the office, I expected Hades to scream at me for getting chummy with his wife, but he chose to ignore me instead.

Then I had to handle distribution to our biggest clients in Greece all night. "You don't have to do that for me. You know that, right?"

"I know. I really liked her."

I liked her a lot too...enough to keep my dick in my pants. "Thanks for doing that. I want her to have an easier life."

"I can tell she thinks the world of you."

"Yeah?" I leaned against my car and grinned. She was always eager for my dick and such an incredible lover that I figured that out on my own.

"She actually thinks you're a good person...which is a first."

I chuckled. "She doesn't know me that well."

"It sounds like it does. She said you've been seeing each other for a while..."

I recognized that tone. "It's not serious, Sofia. I told you that."

"But I know you don't see the same woman more than a few times, right?"

"Doesn't mean anything."

"Sure about that?"

Annabella asked for my fidelity, but she also made it clear it didn't mean anything. She was still carrying baggage from her divorce, still navigating this new life of independence. I was just a rebound —a really good rebound. The monogamy was temporary, and it would allow us to have even better sex—which was good for me. "A hundred percent."

I'D JUST GOTTEN out of the shower when Annabella texted me. *Are you in the mood for pizza?*

I'm in the mood for you.

If you order the Annabella special, you can get both.

I faced the bathroom mirror with a towel around my waist, grinning as I stared down at the phone. *That's one hell of a deal.*

Does that mean I can come over?

I can come get you.

I just left the pizza place. I'll grab a taxi.

I didn't like her getting around on her own because I knew what kind of monsters plagued these streets. To everyone else, it was just a beautiful city with stunning cathedrals and a rich culture. I was one of the few who knew the truth. But I knew Annabella wasn't my problem, that she needed to have the independence to survive on her own because I wouldn't be around forever.

I pulled on my boxers and waited for her to walk inside. Didn't see the point in getting dressed when all those clothes would end up on the floor anyway.

Minutes later, she let herself inside with a pizza box under her arm.

"I'm not gonna be sexy anymore if I keep eating pizza like this."

"I doubt it would make much of a difference." She smiled as she walked up to me and kissed me.

I kissed her back, my mind immediately wondering if she'd completed her tests. I pulled away then reached for the pizza.

"Whoa...not so fast." She kept it out of my reach. "You're gonna have to work for it."

"Yeah? Getting you a job wasn't enough?"

"You said that was all her. And hold on, I got the job?"

I grinned. "Congratulations."

"Yes!" She fist-pumped the air. "I'm throwing my apron in the dumpster when I get home." She moved the box back to me. "In that case, we should celebrate. There's no better trophy than cheese and crust."

"What about sex?" I opened the lid and took out a slice.

"We'll get to that." She grabbed a piece and placed the corner in her mouth so she could take a small bite. "Pizza and sex...sounds like a really good book title."

"I'd read that."

We moved to the living room and sat together on the couch. Our relationship was physical and intimate, but when that wasn't happening, it really felt like we were friends who actually liked each other. I'd been with women I could hardly tolerate when the sex was over. They were either rude or way too opinionated. But when my hormones were extinguished, Annabella was a good friend.

"So...what did she say about me?" She leaned against the armrest on the opposite side of the couch, her knees pulled to her chest as she ate her slice. She was in little cutoff shorts and a pink t-shirt, refusing to let summer leave. Her long legs were tanned from the sunny season we'd just experienced, toned and kissable.

"That's confidential."

"Oh, come on." She gave me a playful nudge with her foot.

"She said you were cute."

She took a bite with her eyebrow raised. "I don't think cuteness was a qualification she was looking for."

"Well, that's what she said. What did you think about her?"

"She was really nice...and very cute."

I grinned at her response. "Do I need to get you two alone in a room together?"

She kicked me again, this time a little harder.

I chuckled then finished my slice. Two pieces was my limit. Anything more than that would screw me over.

She didn't reach for another slice when she finished, and then she turned quiet, like something was on her mind.

I knew her well enough to pick up on her moods now. "What is it?"

"What is what?" she asked quietly.

"Your mood dropped."

"Me not talking means my mood dropped?"

I gave her a cold look. "You can't fool me. What is it?"

She crossed her arms over her chest and considered my question. "This isn't gonna make me look very good, but it's driving me crazy."

I had no idea where this was going. "Alright."

"A few weeks ago, you left your phone on the table and walked away. It lit up with a text message, and I automatically looked at it...and read it."

I stared at her blankly because I got lots of texts from lots of people. What did she see that was so disturbing?

"It was a message from Sofia, and she said something like...talk to me."

I gave Annabella my full attention, trying to work out her point before she got there.

"Was that the same Sofia I just met?"

I answered immediately. "Yes."

"Did you...sleep with her? Because she's married and pregnant..."

I didn't have much of a moral compass, but I had never been with someone who was married to someone else. And I certainly hadn't bedded a pregnant woman either. "No." It surprised me how jealous Annabella was, how much she cared about me seeing other women. She was the one who was solely interested in sex.

"Never?"

I shook my head. "She's just a friend."

"Oh...has she ever wanted you?"

"Are you always this jealous?" I teased.

"I..." Her voice drifted away as she considered it. "No, actually." Her eyes looked elsewhere as she finished her sentence. Eventually, she turned back to me. "I'm not sure why I care so much. Maybe because Liam cheated on me... I really don't know. I'm sorry. I know it's none of my business."

She was right—none of her damn business. "She's married to my business partner."

She looked up in surprise, as if she hadn't expected that elaboration. "The man you've had a falling out with?"

"Yeah. When I was really injured, she was the one who got me back on my feet. We've always gotten along, and instead of seeing her as my best friend's wife or like a sister, I've always seen her as her own person...as the third friend in our group."

Softness entered her gaze.

"She's always fought for me with Hades...even though she was raped because of my stupidity. She's never blamed me for what happened, and she still tries to change his mind about the whole thing. I was an idiot and screamed at her when she tried to reach out to me one day, but Hades had really pissed me off and I was in a bad mood. We didn't talk for a while...and she kept trying to reach out to me. I finally came around and apologized."

"She seems like a good person."

"Yeah...the best." She was even better than Hades. He didn't deserve her. Not sure why the universe thought otherwise.

"I feel stupid now..."

Maybe I would have slept around if I had the time, but ever since I'd met Annabella, I'd been busy every hour of the day. There wasn't time to meet someone else. When I was at the bar, I usually had business to take care of. And then Heath was showing up everywhere I went.

Or maybe I hadn't met someone because I wasn't looking for someone.

I liked that she was a bit jealous, that she wondered where I was when I wasn't with her, that she assumed Sofia wanted me when I doubted she'd ever found me attractive. It was better than indifference.

She stared down at her lap for a while, swallowing her humiliation. She'd put herself on a silver platter, her thoughts as clear as if they'd been written on a billboard. She didn't hide anything, unlike when we first met.

"It's ironic." My arm rested over the back of the couch as I looked at her. "I showed up at your restaurant in the hope of a date, and I had to work my ass off to get anything from you. You shot me down so fast, completely uninterested."

She lifted her gaze to look at me.

"When I finally talked you into it, you told me you would never want me for more than a night, that I would never mean anything to you. And now you're jealous. Now you don't want me to be with anyone else...now you assume every woman I know wants me, which is true most of the time, but not in this case." When she'd sat in that chair across from my desk, she'd made her demands unapologetically. She knew what she wanted and got right down to business. Being the new thing she wanted was a bit exhilarating. "It's funny how things change…"

She watched me for a long time, her eyes shifting slightly as she processed her thoughts and turned them into words. "There was no way for me to anticipate what kind of man you would be…that you would make all the other men I've been with lately look like boys." She averted her eyes whenever she was embarrassed, but right now, she was confident, holding my gaze like there was nothing to be embarrassed about. "If I'd known, I would have been the one chasing you down on the sidewalk."

The hairs on the back of my neck stood up when those sexy words landed on my ears. Lots of women wanted me, albeit for different reasons. Sometimes it was my money, my ride, or my expensive suit. Sometimes it was the drugs…because the danger was a turn-on. But Annabella wanted me for all the physical reasons, when I wasn't wearing my flashy watch and tailored suit. She wanted me in my purest form…naked. My fingertips felt numb when I imagined touching her soft hair. My dick thickened in my boxers, and the bulge was probably noticeable even in her peripheral vision. I broke out in a slight sweat, thinking about the blood that was about to pump from fucking her.

She slowly got to her feet and sauntered toward me, her fingertips loosening the button at the top of her jean shorts. Her painted nails pulled down the zipper, and the little denim bottoms slipped down her long legs.

My arm lowered from the couch, and I felt all the muscles of my throat and chest tighten. Confidence was in her gaze, as if she understood how much she turned me on, and that was sexy to see.

Her panties came next, baby blue. "I got my papers. Did you?"

My hands pushed my boxers over my hips so my cock could come free. My head was so far in the clouds, I couldn't articulate a response with my words. All I did was give a nod as I stared at her slit.

Her knees hit the couch, and she slowly lowered herself onto my lap, her arms hooking around my neck. Chest against chest, we brought our faces together, our quick breaths dancing across each other's cheeks.

My cock was against my stomach, and her lips were on my balls, warm and wet. I could feel her arousal moisten my delicate skin, feel her warmth as it teased me.

She rubbed her nose against mine gently, her eyes looking at my mouth like she wanted to devour me. Both of her hands dug into my hair as she leaned down and kissed me, her soft lips landing against mine like two sides of the same coin.

My hands moved to her hips, and my fingers reached underneath her t-shirt. I inhaled as I felt her hungry lips, felt my fingers dig deep into her flesh like she was a life raft. I tugged her a little closer as I kissed her back and felt my dick twitch when her mouth was on me.

Our kisses continued, loud in my quiet bedroom. Our bodies oozed with desire as the foreplay aroused us both. My knees parted and my feet planted against the ground, my toes digging into the rug because I was already writhing in the pleasure I expected to feel.

Her small tongue danced with mine, the occasional moan filling the charged air around us.

My hand moved across her ass cheeks, getting a nice grip of both of them with a single hand. My middle fingers rested in the crack as I squeezed her, wanting to yank her down my length and take her harshly.

I let her decide when she was ready in case she wanted to change her mind. Fuck, she better not change her mind. I'd never wanted a woman more, and if this were taken away from me, I'd lose my mind.

She ended our kiss and looked me in the eye, her curtain of dark hair framing one side of her face. She arched her back and tilted her hips in the sexiest way, and without breaking our contact, she grabbed my base and straightened it so she could saddle it.

Jesus.

She lowered her slit onto my tip, noticeably soaked and anxious. She parted for me, like a crowd that made way for a queen. Her body divided to take me in, to allow my enormous size to sink into her and claim it.

I closed my eyes for a second and groaned, my fingers squeezing her with absolutely no delicacy. I was only a few inches deep, but it was already the most unbelievable sensation I'd ever experienced. I'd never taken a woman like this, never considered this level of intimacy with anyone.

Monogamy was fucking hot.

She bit her bottom lip as she sank the rest of the way, watching my face match hers. Her fingers loosened on my hair and gripped my shoulders. She slowly fell until she had every single inch of me. She released a shaky breath, wincing with the pain at my stretch, but she didn't seem eager to pull me out.

My mind was overloaded with all the intimate sensations. There was no sheath blocking the sensitivity of my dick. I could feel every single detail, absorb all her moisture, feel all the nerve endings fire off with explicit pleasure. Fucking a woman with a condom was the right thing to do, but fucking her without one was brave.

How would I survive this?

She moaned in my face. "That's a lot better..." Her ass was right on my balls, and she tilted her hips to drag her clit against my hard body. We were combined together, so intimate that we were more than just lovers. She started to move up and down, her face pressed to mine as our bodies slid past each other.

It took me minutes to get used to it, to stop moaning and writhing and focus on what was happening. I'd never felt so weak in my life, paralyzed. I'd been beaten to within an inch of my life, but I was far more helpless now than I had been then.

It took me a while to snap out of the spell. My feet finally dug into the rug, and I thrust up with my hips, meeting her movements so she wasn't doing all the work. The pace was slow because that was more than enough for the both of us. Our slick bodies moved past each other, practically frictionless. My hands gripped her ass, and I helped her rise and fall, showing her I was man enough to be allowed this privilege.

She spoke against my lips. "I can't wait for you to come inside me, Damien..."

Jesus Fucking Christ.

18

ANNABELLA

WHEN DAMIEN'S ALARM WENT OFF THE NEXT MORNING, HE BARELY opened his eyes before he moved on top of me and thrust himself in between my legs. The sheet was over his waist to stay warm, and he gave me lazy thrusts as he woke up to the sensation of being buried in my pussy.

My arms hooked over his shoulders, and I felt him rock me back and forth, my body relaxed because I hadn't fully woken up yet. I was still full of him from the night before, a marathon of fucking that used every piece of furniture in his room. Now, we were at it again...like last night wasn't enough.

It was easy for me to come because the full sensation of his dick was still new. It felt so right to feel the grooves of his dick press right up against me as he sank inside me over and over. My slickness cushioned his glide, and together we made the best sex ever.

He widened my legs with his arms and thrust into me harder, digging my ass into his mattress as he pounded me into the sheets. His head rested against mine, and he breathed hard and groaned with every thrust.

I gripped his arms as I came, my hips thrusting back as my body gave in to the pleasure. My head rolled back, and I moaned long and hard, experiencing so much goodness, I didn't know what to do with all of it.

Watching me come set him off, and he filled me with his final pumps, moaning with every thrust. He stuffed me with another mound of come, adding it to all the previous piles that still sat inside me.

He rested his forehead against mine when he was done, breathing hard as his body spiraled down from the high. He gave me a soft kiss that contradicted the hard and lazy way he'd fucked me then rolled off me. He had to get to the office, so he immediately went to the bathroom to shower.

I turned over and went back to sleep.

HE DROVE me back to my apartment on the way. He parked his car and walked me to the door, even though I told him that was unnecessary.

In his black suit and tie, he looked like the formidable opponent he claimed he was. He handled billions like it was nothing, and he ran the streets as if being a dictator was the easiest job in the world.

And he was so hot while doing it.

I didn't think I had a thing for bad boys, but my ex-husband was a fighter covered in tattoos, and the new man I was sleeping with was a drug lord. I never worried about the risks associated with the men. I just enjoyed the fact that they were strong enough to protect me.

I knew Damien could keep me safe...and I liked that.

When I got the door unlocked, he kissed me goodbye. His large hands gripped my hips, his fingers digging deep into my sides as he held me close. His kiss was sexy, full of eager lips and a bit of tongue.

Now I didn't want him to go.

He released me and pulled away. After a dark look with those intense eyes, he turned around and walked off...without saying a word.

I liked that...because he'd said everything he wanted to say with just that look.

I'D JUST FINISHED lunch when Sofia called me.

"Hey, is this a good time?" she asked, sounding exactly like the bubbly person I remembered.

"Absolutely. How are you?"

"The baby is kicking like he didn't like my lunch, but I'm good besides that," she said with a chuckle. "So, I'm calling to formally offer you the job. Damien has a big mouth, so he probably already told you."

"Yeah...he mentioned it," I said with a laugh. "And I'm very excited."

"Great. Can you start on Monday?"

"Definitely." I'd go down to the restaurant tomorrow and throw my apron in my manager's face. "I'll see you then." Just when I hung up the phone and set it down, it started to ring again.

This time, it was Liam.

He hadn't called me in a long time. After the emotional conversation in my living room, he finally got the hint and walked away. Knowing I had a guy in my bedroom was the straw that broke the camel's back, and he let me go.

But now, he was back.

My first instinct was to ignore his call, but since it'd been months since we talked, maybe he actually had something important to say. Maybe I should give him a chance. I swiped on the phone and took the call. But I didn't say anything...because I didn't know what to say.

He didn't say anything either, his presence enough.

I opened my mouth to say something but changed my mind.

He finally spoke. "I'm surprised you answered."

"Wanted to give you the benefit of the doubt..."

He was quiet again, organizing his thoughts because he'd been expecting my voice mail. "Can we have dinner tonight? I want to talk to you about something."

Were we doing this again? "Liam..."

"It's not about us."

"Then why can't we just talk about it now."

"Because it's not that kind of conversation. Just meet me. Please."

I felt weird going out to dinner with my ex when I was kinda in a relationship now, but if it was platonic, I didn't see the harm. "Alright. Just text me the time and place."

19

DAMIEN

Hades stepped into my office, looking pissed as usual.

"It's way too early for this." I relaxed into the chair, too exhausted for our usual back-and-forth venom. I had been up all night fucking, and I never really woke up. I stared at my computer and saw dots...or flashbacks of my night with Annabella.

"Liam is in my office."

"And?"

"Let's squash the beef and say hello."

"I got him back, didn't I?" I snapped.

"Damien." His eyebrows narrowed. "Seal the deal. You know how this works."

It was hard not to hate Liam after what he did to Annabella, but since he was so important to Hades, I had to be objective about the situation...even though I was fucking his ex-wife. "Fine." I pushed back my chair and walked with Hades down the hallway to his office.

Liam's massive size was in the chair, and he was texting on his phone.

"Sorry to keep you waiting," Hades said as he moved to his chair behind the desk.

"It's fine," Liam answered. "But let's get this rolling because I've got a lot of shit to do today."

I straightened my tie and extended my hand. "Welcome back."

He eyed me for a second before he took my hand. "Yeah…"

"I'm glad we could move past our spat," I said diplomatically. "Hades and I both value your business."

Hades stared at me, and it was the first time he gave me a look of approval.

Liam relaxed further. "And I value your expertise." He turned back to Hades. "Now, let's make some money. I'm having dinner with my ex-wife later tonight." He pulled back his sleeve to eye his watch. "And I can't be late to that."

I stilled on the spot, staring at him with wide eyes.

Hades watched my expression without giving anything away.

Liam didn't catch on to the change in the energy of the room.

Hades cleared his throat. "Then let's get to work. Damien, I can take it from here."

I had to blink a few times before I could regain my composure. Wordlessly, I left the room and headed down the hallway.

When I was back in my office, I felt the wave of anger.

Why the fuck was she seeing him?

Why the fuck didn't she tell me?

My brain boiled with rage, and I felt the betrayal like a knife between the ribs.

But then I remembered she didn't owe me anything. Just because she was having dinner with him didn't mean she was going to sleep with him. She'd had plenty of opportunities in the past and she never did, and our arrangement was going so well, I didn't see why she would need him at all. Whenever we were together, it was obvious she was into me...really into me.

She wasn't my girlfriend, so I let it go.

20

ANNABELLA

IF DAMIEN CALLED AND ASKED IF I HAD PLANS, I WASN'T SURE WHAT I would say. I didn't want to lie to him, but I didn't want to tell him the truth either. He didn't seem like the jealous type, but it might piss him off that I was seeing Liam. Though, he should trust me, because I was committed to him...had been since the moment he'd asked me out. Why would I want to be with Liam again when I already had a man who was a million times better?

A billion times better.

I sat in the restaurant and read the menu by candlelight. It was a nice place, because Liam liked nice things. He would never be seen at the restaurant where I worked or any casual place like that. He said he was too rich "to eat shit."

I'd let him pay because I couldn't afford this place. Just a salad was thirty euro. I'd been wealthy for a long time, so becoming broke was a really humbling experience. I realized how hard it was to get by when you were alone with no experience.

At least I was starting my new job in a couple days.

Liam walked inside, moving to the front because the staff recognized his face. A man in a suit guided him to the table where I waited. Liam didn't look at the chair or the table, his eyes focused on me as if he liked my black dress. Some things hadn't changed... like the way he looked at me.

He ordered a bottle of wine for the table along with an appetizer, running the show like usual. He always issued orders and put people to work because that was how he was...a natural leader.

He was quiet as he stared at me, ignoring the staff as they poured the wine, brought the basket of bread and the appetizer, and barely issued a thank-you when they walked off. His broad shoulders were large in his sports coat, and he stared at me like I was still his, even though I hadn't been his for so long. There were times when I wished I would forgive him because he was the kind of man any woman would want. He was handsome, masculine, and strong. And he always made me feel like a woman. But now that I had Damien, I didn't feel the same way anymore. I was glad I hadn't settled... because I'd met a better man. I'd met a man who made me feel so much, who made me feel safe, who made me trust him without having to try. He put me back together—whether that was intentional or not. He didn't need to take me to a fancy place to impress me. He could do it with a large pizza in his boxers.

"What did you want to talk about?" I wanted to keep it professional because I wouldn't have met him otherwise. I didn't ask how he was because that might open the doors to him saying he was miserable without me...and that whole conversation would start again.

His eyes showed slight disappointment, like he'd hoped for more this evening. But he didn't fight it because he knew I would leave the restaurant. "I'm going back to death fighting."

My heart started to race a little quicker as the fear killed me. He knew exactly how I felt about that, and I wished he'd never told me. We could be divorced for twenty years, and I would still care about his well-being.

He watched my reaction.

"Why?"

His eyes were steady on mine. "Why not?"

"Because you could die," I snapped. "That's why."

He shrugged. "The pot is bigger."

"You're already a billionaire." My voice rose uncontrollably, bringing me from a state of calm to one of hysteria. "Why do you need more money? You have a plane, several homes—what more do you want?"

He hadn't reached for the wine or the warm bread wrapped in the white linen. "I don't have anything else, Annabella. I don't have a wife or a family, so I'm not risking anything anymore. It's a challenge, something to work toward. Regular fights are boring. But when your life is on the line..."

I closed my eyes. "Please stop."

He shut his mouth. "I'm not going to lose. I never lose."

His arrogance didn't give me any assurance. "Why are you telling me?"

It was the first time he broke eye contact, looking across the restaurant at no one in particular. His blue eyes were impossible to read because they were always so hard. He shifted his gaze back to mine. "Because I won't do it...if you take me back."

I inhaled a deep breath into my lungs, appalled that he would put me in that position. He gave me an ultimatum, guilting me into giving him what he wanted, manipulating me by creating a life-and-death situation. "You're an asshole."

He didn't argue.

"How about you not do it out of respect for what we had?"

"Anna." He deepened his tone. "You are my only reason for living.

I'm never gonna love another woman the way I love you. I'm not doing this to coerce you—"

"It seems like it," I hissed.

"I thought you should know how miserable I am without you, that I don't value my life the way I used to. And maybe that will be enough for you to trust me again, to believe me—"

"If you really loved me, you wouldn't do this, simply because I asked you not to—whether we're together or not." Our voices grew louder as we argued across the candlelit table. "You know I'll always care about you, always love you, so you're doing this to be a jackass."

He didn't care about the people who'd started to stare at us. "I *want* to do this. The only reason I stopped was because you asked me to stop. But now that you aren't here anymore, I want to resume. I'm just giving you a goddamn courtesy. If you really want me to stay out of the ring, then you have the power to stop it."

"By doing something I don't want to do."

"No. Something you're *scared* to do. You just said you still love me—"

"Not like that," I snapped. "In an affectionate way, in a fondness for the years we shared together. I told you I'm seeing someone."

"No. You said you were seeing other people."

"Well, I've been seeing one specific person for a few months now, and I don't want to stop seeing him."

His body sagged noticeably, like I'd punched him in the stomach. "Is it serious?"

"I don't know...we aren't seeing other people." Because I didn't want to. Because I couldn't stand the thought of sharing him. Because I wanted him all to myself...every night...for the foreseeable future.

"We just got divorced," he said coldly. "Don't you think that's too soon?"

"We've been divorced for nine months, Liam. And the last three months of that marriage don't count. I was miserable. Every time we made love, all I could think about was you and that other woman. So it's been over a year. A damn year."

He had the humility to look away for a second, still ashamed of what he did.

"So, it's not too soon. I like him...a lot."

He blinked again, as if that hurt. "He'll never love you the way I do."

"Maybe. But at least I trust him."

His eyes narrowed. "It's easier to trust someone when things are good. But what about when it goes to shit? You have no way to predict what he'll do. He's not better than me. He'll fuck up like all men do. At least I actually love you, would die to protect you, would do anything to make you smile."

"Liam—"

"You don't know him well enough to trust him. Who is he?"

I wouldn't throw Damien under the bus like that. Liam still used his bank, and if he knew...he'd burn that place to the ground. "It doesn't matter."

"Yes, it fucking matters. Answer me." He continued to raise his voice, but the staff didn't dare quiet him, not when they knew who he was.

I slightly raised my hand off the table to silence him. "Liam."

He shut his mouth, but his red face showed his rage.

"The answer is no."

His eyes didn't blink.

I got out of my chair because I couldn't stay there any longer. "I hope that you love me enough not to do this...because I would be devastated if you weren't here anymore. But I won't sacrifice my happiness to keep you alive. I won't settle for a man who hurt me, betrayed me at my lowest point, just so he won't recklessly throw his life away."

I WAS low and wanted the one person who took away all my stress. His fingers in my hair always calmed me down, his powerful gaze always made me feel safe, but if I called him, I would have to tell him why I was upset. And I didn't want to talk about it.

But I was sitting in the dark, suffocated by my thoughts.

I texted him. *Come over.* I didn't want to be needy or demanding, but I was anxious to see him, wanted him to drop whatever he was doing to hold me.

He responded immediately, like he'd been staring at his phone when my message popped up. *Want me to pick up something on the way? Anything but pizza. I need to lay off that shit.*

He made me chuckle. *No. Just you.*

Fifteen minutes later, he let himself into the apartment without knocking. He was in jeans and a t-shirt, his jaw smooth because he'd shaved that morning. If he noticed the puffiness around my eyes, he didn't act like it. He took the seat beside me on the couch, his arm moving behind my neck as he held me close. His fingers slid into the back of my hair, the touch exactly what I'd been craving.

I looked into his handsome face, my expression growing soft as I appreciated all those masculine features, especially that hard jawline. My hand reached up, and my fingers rested against his lips, feeling the only soft feature he possessed.

While staring at me, his mouth kissed my fingertips, treasuring them the way he did with the rest of my body.

My fingers moved to his chin and touched his jaw before they dropped to his chest. Conversation wasn't what I needed to feel comforted. It was just...his attention, his affection. I loved how he could convey so much without saying a single word.

"Want to talk about it?" His hand wrapped around mine, and he drew my wrist to his lips, kissing the sensitive area gently, his mouth bringing warmth to my delicate skin.

"How do you know something is wrong?"

He held my hand on his thigh, his expression the same. "Because I know you, Annabella."

———

WEARING HIS T-SHIRT, I lay in bed beside him, the light from the obnoxious streetlight entering through the cheap blinds on the window. I was on my side looking at him, feeling his hand glide over my stomach to the area between my tits.

The muscles of his chest and abs moved slightly as he touched me, as he explored the curves he'd felt so many times before. Sometimes, his gaze would drop to my lips, my chin, and then down to the sight of me in his t-shirt.

I preferred his place over mine, but he made me comfortable wherever I was. He never insulted what little I could afford, and he seemed perfectly relaxed in a place far below his standard of living. Liam would refuse to stay there out of principle. But Damien wasn't like that.

The longer I was with him, the more I wanted him.

We hadn't said more than a few sentences to each other since he came over. He asked what was wrong, but I never answered. We ended up in bed, having slow sex that chased away all the heartache in my chest.

Now I was at peace...because he always gave me peace.

His hand glided between my tits, stroking the swell on either side, feeling my calm heartbeat right below my left breast. He pulled his hand from his t-shirt then cupped my face, pulling away the hair that had fallen in front of my eyes. He tucked it back, his fingers slightly brushing against my cheek.

He was too good to me not to deserve my honesty. I'd told him I didn't want anything serious, just monogamy, but I began to realize how much he meant to me, that I did want this to be serious. He was the only man who made me think about a future, made me scared to picture my life without him. I didn't ever want to risk that. "I had dinner with Liam tonight."

He didn't react at all.

"He told me he had something important to talk about. Otherwise, I wouldn't have agreed to meet him." I wanted to explain that part, so he understood I didn't go out with Liam for the hell of it. "He told me he was going to go back to death fighting, where he and his opponent race to kill the other with their bare hands."

His fingers stopped caressing my cheek as he listened.

"After we got married, I asked him to stop, and he agreed. He still worked in the ring, but only with regular fighting, where the guys beat each other to a pulp, but no one dies." I suspected Damien already knew what Liam did for a living since he was a client. "He told me he was going to go back to death fighting...unless I took him back."

This time, he did react, his eyes widening in obvious surprise.

"It was a terrible thing to do, to put that on my shoulders."

"What did you say?"

I stared at him for a long time, my fingers moving over his bare chest. "I told him I wanted to be with you…"

———

I WORKED with Sofia for the first week, shadowing her and learning new responsibilities for the hotel. My job required me to be in my office most of the time, to process staff complaints and do a bunch of paperwork. It wasn't a flashy job, but it was a big salary increase, so I wouldn't have to stay in that little apartment for long.

And Sofia was great to work with, so that was nice.

We sat together in her office and worked through lunch. She was behind the desk, eating a plate of grilled salmon with veggies. She sliced into the tender meat with her fork while looking at her computer.

I got a sandwich because I wasn't interested in dieting. "Damien told me your husband and he used to be good friends."

She sighed as she typed a few words. "Yeah. It's been a long time since they've been civil to each other. Hades provokes Damien, and Damien is reactive, so he just makes it worse…and it escalates."

I couldn't picture Damien putting up with bullshit from anyone, even a good friend. "That's too bad. It really bothers him."

"I know. I've tried talking to my husband, but he refuses to listen… even though I know he still cares."

"You think they'll work it out someday?"

She shrugged. "Maybe if tragedy strikes…"

Damien comforted me through all my problems, and I wished I could do something to help him. But I'd never even met Hades, so it wasn't like I could change his mind. "That's too bad. Damien has never explicitly said it, but I know he loves him."

"Yeah. I do too. So, how are things going with Damien?"

"Good." I smiled when I thought about him. "He's a great guy."

"He can be when he wants to be," she teased. "So, he must like you."

"I can't imagine him being any different."

"Well, he's a drug lord and a professional money launderer, so he's capable of being a scary man. I've seen my husband get that way. It's pretty scary. But that's not an awful thing. I'd rather be married to the big bad wolf than the innocent lion."

Me too.

"Because good guys only finish last."

———

THE NEXT DAY, I met her husband for the first time. Sofia was in the bathroom when he stepped inside, wearing a dark blue suit and a black tie. A shiny watch was on his wrist, and his wedding band was interesting because it was midnight black. He scanned her desk, and when he realized she wasn't there, he looked at me.

He stared for a few seconds, looking at me like I might be a possible threat to his wife because I shouldn't be there. But then pragmatism set in, and he deduced my identity, turning a little warmer. "Anna?"

"Yes." I got out of the chair and extended my hand. "You must be Sofia's husband."

He took my hand with a firm shake before he released me. "I am. Where is she?" Once he let me go, he slid his hands into his pockets, adopting a harmless stance. He immediately reminded me of Damien, tall, confident, with the same ruthless body language.

"Bathroom. She pees a lot."

He raised an eyebrow at my comment.

"Because of the baby," I quickly explained, trying not to seem weird. Even though he wasn't friends with Damien anymore, I was still uneasy around him, wanting to make a good impression that made me act stupid.

He nodded slightly then continued to stare.

Now I didn't know what else to say. I was supposed to work on paperwork while she was gone, but now I wanted to leave so I wouldn't have to bear the awkward silence while we both waited for her.

He didn't seem uncomfortable with the long silence. He glanced at her desk and the picture frame on top, a picture of both of them with their son Andrew.

"I'm not sure if Damien or Sofia told you—"

"That you're seeing Damien?" he asked. "Yeah, I know. I warned him about it."

"Warned?"

"Liam is my client. Conflict of interest."

"Oh…"

He went back to ignoring me.

"Liam isn't a client of Damien's, so I don't see why it matters. And Liam understands I'm free to see whoever I want—as is he."

He turned back to me.

I didn't have to prove anything to him, but I didn't want anything to come between Damien and me…especially Liam. "Damien talks about you a lot—"

"And I don't want to talk about him." He shut me down so quickly, practically backhanding me with his large hand. His anger toward Damien was obvious in the way he lashed out at me, the way he could barely stand to hear his name. There wasn't just aggression and hatred...but pain.

"For what it's worth, he still feels terrible. And he misses you." Maybe I shouldn't have said that, betrayed Damien's confidence like that, but I knew how much he cared about this man in the little things he said, the way he blew me off because he was too upset to even look at me. He was heartbroken the way I was, nursing wounds after losing someone. His relationship hadn't been romantic like mine, but it was just as painful.

Hades shifted his gaze back to me, and this time, there was a different look in his eyes, less hostility, like he'd actually listened to what I'd said and wanted to know more. But he never asked because Sofia walked back inside.

With her hand over her stomach, she came up behind him. "Hey, sexy."

He turned at the sound of her voice, her compliment immediately inflating his ego, hitting him in his most vulnerable place. His eyes were different when he looked at her, like he was witnessing an angel without wings. "Baby."

She moved onto her tiptoes and gave him a kiss on the lips before she turned away.

He looked like a sad puppy, wanting more love than he'd just gotten.

"You've met Anna?" she asked.

"Yeah." Now that she was in the room, his eyes were reserved for her. I was practically invisible.

She organized a few things on her desk before she grabbed her purse. "We're going to lunch. You want to come?"

I didn't want to get on Hades's bad side, and I was pretty certain I'd already crossed the line with him. The best thing to do was back off. "I brought my lunch today. But thank you."

She didn't question it. "Where do you want to go?" She moved back around the desk and walked up to him.

He stared at her like he hadn't heard a word she'd said, too focused on her beauty to care about the question she'd just asked. "You choose."

"I always choose."

"You're giving me another son. You get to choose."

She smiled before she walked out the door. "Good answer."

He followed behind her, his hand on her ass.

Now that I worked during business hours, my nights were always free.

There was only one way I wanted to spend it. *Are you home?*

Depends. Are you naked?

Even if I said yes, I'd have to put on clothes to get over there.

No, you don't.

I laughed to myself. *Does that mean you're free?*

Get your ass over here, Annabella.

I took a cab to his place and entered his bedroom fifteen minutes later. Dinner for two was set on the table, along with a single white candle.

In his boxers, he walked to me and kissed me in greeting. "You aren't naked."

"I didn't want to get arrested."

He winked. "I would have bailed you out."

I pulled my shirt over my head and immediately got undressed.

His eyebrow rose as he watched me.

I left on my bra and panties. "How's this?"

"Better."

I smiled before I kissed him again, feeling that same electricity every time we touched. My hands moved to his bare chest as I got high off the feeling, leaving all my baggage at the door and feeling nothing but good.

His hand slid into my hair as he deepened the kiss.

"I like it when you do that," I whispered against his lips.

He stopped kissing me so he could stare for a moment. "I know." He rubbed his nose against mine before he kissed me again, his hand digging deeper into my hair. He gave me his breaths and his tongue, his strong arm wrapping around my frame and keeping me tight against his physique.

I had been hungry when I walked inside, but now I couldn't care less about the gourmet meal just feet away. My hand cupped his face as I fell deeper into him, my lips trembling because it felt so good, felt better than it ever did with anyone else. It was spiritual, adventurous, beautiful.

He guided me to his bed and got me on my back, his large size moving on top of me as he pinned me down. He left my bra on but got my bottoms off before he kicked off his own. Then he was inside me a moment later, his hand pinning both of my wrists to the mattress as he thrust, his eyes locked on to mine.

I fought against his hold, desperate to touch him after he'd made me feel so good. "Damien…"

He squeezed me harder. "You want to touch me, Annabella?"

My ankles tightened around his waist, and I pulled him closer. "Yes…"

After a quiet groan, he released my wrists and dug his hand into my hair again.

Once my nails scratched down his back, I moaned loudly, unleashed and enjoying him fully. It was like taking a hit of the most potent drug on the black market, the way he set my nerves on fire and brought me such joy. Sex wasn't always this good, wasn't always this perfect, but with him…it was heaven. "I don't want to share you…with anyone." My fingers dug into his hair, and I rocked with him, lost in those sexy eyes. I didn't know why I said that because he was already mine. It just came out.

"Annabella." He placed a few kisses to the corner of my mouth then on my jawline. Slowly, he made his way to my ear, venturing along my neckline before he breathed against the shell of my ear. "I'm yours as long as you want me."

HE SAT across from me and ate his dinner quietly, making eye contact with me or looking out the window to the darkness outside. An open bottle of wine was on the table, and our glasses were constantly refilled. He relaxed in his chair instead of holding himself with constant rigidness, like he had nothing to hide. When he did look at me, he stared…like he wanted me to know how hard he was looking.

One knee was bent against my chest as I ate the delicious dinner Patricia made. But the most delicious thing on the menu was the man across from me, the quiet man who said more with his expression than his lips. He'd changed my life that day I walked into the bank. He'd helped me when anyone else would have blown me off because of the small balance in my bank account. Then he saw something worthwhile in me and chased me until he got what he wanted.

What did he see in me? He was the sexy motherfucker. He was the man who could have any woman he wanted—have them all at the same time. He knew how to be with a woman, how to connect with body, mind, and soul. He was smart and successful, and he wasn't ashamed to be who he was—to tell the truth unapologetically.

How did I get so lucky?

I wanted to let my words slip out, to tell him how damn special he was, that he changed my life the moment he walked through the door. I thought I would never love anyone again, never thought I would feel something for someone this quickly...but I did. I wasn't afraid to get hurt, afraid that he would go home with someone else when I looked the other way. He was the flame in the darkness, the hope in my destitution. I wanted to say all of that...but I didn't want to chase him away. He'd never been in a long-term relationship before, and maybe the idea was still new to him. Instead of asking him to think about it, I should just let it happen naturally. If he wasn't sleeping with anyone else, that was all that mattered. He was mine...for as long as I wanted him.

"What are you thinking about?" His question broke my internal monologue.

"A lot of things."

"Any of them involve me?"

All of them. "Yes."

"Good things, I hope."

Nothing but good things. "I'm glad I left Liam... I'll leave it at that."

He stared for several seconds before softness entered his gaze. He wasn't a particularly soft man, someone that wore emotion on his sleeve, but his little cues were enough for me, like the one he'd just made. "You deserve better."

"Are you someone better?"

"Even better than me. But let's forget I said that." He grabbed his wine and took a drink.

I thought of the way Hades was so obviously in love with his wife, absorbed in every little move she made. He seemed like the perfect man, hot for his wife as she waddled past him. Damien didn't look at me that way...yet. "I met Hades today."

Instantly, his mood dropped, his playfulness evaporating like a drop of water on a desert rock in July.

"He was...grouchy."

"At least it's not just me..."

"He's in a much better mood when Sofia is around."

"Because he's pussy-whipped."

"I think it's more than that."

Damien averted his gaze to the window. "Because she's his soul mate."

It was a sweet thing to say, and I was surprised it came out of his mouth. "He reminded me of you."

"That's an insult."

"Not really. You carry yourself the same way...talk the same way... exude the same kind of presence."

He continued to look out the window.

"I told him you talk about him a lot."

His eyes flicked back to mine, somewhat alarmed.

"That you still miss him."

He dropped his gaze, as if embarrassed. "You didn't have to say that..."

"I thought if he heard those words from a stranger, they would have a stronger impact. Even Sofia says he's too stubborn and needs to move on. I thought if I could help, I should try."

"I appreciate that," he said quietly. "But you don't need to do that. It's not going to make a difference anyway. Sometimes I think about leaving the bank so I can move on and stop thinking about it...but I'm also too stubborn."

"And he stays at the bank because he's stubborn too."

"Yes. We're like mules."

I chuckled because it was a good description. "Sofia wonders if a tragedy will unite you."

He shook his head. "I doubt it...because he wouldn't care if I died."

21

DAMIEN

I'D ONLY GOTTEN AN HOUR OF SLEEP BEFORE SHE WAS ON TOP OF ME again. I opened my eyes to the sight of her kissing my chest, making her way down to my dick so she could kiss it and make it hard.

My hand moved into her soft hair. "Annabella...I gotta sleep." We'd fucked until two in the morning, and then she woke me up again at four. I glanced at the clock and saw that it was six.

She kept sucking until she made me hard. "I'll do all the work." She crawled on top of me and straddled my hips, her sexy skin touching mine. Then she pushed her tight cunt over my length, sinking until her ass rubbed against my balls.

"Jesus..."

She ground against me hard, rolling her hips so she could please herself exactly as she liked. She used my body like a damn dildo, getting what she wanted without apologizing for it.

It was hot. I sat and tried to roll her over to her back.

She pushed me back and pinned my wrists to the sheets. Her tits shook with her movements, and her long hair fell over one shoulder, her eyes focused on mine with her lips parted from her heavy breathing.

I could get out of this so easily...but it was so sexy. I let her have what she wanted, let her dominate me the way I dominated her. I got so hard watching her, and even though I was dead tired two seconds ago, I was wide awake now, my dick ready to explode.

She only said one word, and that was enough to send a distinct thrill down my spine. "Mine."

I WAS ALREADY AWAKE when my alarm went off.

I grabbed my phone and turned off the obnoxious sound while her head rested on my shoulder. Her hair stuck to my damp body, and her fingers grazed over my hard stomach, letting the drops of sweat stick to her fingertips.

Fuck, I was tired.

But fuck, it was worth it.

She placed a few kisses on my chest before she got out of bed, her perfect ass shaking with her movements as she strutted out of the bedroom and into the bathroom. Her long brown hair hung down her back, the ends clumped together because they were soaked in sweat—hers or mine.

I watched her go, fully satisfied but always hooked.

When she was gone, I spoke to myself. "Damn." I had a heathen in my bed, a woman who liked to fuck like a man, and knowing she only wanted me made it so much better. Liam had given her an ultimatum, but the first thing she did was run to me. Liam was the past, and I was the future.

I finally forced my sore muscles to respond and get my ass out of my bed and into the bathroom. She was already in the shower, helping herself to whatever she wanted. It was the first time she'd done that, brought her things over so she could shower and head to work in the morning.

I came up behind her then got my head under the running water to clean myself off. I smelled like sex and sweat, my dick drenched in the sweet tang of her pussy.

She gave me room, her fingers rubbing shampoo deep into her scalp. Then she grabbed my bar of soap and cleaned herself off, about to smell like me before she went off to work in a tight skirt and pumps.

I'd never had a woman in my life like this, where she was an extension of myself. She was the woman in my bed but also my friend. I supposed it was like a relationship...at least the beginning of one.

"Tired?" She tipped her head back and rinsed everything out of her strands.

"Yes."

"Good. Then I did my job right."

I smiled slightly, loving her confidence. Most women waited for me to take the lead, to do all the work every time. But she wanted to fulfill my fantasies the way I fulfilled hers. She wanted me to be addicted to her the way she was addicted to me. "A million times over."

We finished in the shower, and like a domestic couple, we used the two sinks in front of the mirror, brushing our teeth, styling our hair, and getting ready for the day. A towel was wrapped around her chest, and mine was around my waist. Sometimes I glanced at her in the mirror, seeing the way she plumped her lips before she drew her lipstick along the curves. She rubbed them together before running her fingers through her now-dry hair.

Even watching her get ready was hot.

When we were finished, I grabbed my keys and wallet. "I'll drive you home." I adjusted my tie then checked the time on my watch before I dropped my phone into the pocket of my slacks.

"I'm running late. Could you drop me off at the hotel?" She zipped up her bag and put it over her shoulder.

"Sure." I took her bag off her shoulder and carried it for her.

She gave me the brightest smile I'd ever seen.

We went to my car downstairs, and I pulled onto the road, my engine roaring because it was a souped-up sports car, a two-seater with bulletproof windows and an acceleration that could beat any other car on the road. My arm rested on the center console while my hand shifted the gears, switching up and down, depending on where we were in the city.

Her arm hooked through mine, and her fingers pressed through my crisp suit to my biceps underneath.

I kept my eyes on the road but felt a slight smile enter the corner of my mouth. This woman made me feel like a superhero, with powerful fucking abilities. Hades always treated me like I was garbage, and even Sofia had talked down to me a couple times. My father questioned everything I did, and my sister always gave me a hard time. But Annabella...she made me feel like a goddamn badass.

I pulled up to the roundabout of the Tuscan Rose and put the car in park.

"Thanks for the ride." She leaned over the center console and kissed me goodbye. It was more than just a simple peck, but a deep kiss that probably smeared her red shade all over the corner of my mouth. She gripped my arm as she did it, like she would pull me into the back seat if there were one.

"You earned it."

She smiled before she stepped out of my car, the bag over her shoulder as she strutted to the entryway. She was doing the walk of shame with her overnight bag, but the confidence in her posture and the sway of her hips indicated she didn't give a shit.

And I liked that.

IT WAS difficult to focus at the office because I was deliriously tired.

I'd slept...three hours, maybe?

I owned this goddamn joint so I could leave whenever I felt like it, but I had meetings and other bullshit to take care of.

My phone vibrated with a text message, and instead of it being Annabella like I hoped, it was one of my clients. *Let's meet tonight at 9. The usual place.*

I groaned in disappointment but texted back the answer they wanted. *Alright.*

Hades walked into my office a moment later. "What the fuck is this?" He threw a pile of papers on my desk.

"This should be fun..." I suppressed the yawn that wanted to stretch my jaw open because that would push him over the edge.

"Are these numbers right? Because if they are, we're in trouble."

I kept my cool and flipped through the pages. It took me a few seconds to figure out the problem. "Typo." I grabbed a pen and made the change, adding the zero at the end of the number. "There." I passed it back.

His eyes were vicious, as if my change just made the situation worse. "How could you just drop a zero?"

"Shit happens, alright?"

"Not shit like this." He slammed his hand down on the stack of papers. "That zero is the difference between billions and millions."

"And you knew there was something wrong. Otherwise, you wouldn't have come in here. So calm the fuck down—"

His temper exploded, and he threw the papers in my face. "I'll calm down when you're in the grave, asshole."

SUMMER WAS OVER and fall had arrived, so I wore my leather jacket over my t-shirt and walked up the sidewalk to the bar where I was meeting my client. Some of my guys didn't want to be publicly seen inside a bank, so they preferred these incognito meetings under the cover of darkness for the privacy...and the booze and women.

I opened the double doors and stepped inside.

There was no bass from the music. There were no people.

And the doors behind me were locked by two big guys before they blocked the exit with their size.

It only took me a nanosecond to figure out this was an ambush, and if I didn't call for help, I'd end up in the dumpster outside. I could call my men, but they were on the other side of town. I would normally call Hades first, but he wanted me to die tonight.

I glanced around me and recognized Heath in the center, his arms crossed over his chest with a cruel smile on his lips.

I pulled my wrist and casually glanced at the time. "Isn't it too early for this?" Thankfully, I wore my Apple watch so I picked the person who could help me best...if he honored his debt. I discreetly called then dropped my wrist, hoping he would listen to the conversation, figure out I needed help, and then would trace my call.

It was a long shot...but my best option.

With his head cocked slightly and his bright-blue eyes so cold they looked like maps of the Arctic, he was enjoying this mirthlessly. If he'd just wanted to issue a warning, he would have come alone, but since he brought his boys...there would be a body tonight.

And it was probably going to be mine.

Heath dropped his arms and stepped farther into the center of the room. "I've got an early day tomorrow."

"Brunch?" I asked, keeping it casual, even though nothing about this was casual. "Mani-pedi?"

He turned his wrist and examined his fingernails. "I do have a lot of ingrown fingernails..."

I wanted to slide my hands into my pockets, but I forced them to remain by my sides, so the watch wouldn't be muffled deep inside my pocket. "Well, should we get a drink? Or you want to get straight to the point?"

He chuckled. "You're brave."

"Bravery implies you're afraid of something. I'm not afraid."

"Not even of death?" he asked.

I didn't bother answering.

"Or someone else's death?"

Now I couldn't keep my same indifference.

"I still have hope we can work this out, Damien. So, I'm not going to kill you."

I continued to hold my breath because the worst part was coming.

"But I'm gonna kill someone else...to straighten out that attitude."

The first person that came to mind was Annabella...and all my strength left my body.

He pulled out his phone, made a call, and put it on speaker. It only rang once before someone answered. "I'm ready, Heath."

My breathing increased, and my limbs tightened.

He held the phone close to his mouth. "You got our guest of honor?"

"Yeah, he's tied to the chair."

He? Hades? I was relieved it wasn't Annabella, but this was just as painful.

"Put him on." Heath stood with one hand in his pocket and held out the phone to me.

My night became worse when I recognized his voice. "Son, I'm okay…"

My knees immediately went weak, and the emotion jumped into my throat. I went wild, turning erratic, irrational, broken. "Father…" Tears immediately burned in the corners of my eyes, fueled by self-loathing, hatred, and every emotion in this life. My gaze turned back to Heath. "Touch him, and I swear to fucking god…" I rushed him, ready to break that hard face and tarnish those blue eyes.

His men were prepared for it, so they grabbed me by both arms and shoved me back until I hit the ground.

I couldn't even get close.

I jumped back to my feet again. "Don't do this. He has nothing to do with this. I'm the one you want." I slammed my hand into my chest, already knowing I wouldn't be able to change his mind. I'd never been a crier, but I could feel the burn deep in my throat, feel the moisture flood my eyes. "That's the kind of man you want to be? Going after an elderly man?" I couldn't let this happen, couldn't let that innocent man pay for my stupidity. "Look, I'll pay you. I'll give you every euro. I'll pay your back taxes. Whatever you want, alright?" I clenched my jaw to steady myself, to stop the tears from breaking into my voice.

He smiled. "I appreciate your cooperation, Damien." He didn't hang up or ask the guy to release my father. "But I warned you many times...and you need to learn your lesson."

God. "Heath, come on..."

His smile faded, and he shook his head slightly.

"Kill me and take all my shit. Take my house, my car, take my cash. I'm worth way more than he is."

"Just the opposite."

My father's voice came over the line. "Damien, it's okay... It's okay."

I fell to my knees, desperate. "Heath...please. I'm begging."

He watched me, merciless. "Shoot him."

"No!" I got to my feet again. "Don't."

A loud blow hit the double doors, the sound so deafening it seemed like an explosion.

Heath clearly had no idea what it was, because his eyes flicked to the door in panic. "Hold on."

Both doors flew open and off their hinges, forcing the two men standing in front to fall to the ground. Then Balto stepped through, wearing a long-sleeved olive-green shirt with a couple men behind him. They pulled the pulse device from the door, what they'd used to get inside. He came forward—to honor his debt.

But it meant nothing to me. I wasn't the one who needed to be saved. Now I couldn't do anything to stop this.

Heath stared at his brother then motioned for his men to lower their weapons. He was visibly annoyed, his face hard and his eyes vicious.

Balto placed his body in front of me. "Back off, Heath."

Heath continued to hold the phone. "You can have him. I got what I want." He spoke into the speaker. "Kill him."

A gunshot erupted over the speakers, so loud it hurt my eyes even over the speakerphone.

And I fell...my knees screaming when I hit the hardwood floor. My hands steadied my fall, but the rest of my body gave out. Tears fell from my eyes straight to the floor, the drops in my line of sight. "God..." I listened to my father's death and wished it were me. Instead of feeling vengeance, I felt pain...pain I'd never felt before in all my life. This was all my fault...all my fucking fault. "Father..."

Balto took the phone from his brother's hand. "Hades?"

My body went rigid when I heard the question.

A deep voice sounded over the phone, easily recognizable because I'd heard it every day for a decade. "I've got him."

HEATH HUNG up the phone and stared at his brother for a long time, his rage flashing with just a simple look. He shoved the phone into his pocket then crossed his arms over his chest. "You don't belong here, Balto."

"I know." He stared at his twin with the same intensity. "But that was the last time."

Heath continued to stand there in their silent face-off before he stepped away. He motioned for his men to follow him, and they left the bar peacefully.

I still breathed hard because so much shit had just happened. I got to my feet and stared at Balto's massive back. My fingers ran through my hair, picking up all the sweat I'd just excreted. "Thank you..."

He slowly turned around and faced me, and I could see my gratitude meant nothing to him. "We're even, Damien. You're on your own from now on."

I nodded in understanding.

"Hades...how did that happen?"

His blue eyes were so bright, they seemed fake. It was the softest feature he possessed, and they relayed his thoughts better than his words ever could. "I took your call and listened. It only took me a few seconds to figure out what was happening. The Skull Kings are still loyal to me, and after a quick phone call, I learned everything. But your father was being held on the opposite side of the city, and I couldn't get there in time. So I called Hades."

"And he agreed?" Just that afternoon, he said he wished I were dead.

"Instantly."

I couldn't believe what he'd just said.

"It worked out better that way, because Heath wouldn't hesitate to kill Hades if he showed his face. But me...he wouldn't touch me. I'm bulletproof, and not because of my size."

But because of his blood. "I'm really glad I saved your life." I was still in a daze, unable to believe what had just gone down.

His eyes drilled into mine. "I'm gonna give you some advice. Take it. Because I won't be there next time. You could call me and beg, and I'll hang up on you."

I nodded.

"Give Heath what he wants. Because that wasn't a bluff. He would have killed your father."

I wanted revenge for what he did to my father. He could have given him a heart attack. But I was also scared shitless in that moment, so revenge wasn't my number one choice. "Yeah."

He turned to walk away. "Your father is being held on the top level of the Saint Apartments. Hades will wait with him until you arrive." He walked out first, and like a small militia, the rest of his men followed.

I ENTERED the empty room with the floor-to-ceiling windows and found my father sitting in a wooden chair, visibly unharmed and wearing his favorite blue sweater because he was always cold—even in summer.

A dead body was on the floor, a puddle of dark blood soaking into the carpet. The man's gun lay beside him with his outstretched hand reaching for it. Hades stood near the large windows and looked out across the dark city, his back turned to us.

The only person I cared about in that moment was my father.

Old, frail, defenseless.

Seeing him made me want to kill Heath, to torture him for what he'd done to this elderly man. "Father..." I ran to him and kneeled down so I could hug him, wrap my arms around him and hold him close. I never appreciated my father until I almost lost him, realized I hadn't spent as much time with him as I could, wasn't as good of a son as I could be. I recognized the cologne he'd been wearing for twenty years, seriously outdated and a little musky. He never changed his wardrobe, so the sweater was just as old.

He patted me on the back. "I'm okay, Damien. I wasn't even worried. I knew you would save me."

But I didn't.

"Hades took care of business like he always does." He gripped my shoulder and gave me a slight smile, his puffy cheeks full of wrinkles. "You always have each other's backs. That's hard to find in times like these."

"Yeah…" I swallowed the lump in my throat.

He patted my cheek. "Damien, it's alright. You can calm down."

"I'm so sorry, Father… I'm sorry this happened to you."

"Nothing happened, son. It's a risk that comes with the business. But you handled it beautifully." He patted my cheek again before he rose to his feet. "Let me piss, and then we'll go. All the action excited my bladder." He shuffled his feet and moved slowly until he turned the corner and entered the hallway.

I rose to my feet and stared at the powerful man in the suit. His hands rested in the pockets of his slacks, his watch noticeable on his wrist. He must have been meeting a client on this side of town to be dressed like that. His stoic countenance reflected in the glass as he looked at the lit city.

I came up behind him, at a loss for words. I stared at him for a long time because my mouth couldn't articulate all the thoughts swirling in my head. "Hades…I don't know where to begin." I'd betrayed him and pushed him away…but he was still there.

He slowly turned around and faced me, his eyes hard and his expression cold. His brown eyes looked me over, noticing the puffiness around my eyes and the tears that were still fresh.

"Thank you." My voice choked as I said the words, but I didn't feel shame. "I don't know how to thank you for what you did…"

He pulled his right hand out of his pocket and placed it on my shoulder. "You just did."

All the emotion I'd been holding in for the last year rose straight to my throat, making me feel vulnerable, like a completely different person. I felt the surface of my eyes moisten with tears I refused to shed, but it was getting harder and harder to fight.

"You would have done it for me," he whispered.

All I could do was nod, feeling the tremors all over my body. "I'm so sorry about everything... I miss you." It was the lamest thing I'd ever said, words that should never come out of a man's mouth, but I was more emotional than I'd ever been, and shit was just pouring out.

His eyes softened before he wrapped his arms around me and embraced me. "I miss you too."

My arms grabbed on to him, and I clutched him hard, my hands fisting the material of his suit like I was using it to climb a mountain. My chin moved to his shoulder, and I inhaled a deep breath, feeling the tears escape from my eyes. I could see my pitiful reflection in the glass, and I closed my eyes so I wouldn't have to face my weakness.

He cupped the back of my head, and his breathing increased slightly, like he felt the same emotion too.

I didn't want to let go, wanted to hold him as long as I could. I'd been lost without him, depressed like I'd lost my mother again. He was my family...he was everything. My pain had turned to hatred so it would be easier to handle, but I always knew how I really felt— that I missed him so damn much.

After a few minutes, he pulled away and looked me in the eye, his eyes not wet but filled with emotion. "I'm sorry too." He kept one hand on the back of my neck, his other hand gripping my shoulder.

I wasn't embarrassed that he could see my tears because I wasn't looking at a stranger. I was looking at my best friend, the one person I could be completely myself with, the man I would take a bullet for in a heartbeat. "I love you, man."

He nodded. "I love you too." He squeezed my shoulder before he released me.

My father stepped back into the room. "You can make out with your girlfriend later, Damien. I'm hungry."

Hades glanced at my father and chuckled.

I chuckled too then let him go, quickly wiping away my tears on my jacket. "I'll see you tomorrow?"

He nodded, still smiling. "Tomorrow. And every day after that."

I GOT my father inside and made him a sandwich. "Are you sure you don't want to stay with me?" I placed the plate in front of him at the small round table where he sat.

"I'm not gonna let those thugs scare me out of my own home." He grabbed it with both hands and took a bite.

I stood behind the chair across from him. "Maybe it's time you move in with me anyway. You know I have a big place—"

"No." He took another bite. "I can take care of myself."

"Never said you couldn't. I just think—"

"I said no," he snapped. "I don't need your charity."

"It's not charity, Dad. I just think you'd be safer—"

"I'd rather die."

Fucking drama queen.

"I'm perfectly fine where I am. I'm not going to burden my thirty-year-old son and chase all his dates away."

I didn't roll my eyes in front of him because I'd get slapped. "That's not what would happen. Like I said, it's a big place—"

"The answer is no."

I sighed in defeat. I knew my father was starting to slow down, and after this happened, it made sense for him to live with me. Patricia could help him with whatever he needed, and he would be safe in the house since he never went anywhere anyway. "Alright."

He finished his sandwich, leaving his mess behind. "I'm tired, so I'm gonna go to bed." He got to his feet and patted me on the cheek as he walked by. "I'll see you later, son. You have a key, right?"

I nodded. "Goodnight, Father." I didn't know how he brushed off tonight like it was no big deal, and that made me wonder if he was entirely mentally astute. I turned off the lights then locked the door behind me before I walked to my car.

Then I sat there, finally having a moment to myself to process what the fuck had just happened. I rested my head against the window and let out the breath I'd been holding for the last minute.

I couldn't believe Heath went there...

After an innocent old man.

What would I have done if Hades hadn't saved my ass?

What if it was someone else? Like my sister? Or...

I couldn't even bring myself to think about her.

Annabella.

I sucked in a breath between my teeth, feeling so much pain at the idea of her being tied to a chair with a gun pointed at her head. Heath probably would have picked her if he'd known about her. We'd been seeing each other in private so Liam wouldn't figure out who she was sleeping with. If that hadn't been the case...it could have been her.

And I would have died.

It made me realize how much I cared about her, that she wasn't just some hot piece of ass.

Now I understood why Hades stepped away from the business, because Sofia and his kids would always be at risk. They were easy targets to him, and he would be a terrible husband and father if he didn't put them first.

Made me realize I had to make the same decision—my job or Annabella.

22

ANNABELLA

I WORKED AT MY DESK BUT GLANCED AT MY PHONE A COUPLE TIMES... hoping to see a message from my man.

That's what he was to me, so I would call him as such.

I didn't hear from him yesterday, and since I was trying not to be too forward about my feelings for him, I did my best to keep my distance, not to smother him with obsession. If I had it my way, I'd be at his place every night.

I hated my mattress, and not because it was old and lumpy, but because he wasn't there beside me. I was addicted to his presence, sleeping hard whenever that strong man was beside me. I liked staring at his face as I fell asleep, seeing it again first thing in the morning.

I was so into that man...and he must know.

How could he not? I woke him up several times during the night because I needed more. I grabbed his arm on the drive because I wanted him to know how I felt. I wore my heart on my sleeve, showed him how much I wanted him, so there would be no mistaking my feelings. If I didn't give him everything I had, someone else would...and I would lose him.

I couldn't lose that man. He was my goddamn religion.

Sofia came into my office. "I have good news."

"The board agreed to the remodel?"

"No." She sat on the corner of the desk. "Better than that."

"We're gonna have fresh cookies in the lobby again?"

She chuckled. "Okay, not *that* good. Hades and Damien made up last night."

"Really?" I felt so much happiness because I knew Damien wanted that so badly. "What happened?"

She hesitated before she answered. "Something happened with work, and Hades was there for him...so they buried the hatchet and moved on. I can see how much happier Hades is for it. He's in a much better place."

"That's great. I knew how important that was to Damien. He must be so thrilled."

"Yeah," she said with a nod. "And my husband said you had something to do with his decision."

"Me?" I asked in surprise.

"When you told him what Damien had confided to you, I guess it made him realize Damien was still sorry...after all this time."

I was gonna get some good loving for this. "I'm glad I could help. Now the four of us can go out together."

"Yes, that'll be fun," she said. "I'm just excited to be in the same room with both of them. Every time I see Damien, I feel like I'm having an affair." She hopped off the desk and chuckled. "I'll let you get back to work. Just wanted to share the good news."

WHEN I GOT HOME, I called him.

He answered, but his voice was low like he was trying to speak quietly. "Hey."

"Hey," I said, bursting with happiness. "Sofia told me that you and Hades made up. That's so great. I'm very happy for you."

He didn't reflect my happiness, his mood clearly troubled. "Yeah..."

I turned quiet, trying to figure out what I was missing. "Everything okay?"

He took a long time to answer. "Are you home right now?"

"Yeah. Why?"

"I'll be there in fifteen minutes." He hung up.

My stomach clenched with dread, like I knew something bad was about to happen. There was a warning in my gut, like he was coming by to share terrible news. But I reminded myself that his moods were unpredictable, and he probably just wanted to be comforted after having a hard day...just the way I wanted to see him after my dinner with Liam.

That was all.

HE KNOCKED EVEN though the door was unlocked.

"It's open." I sat on the couch, feeling more uneasy now that he hadn't just walked in like he usually did.

He stepped inside, wearing a long-sleeved maroon shirt that was nice over his muscles. His black jeans were low on his hips, and he wore one of his nice watches on his wrist. He shut the door behind him quietly then stared at me.

Something was wrong. I could feel it.

I got to my feet and walked up to him, my lips aching for his. Even though he wasn't in the best mood, I rose on my tiptoes and kissed him anyway.

He kissed me back—but it was cold.

I leaned back and stared at him, feeling my heart start to pound with fear. This man had only been in my life for a few months, but he became an extension of me, a part of my soul. When I was confronted with the real possibility of losing him, it made me so fucking scared. "What's wrong?"

He continued to stare at me with those dreamy eyes, his jawline covered with a shadow of hair because he hadn't shaved since the last time we'd woken up together. His hands slid into his pockets instead of wrapping around my waist. Then he looked down for a while...so he wouldn't have to look at me altogether.

This couldn't be happening. "You better not be here to dump me, Damien." I issued the statement but felt my sternum crack as I did it. I wanted him to deny my claim, assure me something else was on his mind.

But he didn't. He looked up again, his eyes shifting slightly as he looked at my features.

"No..." I should have kept that plea to myself to save some dignity, but it came out on its own. My heart ached for this man; my body burned for this man. I didn't want to be with anyone else. I'd finally found a diamond in the rough...and I couldn't let it go.

"Annabella." He didn't act cowardly by avoiding my gaze. He knew he was breaking my heart, and he owned up to it. "It's time for us to move on. We've had our fun, but it's over."

I knew the words were coming, but that didn't make them hurt less. I refused to cry, but I knew my eyes would shed a waterfall the second he walked out of my apartment. "Did I do something?"

His voice was slightly wounded. "Not at all."

"Then why?"

It took him a long time to find a response. "I tried monogamy, and it's just not my thing. I'm sorry."

So, he wanted to be with other women... I wasn't enough. Why wasn't I ever enough for the men in my life? Liam hooked up with someone else when I lost our baby, and Damien wanted something new when I didn't please him enough. It fucking hurt.

He waited for me to say something.

I crossed my arms over my chest and thought of arguments to make. I wanted to beg him to stay, wanted to cry until he changed his mind, guilt him into staying. But that wasn't me, and I needed to have some pride. So, I said nothing...used my energy to keep my tears behind my eyes. "Alright..."

He stared at me like he expected me to say something more.

I wouldn't allow myself to speak.

He sighed when the silence lingered long enough. "You'll find someone who deserves you...deserves you more than I do."

But I only want you.

He stepped back toward the door. "I'll let myself out."

Please don't go.

"Goodbye, Annabella." He walked out.

Come back. I watched him close the door then listened to his footsteps as he walked down the hallway.

When I knew he was really gone, I cried.

I cried harder than I ever had.

I CALLED in sick for a few days because I was so distraught.

I felt like a high school girl who'd had her heart broken for the first time. It was the end of the world.

I cried on the couch then in bed. Tissues were piled up everywhere. I ditched the makeup because I would just ruin it. After I let all the sadness pour out of my chest, I finally went back to work.

I worked at my desk and took care of the emails I'd ignored the last few days. I caught up on my paperwork. I normally listened to the radio in my office, but now every song made me feel worse.

If I could write a song, it would be the saddest of all breakup songs.

Sofia stepped into my office, and she probably already knew Damien dumped me. "Feeling better?"

I stared at her blankly, surprised she would ask me that like it was no big deal.

She must have read the horrified expression on my face. "Because you were sick..."

I totally forgot I'd ever said that. "Oh...yeah. I'm getting there." It was hard to look at her and not think of Damien. It was hard not to remember the way her husband kissed the ground she walked on. She'd earned the undying devotion of a man...and I hadn't.

Sofia didn't buy that answer. "You look pale as a ghost."

I touched my cheek, and my fingertips sensed the coldness. "Yeah... just taking me a while to bounce back."

She continued to study me, knowing there was a secret to uncover. "Are you sure there's nothing else?"

Maybe she didn't know. I wasn't sure if I could answer without bursting into tears. "Yeah..."

Her voice grew sterner. "Anna, I know there's something wrong. You can tell me."

I stared at my computer for a second, breaking eye contact to gather myself. When I looked at her again, I answered. "Damien broke up with me..." I let my voice grow quiet so I could keep the emotion out.

"He did?" she asked in surprise. "I had no idea..."

I guess that meant he didn't tell Hades at work. "Yeah."

"Why?"

"Just said he didn't want to do the monogamy thing anymore."

Instead of dropping it and leaving me alone, she shut the door then sat in the chair facing my desk. "I'm so sorry, Anna. I can see you're really worked up about it."

My eyes started to water, and I was scared I might cry.

"It seemed like he was really into you."

I shrugged so I wouldn't have to respond.

"I can talk to him—"

"Please don't." I had too much pride to chase after a man who didn't want me. I shouldn't have fallen so hard, so fast. But before I'd even realized it, I was in free fall. It felt right from the beginning, and I didn't feel like I'd just gotten a divorce. It felt like I was where I was supposed to be.

"Okay," she said quietly. "I won't say anything."

I didn't know Sofia that well, but I trusted her...even though I had no real reason to. "Can I tell you something?" I asked, sniffling because my nose had started to run. "And you promise you won't tell him?" I didn't have any friends to talk to. She was all I had.

"Promise." She leaned forward over my desk so she could grab my hand.

It was a moment of catharsis, to let the truth escape my lips. "I loved him…"

Her eyes fell in heartache.

"I didn't expect it to happen. I got divorced less than a year ago, and I didn't think I was even capable of feeling that way about someone, that I could trust someone after what my ex did to me." My eyes started to water, and the tears came, breaking through the dam and pouring down my cheeks. "But I fell so hard…fell so deep. I fell in love with him so easily, and it just felt right. Like I could do that for the rest of my life." I pulled my hand from hers so I could grab the tissues on my desk and wipe away the tears. "I'm so in love with him, and I miss him…so much."

23

DAMIEN

HADES AND I WERE FRIENDS AGAIN, AND THE PAIN THAT HAD BEEN haunting me for so long had disappeared. He was my family again, a piece of me that had been restored.

But I was also miserable.

I made the right decision when I went to her apartment and ended our relationship. It wasn't easy to cut out something so good, but it was the best option. What kind of man would I be if I didn't?

Selfish.

I thought about her a lot, especially when I was in bed alone. I missed her beside me, and there were times when I reached for her in the middle of the night. When I didn't feel her, I shot up in bed...devastated.

Hades stepped into my office. "How about the four of us get dinner tonight?"

"The four of us?" I turned away from my computer and stared at him as he stood in my doorway.

"My woman and yours."

I hadn't told Hades what happened because I didn't want to talk about it. But I couldn't keep it a secret forever. I was surprised Annabella didn't tell Sofia, who would tell Hades, but apparently she hadn't. "How about it just be the three of us?"

His eyes narrowed like he picked up on the meaning behind my words. "Something happen?" He shut the door behind him and moved to the chair facing my desk. He hadn't sat there for a conversation in a really long time. It was hard to believe he was really there.

"I broke it off." I knew I would move on and forget about her eventually, but for now, I missed her. She was the first woman I'd ever been with that I thought about after we were done.

His arms were on the leather armrests, looking like a titan in that Italian-made suit. He cocked his head slightly as he looked at me, as if my response were a little too complicated for him to understand. "Why?"

"Because it was time."

"If it was time, you wouldn't be miserable."

It was one of those rare times when I wished he didn't know me so well.

"Be real with me."

I dragged my hand down my face before I responded. "I did like her...a lot. But after everything that happened with my father, it made me realize I can't have a relationship like that. I never expected my fling with Annabella to be more, so I never thought I'd have to break up with her. But before I knew what happened...she was more than I realized."

Hades listened without judgment. "You're trying to protect her."

I nodded. "I had to choose between her and my work."

"Are you sure you chose right?"

My eyes moved back to his.

"It was hard to walk away from my life's work, but Sofia was worth it. I don't have any regrets."

"But she's your soul mate."

He held my gaze. "And what is Annabella to you?"

I shrugged. "A woman I like. Not enough to make that kind of sacrifice."

Hades accepted my answer. "I'm sure she understood. Maybe she didn't realize how deep she was in either. If being with you is dangerous, calling it quits before anyone gets hurts is the best decision."

Something told me I did hurt her—and I felt like shit. "I didn't tell her the truth."

"Then what did you say?"

I shrugged. "I wanted to see other people, basically."

"Why not just tell her the truth?"

"Because." I straightened in my chair and rested my arms on the surface of my desk. "If I told her truth, she would want to stay with me..." I knew this wasn't just a fling for her, that she genuinely cared about me, that she would disregard her own safety so we could be together. "And if she said that...I would let her stay."

I WALKED down the street I used to visit on a regular basis. I could navigate the neighborhood with my eyes closed because I'd been there so many times, had a couple drinks on the balcony as we plotted against our enemies.

Now I was back...and it felt like a dream.

I knocked on the door before I let myself in.

Sofia was holding Andrew, so she handed him off to Hades before she beamed and walked toward me. With her arms open, she greeted me like a mother and hugged me tightly. "I'm so happy to see you." She rubbed my back before she squeezed me again. When she pulled away, her eyes were filled with deep affection. "This feels right."

"I'm happy to be here too." My eyes shifted back to Hades.

He walked up to me, holding his son with a single arm. The baby wore a blue onesie with airplanes on the front. "Andrew, you remember your uncle?"

I'd only seen him once, shortly after Sofia gave birth. "He's so much bigger..." His face was more distinguished, he had hair on his head, and he already looked so much like his father. "Wow."

Andrew stared at me, almost like he recognized me.

"You want to hold him?" Hades made the exchange before I even agreed.

"Uh, sure." I took him in my arms and held him rigidly, holding him up the way Hades had just been. "Geez, you're a big boy."

"He loves that milk," he teased. "I have a feeling he's gonna be a big fan of the ladies."

"Don't be gross." Sofia swatted his arm playfully before she walked away.

"So, are you hungry?" Hades asked.

"I'm starving after lifting weights." I looked down at Andrew, who had a curious expression as he stared at me.

Hades chuckled, and we moved to the table.

Hades took Andrew and placed him in the playpen on the floor before he joined us at the table.

Sofia was far enough along now that her stomach was really noticeable in a tight dress. She immediately went for the bread in the center of the table and ripped off a few pieces before she placed them in her mouth.

I grabbed my silverware and started to eat, and even though we hadn't talked much in a long time, I didn't have anything to say. This all seemed too good to be true, sitting there with the two of them...like no time had passed. "How's your pregnancy been?"

"He's just as ornery as the first," she said. "We're gonna have two crazy-ass kids running around."

"We can have a third if you want," Hades said, teasing her.

"Two is perfect. Two is destiny." She glanced at Andrew and kept eating.

Hades looked at me from time to time, not exactly himself because the restoration of our friendship was still a major change for both of us.

Sofia spoke again. "Anna told me the two of you stopped seeing each other." She kept her eyes on her food, digging her fork into her pasta before she raised her head and took a bite. She didn't ask any questions and left the floor open for me to respond in any way I wanted.

"Yeah..." I trusted Hades would tell Sofia the real reason I ended things. "Just wasn't working out." Annabella filled the void when Hades left, and now that she was gone, Hades filled that void in return...but I was never really satisfied.

Something was missing.

"Does that mean you're never going to come to the hotel because you don't want to run into her?" Sofia asked.

"No. I don't have a problem seeing her." I thought things ended civilly. She seemed hurt by my rejection, but not angry. We'd agreed we just wanted something casual, so she couldn't take back what she said.

Sofia finally looked at me but didn't say anything to contradict me. "Are you okay?"

"I'm fine," I said, holding her gaze so she would believe me. "I'm not a one-woman kind of man, and I never will be."

24

ANNABELLA

It was a rough couple of weeks.

After I shed all my tears, I was just numb.

Didn't feel anything at all.

I tried to convince myself that Damien didn't mean anything to me, that I was mixing up lust and love, that I hadn't seen him long enough to have deep feelings...like love. How could it happen that quickly? How could I love someone that fast after Liam?

It wasn't possible.

Right?

I was tired of lying in bed night after night, watching TV late just so I could fall asleep. I ate soup right out of the can and snacked on crackers because I was too depressed to cook or order a pizza.

So I went out to a bar.

Admirers bought me drinks, and I had a few conversations until they went dry. It was nice to feel attractive, for men to notice me when Damien couldn't care less about it. Eventually, I sat with one guy, who thought talking about himself was the best way to impress me. He was self-absorbed and egotistical, but he was polite and interesting.

And I had nothing else to do anyway.

"I'm surprised a woman like you is single." He stopped talking about his job in finance long enough to notice something about me.

"What's that supposed to mean?" I wasn't single by choice. I just kept falling for the wrong guys.

"Beautiful women like you are never single for more than, like, five minutes."

"Well, you caught me in my five-minute window."

"Lucky me." He smiled and tapped his glass against mine.

I tried to enjoy myself, but all I could think about was the man I really wanted...the one who didn't want me. Damien didn't say much, but he was always interesting. Just looking into his confident gaze was enough entertainment. It'd been weeks since he'd dumped me, so he'd probably already been with someone else by now...

"You okay?"

I snapped out of my thoughts and realized what he'd asked. "Yeah... just got out of a relationship, so I'm just not in a good place."

He nodded slowly. "Been there."

When I raised my gaze to look across the bar, my eyes locked on a gaze I instantly recognized. He wasn't blinking, his blue eyes filled with ferocity. I was frozen in place because the look was so frightening.

"You look upset again." He couldn't see the crazy man standing behind him.

I ignored him because my eyes followed Liam as he approached our table. His powerful frame was intimidating to anyone who wasn't blind, and he'd scare off this guy quickly. He stopped at our table and stared at me, like he'd caught me betraying him.

The guy glanced at him, unsure what to do.

Liam didn't look at him. "Take your piss of a drink and leave."

The guy chickened out like I assumed he would, and he vacated the chair so Liam could replace him.

This was going to be fun...

Liam fell into the chair, his large size taking up the whole thing and blocking my view of everything behind him. With annoyance etched into the features of his face, he said, "Please tell me that pussy isn't the guy you've been seeing."

"No."

"Good." He got the attention of the waitress and ordered an old fashioned because he didn't have a drink in hand. "He dropped you, then?"

"What makes you think I didn't drop him?" I held my glass of red wine with my lipstick smeared across the glass.

"Because you wouldn't be wasting your time on a loser like that."

I drank and let the booze warm my throat. Liam had me cornered, and I couldn't lie or pretend he was wrong.

"What happened?"

I told the truth. "He ended it."

He didn't pretend to be apologetic or sympathetic.

I kept drinking my wine.

"He'll regret it." He grabbed his glass and took a drink. "I promise you that."

It'd been a couple weeks, and that hadn't happened. Doubted it ever would. He'd treated my apartment like a pit stop before he went to the next event. I'd had enough wine tonight, and I needed to stop drinking. Otherwise, I'd have to crawl home. "Thanks for stopping by..." Liam could go back to whatever woman he was trying to impress.

He didn't move. "You really want to keep doing this?"

My gaze turned back to his, unsure what that meant.

"There's no guy in this bar who deserves you. That asshole didn't deserve you."

"And you do?" I asked coldly.

His eyes narrowed in offense. "I'm in love with you, aren't I? A real man isn't afraid to feel shit. Your guy is a pussy. He'd rather waste his time on women who will never mean anything than actually have the real thing." His intense gaze burrowed into mine. "I want to take care of you. I want to provide for you. I want you to live in that big-ass house with me. I want you to take my money and buy pretty things. Why waste your time out here when I can give you everything you want?"

"I never wanted you for your money, Liam. I wanted loyalty, fidelity, honesty—"

"And I was honest." He placed his hand over his chest. "You never would have known what I did if I hadn't told you. I couldn't live with the guilt or the shame, so I came clean. I couldn't lie to your face every day. You act like that doesn't mean anything, but it does." He slowly lowered his hand. "I know what it's like to live without you, and I promise I will never do that shit again. I'm tired of chasing the loneliness with women in my sheets when the only person I want is my wife." He spoke loudly before the music and conversation drowned him out. "I won't break your heart. I won't hurt you. You don't have to put yourself out there again. I'm the one earning your trust. You have all the power, Anna."

Damien broke my heart so much that settling actually sounded nice. I knew Liam's apology was sincere, and he would probably never betray me again. It'd been almost a year since we went our separate ways, and he still wanted me back. He wouldn't feel that way unless I was important to him. He could have any other woman he wanted, and he could have moved on by now if he wanted. Being single sucked. Most of the guys I met were losers, and the one I actually liked was a player who ripped me to pieces. Could I ever put myself out there again?

Liam studied my expression like he hoped I would finally give him what he wanted.

I picked up my clutch and fished out the cash to pay for my drink.

Liam quickly threw a ton of cash on the table. "Let me take you home."

I didn't bother with the money dance even though I didn't want him to pay for my shit. "Thank you, but I'm okay." I excused myself from the table and walked out of the bar, not looking back as I craved the cool air outside the double doors.

When I reached the sidewalk, I realized he was right behind me.

"Anna." He moved around me and blocked my path. "Come on."

"I don't need a ride, Liam—"

"Then I'll walk with you. But I'd rather drive."

I knew this confrontation would only end in one way—his way. "Fine."

He drove me to my apartment, and of course, he insisted on walking me to the front door. He didn't accept my arguments and just did whatever he wanted.

I got the key in the door and opened it.

He didn't try to come inside. With his hands in his pockets, he leaned against the doorframe, halfway inside my apartment and halfway out. "Moving anytime soon?"

"Yes, my place is a dump. You've made that clear, Liam."

"That's not what I said."

I set my clutch and keys on the table and turned back to him. "I got a new job a couple weeks ago."

"Yeah?" He smiled slightly. "Good. I hated knowing you were waitressing."

"What's wrong with waitressing?"

"Nothing. I just don't want you to do it." He crossed his arms over his chest. "Where's your new gig?"

"I work in the office at Tuscan Rose."

He nodded in approval. "That sounds nice."

"I like it. I'll be able to afford a new place soon."

"You know...you could afford a new place now." The intent in his eyes was obvious.

"Liam."

His expression hardened.

"Why do you keep trying? And don't say it's because you love me or miss me." I'd rejected him plenty of times, and it gave me no pleasure to do it. But just when I thought he was really gone, he turned up again. He refused to go away.

His gaze moved down the hallway for a minute as he pondered the question. When he had a good response, he turned back to me. "You don't realize what you have until it's gone, you know? I've lived in that big house alone, your ghost haunting every room, every lonely night. Sometimes I would spray your perfume just so it felt like you were in the house. And when you refused my money...it hit me hard. The women I meet want my money. They want me to go back to death fighting because they think it's sexy. The fact that you don't want anything from me just makes me realize...you loved me for me. I'm never going to find that again."

I'd loved him before he was rich. I'd loved him when he was just like everyone else. When the money poured in, it didn't change the way I thought about him. I loved him exactly the same, wanted to have his kids because of love, not because he could provide for them or give them a good life.

He looked at the ground for a while, his fingers moving over the back of his hair. "I shouldn't have had to lose you to really understand that, but that's how we learn the hardest lessons...with the most pain." He raised his head and looked at me again. "And I think you've learned the same thing. That there's no man out there who's gonna love you as much as I do, because I'm still here, still fighting for you, and that other guy has already forgotten you."

His last statement hit me the hardest because I was terrified it was true. Every night together...did that mean more to me than it ever did to Damien? He hadn't contacted me since the night he'd dumped me, so it did seem like he'd forgotten about me. "Good night, Liam." I should brush off Damien and stop caring about someone who didn't care about me, but it was hard...really hard.

Liam straightened at my dismissal, the disappointment obvious in his eyes. "Good night, Anna." He stepped back from the doorframe and walked down the hallway.

I shut and locked the door and immediately moved to the couch, the red wine still potent in my blood. I was upset that I'd lost my husband, that he cheated on me in the first place, but I was really miserable over that beautiful man.

I missed Damien's intense gaze, the way his fingers brushed through my hair. I missed those good kisses, the way he made me feel loved without even trying. I still reached for him in my bed even though I knew he wasn't there.

I still hoped.

I pulled out my phone and stared at his message box. Texting your ex late at night after a couple drinks was stupid. It never ended well. But I was sad...really sad. *I miss you.* My thumb hit the button and sent it right away.

Damage was done.

I stared at the phone and waited for those three little dots to pop up.

They never did.

And he never texted me back.

25

DAMIEN

"I can do half a billion by noon tomorrow." I rested against the leather seat of the booth, a new client sitting slightly across from me.

Hades was there too, positioned on the other side of the round booth.

"Really?" Victor asked. "By tomorrow?"

I nodded.

"If that's the truth," Victor said, "you boys got yourselves a deal."

My phone vibrated on the table, and I quickly glanced at it in case it was something important.

It was Annabella. *I miss you.*

I stared at it for a long time, blood draining from my face.

"Can you do more?" Victor asked.

I didn't even notice he'd spoken.

Hades interceded on my behalf. "Let's start small and work our way up. Meet us in the office tomorrow."

"You know I don't like to show my face in public," Victor said.

"We'll work something out over the phone, then." Hades shook his hand before he nudged me in the side.

I snapped out of it and shook Victor's hand before he slipped out of the booth. I let my phone go dark and didn't look at the message again because I didn't need to. Those three little words were ingrained in my mind now. It didn't fill me with any kind of elation, just made me feel like shit.

Because I missed her too.

But I would never tell her that. I wanted her to move on, to forget about me.

"What is it?" When Victor was out of earshot, Hades addressed my aloofness.

I opened the phone again and slid it to him, unafraid to share the intimate details of my life.

He picked it up and looked at her message. His expression didn't change before he slid it back to me. "She has it for you bad."

"Yeah." I slid my phone into my pocket.

"What are you going to say?"

"Nothing."

"Just leave her hanging?"

I swirled my drink before I downed some of it. "I don't want to lead her on."

"It's not too late...if you want to change your mind."

I wasn't going to sacrifice my lifestyle for a woman I hardly knew. That was how Hades's story ended, but it wouldn't be the same with mine. He had a soul mate, and I didn't. I wasn't looking for one either. Now that I had him back, I didn't need a woman to fill the void anymore. "No."

He stared at me for a while but didn't press it. "Have you decided what you're going to do about the Skull King?"

"I'm gonna pay him."

"Good. Diplomatic choice."

"But I'm still gonna kill him."

Hades was about to drink from his glass, but when he heard what I said, he set it down again. "Not the diplomatic choice..."

"He was going to execute my father, Hades. How can I ever let that go?"

"It wasn't personal."

"Bullshit, it wasn't personal," I snapped. "It was entirely personal. That was why it worked."

He drank from his glass, his eyes on me.

"What if it was Ash? Sofia?"

"Sofia doesn't apply, but I get what you're saying." Because Sofia meant far more to him than his brother ever would.

"And I just sweep it under the rug?"

"Your father seems to have."

I rolled my eyes. "He's too old to really understand what happened."

He swished his drink before he set it down. "Don't expect me to participate in your vendetta. I saved your father because that was a special circumstance, but my attitude about my distance hasn't changed. I have a family to prioritize. You're alone in this."

I hadn't expected anything from him. "I understand."

"Then think this through. Because Heath is a serious opponent, and if you make a wrong move...you could end up dead."

I DESCENDED INTO THE LAIR.

The Skull Kings operated in plain sight. Pedestrians walked past the building, assuming it was an old factory that may or may not be in operation. The police knew where it was and always avoided the streets surrounding it.

With a few men, I got past security and descended to the bottom floor, where the Skull Kings preferred to linger with their booze and women. All the men at the tables glanced at me when I entered, their laughter dying away when they recognized who I was. Women sat on the laps of the generous tippers, their tits hanging out in their barely there clothing.

Heath sat on the wooden throne, skulls carved into the black wood, his knees far apart and his slouched frame sunk into the large chair. His elbow was on one armrest, and he stared at me with a sense of boredom.

I dropped my bag of money on the ground. My men did the same.

It was dead silent as Heath stared at me, all the men holding their breaths to see what their leader would do. He was still as a statue, frozen in that seat. His fingers rested across his lips as he stared at me with those crystal-blue eyes, like a predator deciding what to do with his prey.

He finally dropped his fingers from his lips. "I'm glad you changed your attitude."

Oh, my attitude was exactly the same.

His hands pushed against the armrests, and he rose to his feet. "I'm sorry it had to be this way, but you know how it is. Just business." He stepped toward me, his tattoos running down both forearms.

"It's all there—past and present royalties." I had more money than I knew what to do with, but handing over this much cash made bile flood into my mouth. I'd violated my principles, caved to an opponent when I'd never done it before. I bent the knee when I shouldn't have to, and that wounded my pride.

"I'm sure it is." When he stopped in front of me, a vicious smile entered his expression, as if he was enjoying every single moment of this. "I look forward to our new partnership." He extended his hand to mine.

I saw the skull diamond sitting on his ring finger, the same one Balto wore. It was enormous, rumored to be the most expensive diamond in the world. It was pristine, flawless, and uniquely carved into the special ring. The twins wore the same ring but on different hands. It was the only way to tell them apart—because Balto used it as his wedding ring.

Heath waited for me to take his hand. "I like you, Damien. So, I hope this is real, that you take my mercy with gratitude. Because if it's not...I know Balto won't help you. And your father isn't the only person in your heart."

He'd just threatened me—again. How could I take his hand after that?

His eyes drilled into my face as he waited. "I'm not a patient man."

I finally sealed the deal and made the gesture.

He squeezed my hand hard, threatening my wrist bone.

I gripped him just as tightly.

He smiled before he dropped his hand. "I'll see you next month. And don't lie about your numbers. I'll know." He moved back to his throne and sagged into the chair, his hands returning to the armrests.

I wanted to kill this smug son of a bitch.

I motioned for my men to leave. We turned around and headed to the stairs, showing all the men that their leader prevailed—again.

Like I had a target in my back, Heath fired off a last shot. "Give my best to your father, would you?" Humor was in his voice, getting his revenge after I'd humiliated him with Balto. Maybe he wouldn't hurt me, but he would make this relationship as difficult as possible.

I halted on the spot but didn't turn around. I had to close my eyes and let the rage circulate through my body then escape as breath. If I responded to the taunt, I'd end up dead. I had no chance here.

Keep walking, Damien. Hades's voice came into my head.

I sighed and kept going.

My time would come...soon enough.

26

ANNABELLA

A WEEK HAD PASSED SINCE I'D STUPIDLY TEXTED HIM.

God, I seemed desperate.

But I was desperate...for one man. I could go back to my ex-husband or find someone else, but that wasn't what I wanted.

I wanted Damien.

Like always, I sat at my desk and let my thoughts drift into the past, when we'd made love on the couch while the fire burned in the hearth. I was on his lap, slowly riding his bare length as I looked into those intense eyes.

I wanted to do that every night.

"Anna?" Sofia stood on the other side of my desk, slowly waving her hand in front of my face.

"Oh, sorry." I snapped out of it, missing the heat of the flames the second I was pulled from the memory.

"Where were you?"

"You know...thinking about my grocery list."

Sofia didn't seem to believe me, but she didn't call me out on it. "How have you been?"

"Good...good."

Sofia lowered herself into the chair. "Honestly, you look just as pale as you did three weeks ago."

It'd been three weeks? It felt like a day. It felt like he'd just let me go. "Yeah...it's been rough."

"Have you talked to him?"

I wanted to keep my secret because I was embarrassed, but he could tell her at any time. "I did something stupid. I went out, had a couple of drinks, and then texted him..."

"What did you say?"

"That I missed him." Oh god, the shame. Chasing a man who didn't want me wasn't me. I had too much pride for that shit. But this man...was *the* man.

"Did he say anything back?"

I shook my head.

Her eyes flashed with sympathy. "Damien is a good friend and I love him dearly, but don't waste your time on him. If a man drops you like that, walk away. I know it's hard but...you deserve better. You're gorgeous, Anna. You're smart, outgoing, everything a man would want."

"Has he said anything about me?" I hated myself for asking.

She shook her head. "I mentioned that you'd told me you stopped seeing each other, and he didn't say much...just that it didn't work out. That was the end of it."

Just like that? And he moved on?

"Damien has never been a one-woman kind of guy. He saw you for so long, I thought this time it was different. But I guess not. I'm not trying to make you feel worse. I'm trying to help you."

"I know."

"And I care about you, so I don't want to see you suffer. You're too good of a catch."

I gave a weak smile. "Thanks... I appreciate that."

———

I WAS SITTING on the couch when a knock sounded on the door.

I was enjoying a bottle of wine by myself, along with cheese and crackers. The spread made it seem like I was entertaining, but nope...it was all just for me.

After I got to my feet, my heart started to race because I hoped it was Damien, that something had snapped in his head and he realized he wanted to see me again. It was what I wanted more than anything...and I couldn't control the impulse.

When I looked through the peephole, I was disappointed.

It was Liam.

Now that he knew I was depressed and alone, he'd started to come around again.

I opened the door but stayed in the doorway so he wouldn't come inside.

He read the irritated look on my face. "I come in peace."

"And what peaceful offering do you bring?"

"Dinner?" He was in a long-sleeved black t-shirt, the color a stark contrast against his fair skin. His blue eyes seemed harmless, soft like they used to be.

"I had dinner."

He glanced over my shoulder and saw the wine and cheese. "That doesn't constitute dinner."

"You know I'm not a big eater."

"Come on." He stepped back. "You should get out of the house."

I eyed him suspiciously.

"It's just dinner, Anna."

I didn't know why I agreed. Maybe it was loneliness. Maybe it was because I'd stopped caring. "Alright..."

I GOT to pick the restaurant, so we went somewhere casual, a little bistro close to my apartment. We sat across from each other at the small table near the window, sharing my favorite bottle of wine while we both ordered salads.

Liam kept the conversation light, asking about work and what I'd seen on TV lately.

But I knew it was coming.

"Did he text you back?"

There it was. "No."

He didn't hide his relief. His response was subtle, but I knew him well enough to detect all the little expressions he made. "Seeing anyone else?"

I didn't want to meet someone else and start over. He would probably be bad in bed like most of the others. That was way too much work, and I was exhausted. I wasn't looking for my next husband, but I wasn't looking to waste my time either. And every man I met was a waste of time—except Damien. "No."

"I'm not seeing anyone either."

I pushed the kale around on my plate because I was full. Now I just played with my food so I had something to do. "I didn't ask."

"But I wanted you to know...if you ever want to stop by."

Did he just invite me over to screw? My eyes lifted at his absurdity.

"It seemed like that was what you were interested in, something casual and easy, and I can provide that. And you know exactly what to expect..." He sat with his arms on the table, holding my gaze without a hint of shame. "It's better than being disappointed over and over, right?"

Ain't that the truth.

"At least, that's what women tell me..."

I wasn't jealous, but I didn't like thinking about all the women he was screwing. "Have you been fighting lately?" I sidestepped the awkward conversation and moved on.

He let it go. "No. But I've been working out a lot."

"I can tell."

"You could tell better if I weren't wearing clothes."

Now I shot him a pissed look.

He smiled like he enjoyed getting under my skin. "Just saying..."

"I'm not going to sleep with you, Liam."

"Why not?" he asked. "You're lonely. I'm lonely."

"Our relationship is already so complicated."

"Then what's the harm?" He dropped his smile and stared at me with that intense expression, just the way he did before he cornered me and ripped off my blouse. It'd been a long time since we'd been together, but those things hadn't changed.

I dropped my gaze and looked at my salad again. "I'm not going to sleep with you to get over someone else. It's rude."

"It's not rude if I don't care."

"Well, I care."

"You could—"

"I don't want to talk about this anymore." I shut down the conversation and raised my hand to catch the waiter's attention. "Thank you for dinner, but I think it's time for me to go home."

He didn't argue with me even though it looked like he wanted to. "Alright. I'll walk you home."

27

DAMIEN

"What the hell are you wearing?" I took the seat across from Catalina in the restaurant, looking at her short blue dress, enormous sunglasses, and pulled-back hair. "It's almost October."

She took off her sunglasses and gave me that ferocious look she'd been giving me since she could crawl. Her thick lashes were full of mascara, and her bright eyeshadow made her look as if she were ready for a pool party. "I'm not ready to accept fall. I want to hold on to summer a little longer."

"Well, summer is long gone. The first official day of fall was last week—"

"Shh." She leaned over the table and placed her forefinger against my lips. "Don't talk like that." She leaned back and picked up her menu, as if she hadn't just shoved her hand in my face. "I know I should get a salad, but I don't want to... I can dance if I'm a hundred pounds heavier, so I don't get all the rules."

"Stop dancing."

"I don't want to do that either. I'll retire when I turn thirty and order whatever I want then." She closed the menu and dropped it on the table.

"Why will you stop at thirty?"

"Because I'll be old and have to pop out some kids. We both know you aren't going to do it. The responsibility falls to *moi*."

"*Moi*?" I cocked an eyebrow, surprised she still behaved like a diva. "I doubt you'll find a guy who wants to have kids with *moi*."

She flashed me another glare. "So, what's the reason for this special occasion?"

"I've asked you to dinner before."

"Maybe on my birthday. And that's fine, I don't like you either." She stuck out her tongue at me.

"That isn't why I don't call more often. I'm just busy…"

"I'm busy too, but I always text."

I couldn't argue with that because it was true. She did check in with me pretty often, even if it was just sending a stupid animal video she thought was funny. I was the older brother, so I should do a better job of acting like one. "Are you seeing anyone?"

"Are *you* seeing anyone?" she countered.

"No need to get defensive. I was asking about your life."

"Do I ever ask about yours?" she asked. "Because it's personal, and I know you'll tell me if there's something worth telling me about."

"So, nothing worth telling me about, then?"

She shook her head. "Nah."

My sister had always been a character, and I loved her for it—when she didn't annoy me. "So, some stuff happened with Dad…"

"Oh my god, is he okay?" She dropped her diva persona and turned into a real person again.

"He's fine. I should have led with that. But I think it's time he moved in with me, and he's being stubborn as hell about it."

"Now you know where you get it from," she teased. "So, what happened?"

I didn't want to scare her, so I lied. "Some guys broke in to his apartment."

"Fucking assholes." She slammed both of her fists onto the table.

"I took care of them, so it's resolved. But I don't think he should live alone anymore."

"I've been saying that for years. I tried to get him to live with me, but he said he'd rather die." She rolled her eyes. "Rather die? *Really*?" She rolled her eyes again. "He was never this dramatic when Mom was around."

"I think that's *why* he's dramatic."

"Man, I miss her," she said with a sigh. "Everything changed the day she was gone."

"Yeah..." It felt like yesterday. "I thought maybe we could both talk to him. Maybe if we gang up on him, he'll cave."

"That could work."

She took a sip of her water. "But are you sure you want him to live with you? It's not like you can just kick him out if you don't like it. He could live with me too."

"It's a big place. It'll be fine."

"That's right, you're a rich boy."

It was my turn to roll my eyes. "He also has Patricia for help and company."

"Her cooking is good. He'll be happy just with that. That works out better because I don't want him to live with me."

I cocked an eyebrow. "Then why did you offer?"

"Because he's my father, and I'm happy to take care of him. It's just a small apartment, and it would get awkward with sleepovers. I'd have to stay at their place all the time, and that would be just as awkward."

"Yes...awkward." Like this conversation was.

"Get over it," she said when she picked up on my tone. "I'm a grown woman with needs."

I cringed and grabbed the menu. "This is why I don't check in more often."

"Because your grown-ass sister has the same lifestyle you do? Sexist."

"No. I just don't want to hear about my sister's conquests. So, let's just order and leave."

She stuck out her tongue at me again. "Whatever..."

28

ANNABELLA

Go home, Anna.

But the cab stopped at the curb, and the driver waited for me to get out.

I could just tell the driver to go back, but I didn't want to leave.

I finally got out of the car and moved to the front door. My finger dug into the cushioned doorbell, and I waited for someone to answer.

Patricia opened the door, visibly surprised to see me standing there. "Annabella? How are you? I haven't seen you in a while."

I shouldn't have expected her to know anything. I didn't see why Damien would explain himself to his maid. "I was wondering if I could see him."

"Sure." She invited me inside then grabbed her phone. "I'll tell him you're on your way up."

There was no going back now.

I entered the room with the grand staircase and started my ascent to the top floor. It was a spiral stairway, the kind that went round and round until it reached the chandelier at the top. The crystals were bright with the light, and the white banister was smooth under my fingertips as I glided up.

My heart was in my throat.

My pulse was heavy in my ears, thudding like a war drum.

I kept moving, my heart in the driver's seat.

I reached the top and the hallway that led to his bedroom. My long coat was unbuttoned, and my fingertips were sensitive from the heavy pulse throbbing in every single vein in my hand.

Insanity had driven me here. Desperation. Longing...deep longing. Maybe he didn't need more to say goodbye...but I did. Moving on from him was harder than moving on from Liam, even though that made absolutely no sense.

When I reached his door, he opened it.

In black sweatpants without a t-shirt, he stood there, his eyes impossible to read. They were intense, just the way they used to be when he looked at me, but they were also disturbed, like he was afraid.

I stopped in front of him...and just stood there.

I couldn't believe I was looking at him.

He was as handsome as he was the last time I saw him. It'd been a month, but it felt like a second. A shadow was on his jawline from his scruff, and his lips looked like they hadn't been kissed since me. His green eyes were those of an old soul, a man who had lived many lifetimes in very few years. He was better than I remembered him, so strong and beautiful.

He said nothing, probably in utter shock to see me standing there.

I'd prepared a speech, but now that our eyes were connected like this, every word left my brain as if it'd never been there in the first place. I couldn't tell him I loved him, not when I knew he didn't feel the same way. I couldn't beg him to come back to me, not without hating myself. All I really wanted was a night...even if it was the last.

I moved into him, seeing the way he didn't step back. I gained more courage with our proximity, knowing he wouldn't turn away. When my lips were almost on his, my fingers finally reached out and cupped his cheeks.

My hands burned.

I tilted his chin to mine and kissed him.

The touch ignited my senses, reminded me that I hadn't been crazy, that it was as good as I remembered. My fingers moved farther, sliding into his hair as I took a deep breath at our connection. My chest pressed against his, and I backed him up into the bedroom, returning to the place where I'd fallen in love with him.

He kissed me back, his hand brushing through my hair like old times.

It was better than I remembered. I kissed him harder, felt the fire from our raging passion. It pulled me under and burned me alive, brought me to a higher plane of existence that I hadn't touched since he'd left.

I wanted this...so much.

His arm circled my waist, and he tugged me into his body as he kissed me, as he felt my cheek with his hard fingertips. His lips were seductive and soft but full of the masculine aggression that made me feel so desirable.

I pushed my jacket off my shoulders and let it fall to the ground without skipping a beat.

But that action made him pull away.

He ended our kiss, took away the fire that had finally thawed my frozen soul. He stared at me with incredulous eyes, as if he couldn't believe what just happened. His hands slid from my body, and he stepped back. He inhaled a deep breath then dragged his hand down his face, persecuting himself when he wasn't guilty in the first place. "Annabella—"

"I just want one night." No one on this earth called me Annabella but him...and I missed that. He took the time to say every single syllable instead of needing to rush and go by a nickname instead. "I know you said you don't want monogamy. But that doesn't mean this can't happen..." Why was I settling for less than I deserved? Why was I showing up here like a crazy person? I was the one who'd told him I didn't want anything serious. Now I was the one who was so desperately in love, I'd completely lost control.

"Annabella." His eyes stayed on the floor while his hands moved to his narrow hips. He was quiet for a while, processing what he wanted to say before he lifted his gaze once more. "It's over."

My lungs were both punctured by his knife, and I couldn't breathe. His rejection stung like a swarm of wasps. Once again, I was embarrassed...and I had no one to blame but myself. Why did I have to come here? Why did I have to chase this man like my life depended on it?

His gaze turned hard, ice-cold. "Don't come here again."

I was gonna cry...cry my eyes out again.

"Go." He walked past me to the door and opened it wide.

I didn't turn around right away. I tried to understand what had happened. I walked through the door and kissed him...and he kissed me back. He kissed me back with the same passion and desire. But then he quickly changed his mind and kicked me out.

Why?

I finally found the courage to face him and walk out the door. I turned around again.

He kept his hand on the knob so I couldn't slip back in.

"Why?" My humiliation was enough closure for me to move on and try to forget this happened, but I still felt like I was missing a piece of the story, like he was hiding something from me.

"I told you why, Annabella."

"But I'm not asking for—"

"I just want to move on, alright?" He turned harsh again, treating me like a stray dog that wouldn't stop coming around for extra scraps. "I'm sorry I hurt you. But I've moved on, and you need to do the same."

THE CAR RIDE happened in the blink of an eye.

I stared at the streetlights through blurred vision. Red. Green. Red again. The shame and heartbreak mixed together and caused a burst of pure humiliation. He'd rejected me because he didn't want me anymore. That connection I felt...it was all just me. That good sex...was just sex. I saw something that wasn't there, fell for a man who couldn't care less about me.

God, I felt stupid.

Tears streamed down my cheeks, but I didn't even notice them. Didn't even care.

I should have listened to Sofia. Why didn't I?

Damien would tell her what I did, and then she would look at me like I was a crazy person too.

Maybe I was a crazy person.

Love made me crazy...and I wondered if I'd ever really loved Liam at all.

I sure as hell hadn't loved him like that.

When he'd cheated on me, I didn't fly off the rails and throw dishes across the room. I didn't hunt down the woman so I could bitch-slap her. I didn't throw his clothes out the window. I wasn't spiteful. I was calm...totally calm.

I wanted to be calm again. I wanted to be confident, self-assured, elegant. I wanted to be indifferent, to be chased instead of doing the chasing. I wanted a simple life, because reaching for something more...was stupid.

And I would never be stupid again.

The cab pulled up to the house and stopped.

I stared at it for a few seconds before I handed over my cash and walked to the front door. It was dark, and the distant sound of thunder vibrated against the clouds. Rain had been in the forecast, and it began to sprinkle.

I made it to the front door and knocked. This time, I didn't feel embarrassed because there would be no rejection. I would be welcomed with open arms, be appreciated for the woman, the diamond I was told to be.

The door opened, and Liam stood there, his eyes filled with unmis-takable surprise. He'd pictured this moment a thousand times but never thought it would actually happen. I'd been gone for so long, and with every passing month, his chances dwindled. But I was there now...and he could hardly believe it.

I'd cried over another man, and those tears stained my cheeks. I didn't hide them because I couldn't feel any more shame than I already did. Liam wanted me so much that he didn't care about the conditions.

As long as he got to have me.

I moved into his chest, and he leaned in and kissed me.

He didn't respond right away, his lips soaking in my kiss until he understood what he was feeling. Then his hands were on me, his arm hooked around my waist as he kicked the door shut behind me. He backed me up into the wood and kissed me with the passion I was looking for, like I was the only thing in the world that mattered to him. His hands cupped my face, and he pulled back to stare at me, to appreciate the sight of my face in the dim entryway light. "I'm not gonna let you go this time..."

29

DAMIEN

I GOT INTO THE OFFICE LATE THAT DAY.

Because I didn't want to get out of bed.

I never thought I could hate myself so much.

But I did.

Hades knocked on the open door before he stepped in. "You've got those numbers? And if you do, I hope they're right this time." Instead of talking to me with pure loathing, there was a teasing tone to his voice.

"I'll get them to you in an hour."

He stopped in front of my desk, his hands in his pockets. "What happened now?"

What didn't happen?

"You pay Heath?"

"Yeah. He got his money."

"Gonna take my advice?"

I shook my head. "Probably not. He was a dick to me."

"You did turn his brother against him."

"Just for the night."

"Either way, it probably rubbed him the wrong way."

That was the least of my problems, ironically.

"Something else?"

"My sister and I agreed that my father should move in with me."

He sighed loudly. "That's rough. Maria is a nice lady and she's great with Andrew, but...not a fan of living with my mother-in-law. Sofia is my wife, but I feel like I'm the one crossing the line by sleeping with her every night."

That wasn't what I was worried about. "There's plenty of room for him. It's getting him there that's the problem."

"Yeah, he's an asshole just like you."

I wasn't in the mood for jokes.

"Anything I can do to help?"

I shook my head. "Thanks anyway."

He turned to walk out of my office. "I'll be waiting for those numbers."

"Hades?"

He turned back around.

"Annabella came to my place last night."

He leaned against the door, both of his eyebrows rising. "And?"

"I asked her to leave."

"What did she want?"

I didn't answer.

Hades picked up on my silence. "She wanted to sleep with you, and you said no?"

I nodded. "If I go down that road again, I'll get stuck. I'll never be able to leave."

"You're stronger than I give you credit for."

Strong wasn't the right word. "I felt like a jackass, asking her to leave. She was devastated... I could see it in her eyes."

"She'll get over it...eventually."

I knew she would find someone else, and I would be a distant memory. She would be happy with a good man, and I'd be content knowing I'd stepped aside so she could have a better life. But that didn't mean this was easy for me.

Hades continued to stare at me.

"Yeah...she will."

30

ANNABELLA

A MONTH HAD PASSED.

And it was all a blur.

I'd arrived on Liam's doorstep in a desperate attempt to fight the loneliness, to heal the latest set of wounds Damien had created, to feel loved when all I'd felt was used. It wasn't my finest moment, but who would dare judge me.

Now I was done thinking about Damien. He didn't want me?

Fine. I didn't want him either.

I opened my eyes and stared out the large window, seeing the sunshine stretched across the carpeted floor. The curtains were open because they'd never been closed. Hours ago, only starlight shone upon the floor.

I used to wake up like this every morning...once upon a time.

I wiped the sleep from my eyes and grabbed my phone off the nightstand. It was Saturday morning, so I wasn't expected at the office. There were no emails waiting for me. No texts either.

I returned it to the nightstand and lay down again, so comfortable in this bed that I didn't want to leave. I used to sleep there every single night, used to listen to Liam's even breathing like a lullaby. Now I was back...and it felt like my castle once more.

"Morning, baby." Liam walked through the door in his workout shorts, his chest soaked with sweat because he'd just finished his workout. He was nothing but hard muscle and tattoos, a beast. He came around the bed and leaned down to kiss me on the forehead. "Good afternoon would make more sense, actually." He smiled down at me, teasing me.

"Yes, I'm lazy." He worked out first thing in the morning, then had breakfast. A productive couple of hours while I refused to gain consciousness. "You made your point." When I was a housewife, I did this every day, getting to the gym only when I talked myself into it.

"I think it's cute." He stared at me with that soft gaze, like he was the happiest man in the world. Once I stepped into the house, he didn't let me go. He constantly pestered me to come over, and sleepovers always stretched into week-long stays. I was hardly at my apartment anymore, only stopping by to grab more clothes.

My life had become uncomplicated...and it was nice. "I'm glad you find my lack of motivation cute."

"It's not a lack of motivation." He kissed me again. "I just like seeing my woman taken care of." He dropped his bottoms and walked into the bathroom to shower.

I was about to get up, but after his words, I didn't intend to go anywhere.

———

I cooked dinner in the large kitchen, having all the space I needed to whip up one of my favorite meals. I wore his t-shirt as an apron as I tilted the hot pan and dished up the food onto the plates.

Liam walked in wearing sweatpants. "Smells good." He sat at the bar and stared at me, watching me work the kitchen the way I used to before I left. His blue eyes were focused in their stare, watching every movement I made like it was fascinating.

I served him his plate and a glass of ice water.

"Thank you." He grabbed his fork and immediately took a bite.

I stood across from him, pushing my food around before I took a bite. We never talked about the night I'd shown up on his doorstep with tears on my cheeks. When he didn't ask me why I cried, I assumed he already knew why and didn't want to hear about it. So, we'd spent the last month not talking about anything at all.

He didn't seem to mind.

We ate quietly, exchanging subtle looks while the silence surrounded us.

He was an animal, so he ate his dinner in just a few bites.

I was a slow eater. That was probably why I didn't eat much.

"I have an idea." He pushed his plate away and rested his elbows on the counter.

"Yeah?"

"Live with me." He let his words echo off the high ceilings, let them wrap around us both with heavy anticipation. With confidence in his gaze, he stared at me hard, as if he hoped his presence was enough to influence me. He sat in the spot where he'd been many times over the years, staring at me like I was the only person who mattered to him. He kissed the ground I walked on, treated me the way Hades treated Sofia, and that was what I wanted. He seemed to mean his apology, seemed to be a better man because of his mistake. Losing me made him love me more, made him obsessed with getting me back into his house.

There was nothing for me at the apartment. There was no special guy out there waiting to meet me. And Damien was officially an asshole who'd played me for a fool. I wouldn't waste another moment thinking about him. "You don't think it's too soon?"

He shook his head. "I would have asked the first night if I'd thought you'd say yes."

"But you haven't asked me anything." Like if I was still hung up on Damien, if he was the man I pictured when we were in bed together, if I was only there to use Liam to mask my pain like a drug.

He shrugged. "I want you as you are...even if you're broken from someone else."

Never thought Liam could be so romantic.

"I want you so much, I don't care. I don't give a damn if I'm a rebound." He rose from the barstool and planted his hands against the island, his powerful arms visibly sculpted under the lights. He slowly made his way around the island and came toward me. "I'll make you forget about him." He stopped in front of me, staring at me so hard, I thought I might catch on fire. "Let me make you forget about him."

Damien's rejection had forced me to have a moment of self-reflection, to examine my ridiculous behavior, my irrational response when I couldn't have what I wanted. I knew it was a type of love I'd never experienced before, where you lost your mind to insanity. It was powerful, crazy, beautiful...but it wasn't real.

How could it be real if he didn't feel the same way?

If I could go back in time, I would have changed my decision. I wouldn't have gone to his place, wouldn't have texted him and said I miss you. I would have held my head high and walked away. "I think you already have."

His eyes darkened noticeably, like those words were pure joy to his ears. "Is that a yes?"

"Yeah." I shouldn't be with a man who cheated on me in the first place, but the perfect man didn't exist. I wanted to be with someone who cared about me, who would fight for me rather than push me away.

He didn't smile at my answer. "Then let's take it a step further." He reached into his pocket and pulled out my wedding ring. It was pristine and shiny, like it'd been cleaned since I left it behind. He grabbed my left hand, and without waiting for an answer, he slipped the ring onto my finger.

I didn't say anything because I was still in shock. I didn't fight him. I felt the weight on my left hand, felt the weight of my old life. I'd left him because I deserved more, and maybe I would say no if Damien hadn't broken my heart. Maybe I would keep going and refuse to settle. But I did meet Damien...and he crushed all my dreams.

"Marry me. Again." Liam's hands cupped my face and forced my gaze on his, commanding me to give the answer he wanted. "I've lived without you. I know how fucking unbearable that is. I want to be here, every day, until we're both dead in the ground. Give me another chance. I won't fuck this up again."

My fingers wrapped around his wrists, and my answer came out as a whisper. "Okay..."

He rested his forehead against mine and closed his eyes. A loud, happy sigh filled the kitchen around us. "I can't believe you said yes..."

Neither could I.

31

DAMIEN

My assistant spoke into my intercom. "Sir, Liam De Luca is here to see you."

The last thing I wanted to do was deal with that asshole. Fucking worthless. I slammed my finger onto the button. "Send him to Hades. He's not my client."

She responded immediately. "He asked for you."

I closed my eyes and breathed through the annoyance before I hit the button again. "Fine. Send him in." Why did that fucker want to work with me anyway? We'd buried the hatchet, but we weren't friends.

A moment later, he stepped inside, dressed in a sports coat with a gray sweater underneath. His hair was shorter than the last time I saw him, which had been a couple of months now. He blocked the doorway with his size and approached my desk. "Damien." He extended his hand to shake mine.

I took it. "Liam, what can I do for you?"

When Liam stepped aside, I realized he wasn't alone.

Liam sat in one of the two chairs facing my desk. "You remember Anna."

She emerged once he stepped out of the way, wearing a deep-blue button-up blouse with her beautiful hair pinned back in a shiny updo. Bold diamonds were in her earlobes, and her makeup was dark around her eyes, making her ready for the runway rather than a boring bank meeting.

I was fucking speechless.

She held my gaze for a nanosecond, but she quickly averted her eyes because she didn't want to look at me. Without extending a hand to shake mine or giving some kind of greeting, she sat in the chair beside Liam and continued to ignore me.

"Yes...nice to see you again." I recovered, but my voice was weak and clearly different than usual. She floored me, not just with her stunning appearance, but with her company. What the fuck was she doing with him? Did he talk her into taking his money? Did she need help? Because I could help her.

I returned to my desk, my eyes glancing at her expression over and over, disappointed that she was more interested in her heels than my face. "Where should we start, Liam?" All I wanted to do was stare at her, to get her to look at me, but she wouldn't. I turned to her ex-husband.

He didn't seem to notice the burning tension in the room. He never would have come here peacefully if he knew I was the man who used to bed his ex-wife. She'd obviously never told him. "Anna needs to be returned to all my accounts."

I looked at her, waiting for an objection. "Is that what you want?"

Even when she spoke, she still didn't look at me. "Yes." Was it embarrassment from the last night we saw each other? Or was it hatred? Did she hate me for what I did for her?

Liam reached for her hand and held it on the armrest. "We're getting married."

That was when I noticed the enormous diamond on her left hand, the claim that Liam had put on her. And my heart sank...so deep, it hit my feet. I looked at her again because I wanted her to say it wasn't true—that she wasn't taking this cheater back.

Liam rubbed his thumb over her diamond ring, looking at her like she was the bigger jewel than the one he'd bought for her. He was elated, clearly in love.

But what was she?

Liam turned back to me. "I want her on everything. And put it under De Luca—because that will be her name in a few weeks."

———

ANNABELLA IGNORED me through the entire meeting, and when they left, she didn't say goodbye before she walked out. There had been no eye contact from the moment she'd initially looked at me, like she needed to make sure it was really me.

Then I was dead to her.

Now I sat in my office, letting the light disappear from the windows. I didn't have any more appointments or meetings for the day, so I could have gone home hours ago...but I was stuck in place. I hadn't moved from my chair since she'd walked out, and everyone else at the office had already packed up and gone home.

She was marrying him?

Why?

I broke up with her two months ago, and when she couldn't get me back, she went to him?

That cheating asshole?

What the fuck was she thinking?

Hades passed my office on his way out of the building, and when he noticed I was still inside with the lights on, he stopped and entered my doorway. "I've never seen you stay late in my entire life."

I wasn't amused by the joke, so I didn't look at him. My feet were up on the desk, and I had sunk into the leather chair, my hands folded on my stomach. I stared at the fluorescent lights for a long time, trying to make sense of the chaos I'd just witnessed.

He approached my desk. "What happened?"

My eyes shifted to his, and I stared at his hard expression for a while before I lowered my feet to the ground and straightened in the chair. "Liam stopped by."

"And you didn't send him to me?"

"He wanted me to put his fiancée on his account."

His eyebrows slowly rose. "He's getting remarried?"

I nodded. "You won't believe who it's to."

Hades was a smart guy, so he jumped to the right conclusion within a couple seconds. "Anna?"

I nodded again. "She sat in that chair and wouldn't look at me..." I glanced at the armchair that probably still carried her perfume. I still remembered the taste of her lips, the taste of her everywhere. "Didn't say a word."

Hades slid his hands into his pockets and stood there. "Are you okay?"

I shrugged, as if that was a sufficient answer.

"He's strong and rich...there are worse guys she could be with."

I lifted my gaze to meet his. "He fucked someone else when she lost their baby. Fuck him."

He didn't react to my hostility.

"I don't fucking understand." I slammed my hand on the desk. "Why did she go back to him? Why would she want to be with someone she'd already left? She deserves better than that piece of shit."

He dropped his gaze.

"I just don't understand..." I dragged my hand down my face, closing my eyes for a second to shut out the world.

"Maybe you don't have a problem with who she's marrying. Maybe your problem is that she's marrying someone at all."

"We've been broken up for two months." Our relationship wasn't serious, but marrying someone that soon? It didn't make sense. "She was in my bedroom a month ago...begging me to be with her."

"Maybe that's exactly why she's doing this."

I stared at him.

"She doesn't want a risk. And Liam isn't a risk."

AFTER SLEEPING ON IT, I'd thought I would feel a lot better about the whole thing. I was just caught off guard when Anna entered my office with Liam. It was unexpected, so I had to process all of that in a very short amount of time.

But I didn't get any sleep.

And I felt exactly the same way when the sun came up.

Why was she doing this?

She shouldn't do this.

It was none of my business what she did, and I'd imagined she would end up with someone else at some point...but it wouldn't be in my face like this. And it wouldn't be Liam De Luca, the jackass she'd already divorced once.

I wanted to go to work and brush off the whole thing.

But I couldn't focus at work. I was exhausted from my long night of staring at the ceiling, and I couldn't concentrate on anything I was doing. This distracted, I could transfer billions of dollars into the wrong account, and Hades really would kill me.

I grabbed my coat and walked into the hallway.

Hades happened to be passing. He looked me up and down, seeing me put on the heavy coat to battle the frost that formed in the corners of all the windows. "Can I talk you out of it?"

"I wish you could. But you know by now I never listen."

He gave me a gentle pat on the shoulder before he continued on his way. "Good luck."

"Thanks..." I drove to the Tuscan Rose and threw my keys at the valet before I stepped inside. I'd never seen her at the hotel before, but I knew her office was next to Sofia's, so it wouldn't be difficult to hide.

I moved down the hallway and crossed paths with a few staff members, all of whom glanced at me like they had no idea who I was. The women stared the hardest. I peeked into the first office and saw an older lady. I went to the next door and stilled when I spotted her.

She stood behind her desk, wearing a long-sleeved black dress with a diamond necklace around her throat. Her shiny hair was slightly wavy, thick and with enormous waves gliding down her strands to the ends. It was pinned over one shoulder, making that side voluminous. Dark makeup was on her eyes, and her favorite shade of deep lipstick outlined the beautiful plumpness of her lips. She stared down at a few documents in her hand, as if she were about to leave her office to take them somewhere.

I stared at her, enjoying the sight as long as I could. She was stunning...more stunning than I remembered. I just saw her a few days ago, and she didn't glow like this. My hand missed fisting that sexy hair, missed feeling the small muscles of her back. Now that I was there, I didn't know what to say.

Why had I come here again?

She stepped away from her desk toward the door, about to run into me after a few more steps.

"Annabella." I wouldn't mind if she crashed into my chest—because I would get to rescue her from the fall.

She stilled at the sound of her name, her head popping up so she could stare at me. Now, she was the one caught off guard. Now, she was the one who couldn't feign indifference. The papers she held slipped from her fingertips and fell to the floor, as if she couldn't fathom the reality of my presence.

I stepped farther inside so I could shut her office door.

My movements snapped her out of her daze. "Why are you here?" She stared at my face with such concentration, as if she wanted to memorize my features because she couldn't look at me again. She hardly blinked as she took me in, that ferocity mixed with a subtle hint of longing.

I stepped closer to her, stalling for time because I didn't know what to say. "What are you doing?" Now that I was this close to her, I could smell her perfume. It wasn't the way she used to smell, like she'd upgraded to something fancier now that she had Liam's money again. That would explain the diamonds in her lobes as well as around her neck, in addition to that big diamond ring. "That asshole cheated on you. You left him and moved on. Now you're right back?"

Her eyes narrowed in anger. "So?"

"*So*?" I lifted my arms and threw them down again. "You deserve better, and you know it."

"Yes, I do deserve better. But better isn't out there."

She'd slammed her fist into my heart. "Annabella, there is better out there. Don't settle."

Her hands moved to her hips, her fingers digging into the fabric of her dress. "I've been single, and it sucked. I met a lot of guys who were really just boys who hit puberty early. And the one guy I actually liked dumped me. I don't want to waste my time anymore."

"And Liam is the solution?" I asked incredulously.

"He loves me."

"When a man loves a woman, he doesn't cheat." I threw my arm out. "Ever. No matter what the circumstance is. Even if she cheats on him first, he doesn't do that shit. Because a real man is loyal, devoted, and will be committed until those goddamn papers are signed."

"Maybe real men don't exist." She spoke with defeat.

"Yes, they do. Look at Hades. I've been with him to every bar, and every time Sofia would never know if he fooled around. And trust me, he doesn't even fucking look. And there've been offers. When times got tough, it didn't change anything. He was there—every fucking day. So yes, they exist." I placed my palm over my chest. "I'm a real man. I'm honest and loyal—"

"But you didn't want me." Ferocity was in her eyes, as if she'd never forgiven me for what I'd done, as if she wasn't over it. "You dumped me. And you knew how I felt, Damien."

All my confidence went out the window when I heard those words, when I was confronted by this level of intimacy. I'd never spoken to a woman like this, listened to her speak to me like this. It was the first time...in my thirty years.

"Don't be a coward. Don't act like you don't know what I'm talking about."

I breathed hard, feeling the vest of my suit stretch over my rib cage with every breath.

"I loved you." She didn't drop her gaze like she had in the bank. She looked at me head on, fearless, and confessed, "I fell in love with you, and you broke my heart."

"I didn't know—"

"Yes, you did." She dropped her hands from her hips. "It was obvious every time I'd wake you up in the middle of the night to have you. Every time I climbed on top of you and said you were mine. Every time I'd reach out for you in the middle of the night because I felt so safe with you there."

Paralyzed, I just stood there, listening to this gorgeous woman tell me these terrible things.

Tears formed on the surface of her eyes, growing wet and reflective with her speech, but she didn't let them well up and fall. "I still don't know how that happened. I expected it to take years to feel that way about someone, especially after the losers that came before you. But you were special...and I knew it. I'm tired of getting my heart broken, and I don't have the energy to put myself out there again. I know what's out there—nothing. Liam loves me, would do anything for me, and I know he's sorry for what he did. He knows what it's like to live without me, so he'll never do that again."

"Once a cheater, always a cheater."

Her eyes narrowed farther this time, furious about my reaction. "After everything I just said, that's the only response you have?"

It was the only thing that came out, but it wasn't the only thought I had.

"Why do you even care, Damien?" She threw her arms down. "You don't want me, so why do you care who I want to be with? What Liam did was wrong, but he's a good man in every other way. He made a mistake, and I'm not going to vilify him forever—"

"But you don't love him." I really needed to shut up.

She crossed her arms over her chest. "Well, I can't be with the man I love..."

I was the first one to break eye contact because the self-loathing was too much. I wanted to tell her the truth, that I left to protect her. I could tell her the reason right now, but she would try to convince me that she wasn't afraid, that she didn't care about the risk. And I would cave... I knew I would. And if I loved her and truly cared about her, I would give up everything to be with her, but I didn't feel that way. We weren't Hades and Sofia. We weren't soul mates. I hadn't even been with her long enough to develop intense feelings like that. She was just a woman I liked...and that wasn't enough.

"Unless I'm wrong?" she asked hopefully, her voice breaking with emotion. She blinked a few times to chase back the tears, to maintain a strong expression that contradicted the emotion building inside her chest.

No. She wasn't wrong. "No." I lifted my gaze and looked at her again. "I do care about you...deeply. And I want you—"

She raised her hand, doing her best to keep her tears at bay. "Leave."

I stood rooted to the spot because I didn't want to leave her like this.

"This conversation is over." She slowly lowered her hand. "I'm going to move on with my life. And I'm going to do my best to forget you. Let me forget you."

32

ANNABELLA

I HAD MY OLD CAR, BUT I TOOK THE LONG WAY HOME.

I didn't want to walk in the door with all this baggage on my shoulders. Liam would be there, and he would see right through my poor attempt to mask the shitty day I just had. He didn't want to hear about the guy who still held some real estate in my heart. He didn't deserve that.

But I couldn't shake the feeling.

And I couldn't lie either.

So, I finally walked through the front door and hung up my coat in the entryway.

The sound of someone working in the kitchen was audible, heavy pans hitting the bottom of the sink. "Baby, is that you?"

I sighed as I slipped off my heels and left them by the doorway. "Yeah."

"You're home later than usual."

Because I was wandering around the streets with my music blaring.

I moved down the hallway and entered the large kitchen, seeing him plate the food and set it on the kitchen island. "Paperwork."

His back was still turned to me so he couldn't see my face. "You can quit whenever you want. You know that."

I wanted to keep working. It was nice to have something to do, something that got me up in the morning and kept me active. "I like my job." I sat on the barstool.

He turned around and put the plate in front of me. When he read the expression in my eyes, he said, "Doesn't seem like it."

"Well, today wasn't my favorite."

He grabbed a couple forks and set them between us. Then he stared at me again, reading my expression like words on a page. "It's more than just work. I can tell."

He knew me better than anyone. "I don't want to talk about it..." I started to push my food around so I could keep my eyes averted.

He grabbed my fork and set it down. "I'm your husband, so you're going to talk to me about it."

Not yet.

"Annabella." He used that deep tone to get me to look at him.

"Trust me, you don't want to hear about this." I didn't want to hurt him because I cared for him. Some would say this was karma, but even then, I had no desire for payback.

When he understood my meaning, he sighed quietly. "Yes, I do. I want to hear everything about your life...even the shit I don't like." He was trying much harder to be a good husband this time around. He hadn't been nearly this attentive and emotionally available in the past. Losing me had really changed him.

I stared at my plate again. "He found out I was getting married."

Liam didn't say anything, but his body tightened in anger, as if he was afraid I was about to leave him. His response to any situation was violence, but that wasn't applicable here.

"Told me I shouldn't...that I deserved better."

He closed his eyes.

"We argued for a while, and then I asked him to leave."

"You didn't take him back?" He lifted his gaze to look at me.

"No...but he didn't ask. He still doesn't want me. He just doesn't want me to be with you."

He gripped the counter with both hands and sighed. "What is it about this guy?"

"I don't know...he says he cares about me—"

"No." He sighed again. "Why are you still on his hook?"

I hadn't thought about Damien much in the last month, probably because I didn't have to see or talk to him. But the moment I saw his pretty eyes and hard features, I was sent back in time to all those nights we'd spent together. Feelings rushed back like no time had passed at all. "I don't know..."

"Are you in love with him?" Liam had never asked me details about my former lover because he preferred to avoid the elephant in the room, but when the problem wasn't going to go away, he couldn't ignore it anymore.

I couldn't look him in the eye as I answered. "Yeah...I loved him."

He couldn't hide his hurt. "I asked if you loved him now."

"I...I guess. But I don't want to. I hadn't thought about him much lately, but when I saw him...everything started again."

Liam had clearly lost his appetite because he didn't even look at his food. "Is it done now?"

Damien had said what he wanted to say, and now it was over. I'd told him how I felt, and he didn't reciprocate. He hurt me all over again. Now there was no reason for us to ever speak again. "Yeah. It's done."

"If he wanted you, would you go back to him?"

I wanted to lie to spare Liam's feelings, but I couldn't. "Liam…"

"I think I already know the answer, but I want to be sure."

I stared at my plate. "Yeah…"

He dropped his hands and stepped back for a second, unable to hide his disappointment.

"We don't have to do this, Liam. I understand if—"

"You're the only woman I want to be with." He came back to me, his arms crossed over his chest. "None of this would have happened if I hadn't fucked up everything. We'd still be together right now, maybe even have another kid on the way. I'm the only one to blame for this, so I accept the consequences. I know in time you'll really forget about him…and I can be patient."

33

DAMIEN

Weeks had passed since Annabella and I had spoken.

Since she'd told me she loved me with tears in her eyes.

And I'd just stood there...and felt worthless.

Time had passed, but the wound was still fresh. When my thoughts wandered, they always wandered to her. Now I sat in my office at the lab, my feet on the desk as I stared at the weird painting on the wall. It had been there when we'd moved in to the place, but Hades and I thought it was so stupid that we had to keep it.

A knock sounded on my door. "The Skull King is here."

I took a deep breath and steadied my temper. I wanted to pull out a rusty knife and stab him right in the throat, let the blood spill and the rust enter his veins. "Send him in."

A moment later, the arrogant son of a bitch entered my office. "Nice place."

I dropped my feet and righted myself in my chair. "The money is on the table." In a black duffle bag were the royalties that he was due. "Paperwork is inside."

He grabbed it with one hand and tested the weight.

"You can count it if you want."

He lifted it over and over. "I am." When he was satisfied, he put the bag on his shoulder. "It's always nice to see you, Damien." He stood at my desk and grinned, enjoying every second of my submission.

I'd get my chance.

He continued to linger. "Why the sour face?"

I rose from my chair and faced him. "You got your money. I don't owe you anything else."

He chuckled. "We could be friends, you know."

"I have enough friends."

"Well, Balto doesn't owe you anything, so he doesn't count. So, Hades is all you've got, but he's out of the game, so he's useless to you."

"He doesn't need to do anything for me to be my friend."

"True. But he'd be a much better friend if he could save your ass. I could do that for you. It's what you're paying for, right?"

I'd never ask for help, even if I desperately needed it. "Goodbye, Heath."

He grinned again before he walked out.

———

When I opened the door, Hades stood there.

In a nice suit with his watch on his wrist, he stood with his hands in his pockets. "Damien."

"I told you I'm not going." I left the door open and walked away. I was in my sweatpants, and I hadn't showered. It was too early in the day to drink, but that hadn't stopped me. I moved to the couch and fell into the cushions.

He stood near the roaring fire. "You have to."

"I don't have to do anything, asshole." I poured myself another drink.

"Damien." His voice turned cold.

I shook my head.

"You know he's an important client—"

"He's *your* important client."

"Damien," he repeated. "We know how this is going to end, so don't make it difficult. Waste of time."

I shook my head and dragged my hand over my eyes, so frustrated I could explode.

"I know this is hard, but you have to go."

I grabbed the glass and took a drink. "I shouldn't have to watch her marry that jackass."

"I know," he said gently. "But that's how it has to be."

"If he knew I'd fucked her, he wouldn't want me there."

"Or maybe he'd want you there more."

I gave him a glare.

"Damien, you had your chance—twice. You said no. Be a man and move on."

"Just because I don't want to be with her doesn't mean I want to watch her be with someone else, especially a jerk who cheated on her."

"Damien." He spoke to me like a child. "I got here early because I knew you'd be like this. You have an hour to shower and get ready. Don't make me rip off your sweatpants and throw you in the shower —because I will."

I groaned.

"Liam is going to make us a lot of money very soon. This is important to me—so I'm asking you to do this for me."

I groaned again. "You can't do that—"

"I just did." He flashed me his irritated look. "Now, get your ass up."

THE CEREMONY WAS in an old cathedral.

Interesting choice since Liam had killed people with his bare fists...

I sat beside Hades on the wooden bench, sitting on Liam's side even though I had no affinity for the man. There weren't very many people, maybe a couple dozen. Everyone there knew why they got divorced, so I was surprised they were so supportive of this.

Annabella deserved better.

How hard was it not to cheat on your wife? Just don't fucking do it.

And why the fuck would you cheat on a woman like Annabella?

I sighed in my seat and glanced at my watch, wanting this nightmare to end.

Hades didn't say anything. Sometimes he gave me glances to make sure I wouldn't explode where I sat.

Then the music began.

Unlike a traditional ceremony, there were no bridesmaids or flower girls. Liam walked down the aisle in his suit, bulky and massive as he headed to the place where he would wait for his bride. He turned around and brought his hands together at his waist and waited.

Hatred exploded inside me as I stared at him, as I saw the genuine affection in his eyes, the excitement that Annabella was his once more. Maybe things would be different this time around, maybe that was just a one-time mistake. It seemed like he loved her...really loved her.

And then she came.

Fucking angel without wings.

In a long-sleeved wedding gown made of lace, she glided across the stone floor carrying a beautiful bouquet. Pops of color—pink, white, and green—were in her hands, the colors complementing the simple pink ribbon tied around her small waist. Her eyes were straight ahead, looking at the man who couldn't wait for her to reach him.

For an instant, I wasn't sick. I was at peace...in awe of her heavenly glow. Her brown hair was scattered around her shoulders, and she'd chosen to go light on the makeup, letting her natural beauty fill that cathedral to the very top. With her rosy cheeks, painted lips, and gorgeous eyes...she really was the most beautiful woman in the world.

And I watched her go.

She passed me without knowing I was there, and that was when the nausea returned.

The sadness. The despair. The regret.

I'd made my choice, and I stood by it. There was no other possible outcome, so there was no past to rewrite. I was where I was supposed to be...as was she. But that didn't make this pill easier to swallow, didn't make me less angry.

But I couldn't stand there and watch.

I shifted down the row of people, disturbing their view for a moment before I finally made it to the aisle. The music still played over the speakers as the ceremony continued. I made it to the main doors just when the music cut off and the priest began to speak. "We're gathered here to—"

I walked outside into the cold winter air, the intense sunshine, and moved to the balcony that overlooked the street. My hands gripped the rail like an old man gripped a walker. I wasn't the strong man who could be bled dry and still fight. Now I was reduced to a weak, skeletal frame, a dead person without a beating heart—because it had been ripped out of my chest.

A hand touched my shoulder, strong fingers squeezing into the crispness of my suit.

I knew who it was without looking.

Hades released his hold then stood beside me. He looked out at the city instead of scrutinizing my face. Then he reached inside the jacket of his suit and pulled out two cigars. "Thought we might need these." He lit one for himself and handed mine over.

I lit up then puffed a deep breath from the tip, getting the smoke into my mouth. Hades and I only smoked for the best occasions— or the worst. His wife was strongly against the activity, so he'd have to pay for his choice when he got home—because he would reek of the smell.

Hades leaned against the rail as he enjoyed his cigar and the view instead of grilling me about what just happened.

The last thing I wanted to do was to talk, to try to understand what the fuck had just happened. I shouldn't care that she'd married someone else. With tears in her eyes, she'd told me she loved me, and I didn't feel the same way. I shouldn't feel anything at all right now...not a single thing. But I couldn't face the reality...like a fucking coward.

"I'll drop you off and come back."

"No." I tapped the shaft of the cigar and let the ash fall before I put it in my mouth again. "I'll go back in there. Just need a second."

Hades moved his hand to my shoulder and stared at me. "You don't have to prove anything to me, Damien. I'm the one person in the world you don't have to pull that shit with." He dropped his hand. "I'll tell Liam you were ill."

"You sure?" I asked, my gaze still on the ground.

He patted my back before he finished his cigar. "I got your back." He tossed the ashy remains of the cigar in the trash as he walked back into the cathedral. When the doors were open, I could hear the sound of cheering, the moment where they were pronounced husband and wife.

I had to get the fuck out of there.

I headed down the steps and reached the street before I waved down a cab. I got into the back seat, finally taking a breath now that I was away from the cathedral.

The driver turned his head slightly. "Where to?"

My eyes moved to the double doors as they opened, and Annabella stepped into the sunlight in her glowing white dress, pieces of rice in her dark hair and against her tanned skin. She held Liam's hand, smiling as she gripped her arrangement of flowers. I took a deep breath as I stared at her, feeling time slow down to appreciate every second of the anguish. She'd never looked so beautiful...and that just made the torture worse.

When I didn't answer, the driver turned to look at me. "Where to?"

I pulled my gaze away because I couldn't stand the sight of her a moment longer. "Just get me the fuck out of here."

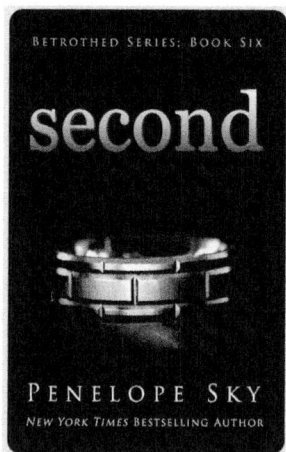

Printed in Dunstable, United Kingdom